THE OFFICE BET

EDEN FINLEY

Chapter 1

Fox

There are only three things I've ever been passionate about in my life: my family, sports, and hating Archer Holloway.

He's been a pain in my ass ever since he transferred from the New York office, where he interned four years ago. I was lucky enough to be chosen to be the sole intern here in LA, so I see this as my turf, and he's done nothing but encroach on it since the day he stepped foot in this office.

Most sports agents are dude bros who are all about pranks and picking on the little guy. The majority of agents are failed athletes themselves, so they're used to that kind of toxic environment where putting down someone else makes them feel like some kind of alpha male. King Sports is supposed to be different, and mostly, it is. I have loved working here. My bosses are great, the CEO is an inspiration, and with it being an inclusive agency, working here has been a dream.

Until him.

I'm used to being the picked-on kid. I'm not athletic and never have been, but that doesn't mean I can't love sports. I may have never been able to play the games I love, but getting paid to watch my athletes thrive is the next best thing. They do the hard work, like diet and exercise and keeping in peak physical form, while I get to sit behind a desk and put my MBA to good use.

I originally went into sports journalism in college, but my sophomore year, I realized I could make bank by becoming an agent.

I worked my ass off to get here, and here I am, doing it. Loving it. There's only one thing I hate about it, and that's Archer.

I've learned to expect him to try to snipe my clients, to beat me to meetings with athletes—even though we don't have a lot of overlap with the kinds of clients we rep—and to backstab anyone and everyone to get ahead, but this latest move? This is too far.

A new shipment of business cards came in today, and instead of mine saying Lincoln Fox, Associate Agent, it has Lincoln Fox, *Future Mr. Holloway*, and in small print says, "Just fuck already."

It's like he wants me to report him to HR.

This is exactly the type of thing he'd do to try to get in my head to throw me off my game. Does he think it's funny? I'm failing to see the humor. Then again, I fail to see a lot of the "good qualities" Archer supposedly has. His charisma comes off as slimy, and I always feel like his mask is hiding deep-seated issues of childhood trauma. Textbook bully persona. They hide their insecurities by exploiting others'.

I might have also taken psych classes before deciding on sports management as my major, so I know what I'm talking about. Sort of.

My point is, Archer sucks, and this time, I'm going to let him know it. I usually try to ignore him because if he gets a rise out of me, he wins. If I show that he gets to me, he wins. But this is so much more than petty competition for clients. This is ... It's bull-shit is what it is.

I storm out of my office and cross the bullpen, where our interns and junior agents are laughing and goofing off, but I ignore them and keep moving toward Archer's office.

The layout of the LA office has always had an "us and them" kind of vibe. The managing partners, Camden and Xavier, aren't only managers of the LA office; they're actual live-in partners. But, like Archer, they're competitive as fuck, and apparently, it dates to before they were even together. Even now, as life-partner kind of boyfriends, they still have that competitive edge. Xavier takes care of PR, and Camden is the Damon King of the LA office—agent extraordinaire. Together, they make a good pair, but I don't think it's a coincidence that the offices are split. Instead of two offices together, they have them at different ends of the floor with reception, bullpen, and then associate offices in between. I'm on Xavier's side of the office. Archer is on Camden's.

I thought the walk would give me time to calm down, but unfortunately, the building isn't that big. My work email alert sounds from my pocket, but it can wait in my inbox with the rest of the emails I haven't yet read this morning.

I enter Archer's office without knocking, which I wouldn't normally dream of doing to anyone because it's disrespectful, but I'd have to respect Archer to care about that.

Archer has his bleach-blond head buried in his screen, a smile on his plump lips, and his shirtsleeves rolled up to his elbows to show off his tattoos. They're also peeking out above his top button too.

I hate those tattoos. Hate that my gaze is always drawn to them. Hate that I want to see what the ink is that's hidden by his button-up shirt. But mostly, I hate them because I find tattoos irresistibly hot on a man, and these tattoos are on a man who doesn't deserve them. They're too good for his skin.

Archer lifts his head and then tilts it to the side like a dog. "What are you here to yell at me for this time?"

I wish I could say I come to his office for other reasons and had a right to be mad at that greeting, but I don't. On either account.

"This." I throw one of my business cards at his desk. It misses, and I internally sigh. Because God forbid I look cool while throwing something for once in my life. I step closer and pick it up, placing it in front of him this time with a firm hand. "What the hell is this supposed to mean, and why would you do it? Are you serious or purely delusional?"

Archer picks up the card and chuckles. Legit lets out an immature chuckle like someone just said sixty-nine and he can't help himself. "I mean, the thought of you marrying me is pretty funny."

"What is your issue with me? Are you playing childhood games to get me to blow up at you in front of everyone and get fired? Stooping to sabotage so you can sign all of my clients to your roster? If you need to do this shit to get accounts, you're not as charming as you think. Whatever you have against me, let it go. I'm not going anywhere."

Archer puts his hand on his heart and says in the driest tone to ever exist, "It hurts so much that you don't want to be the next Camden and Xavier of this office. It hurts so bad."

I go to lose my shit at him even more when he beats me.

"It wasn't me, jackass. Do you really think I'd spell my name wrong on my own cards?" He takes one of his cards out of the box sitting on his desk and slides it over to me.

Archer Halloway

Competitive PITA

His last name has an *A* instead of an *O* in Holloway. He makes a good point, but maybe that's to throw everyone off so he doesn't get in trouble for pranking my business cards. Make himself look like a victim too.

"At least yours is true," I mumble.

He laughs for real this time.

"But it also doesn't mean you didn't have—"

"Also, you might want to check your work email."

Uh-oh.

Swallowing hard, I pull my phone out of my pocket and open the inbox I've been ignoring since I first saw my new business card.

From: Damon King

Subject: Check your business cards

Hi all,

Due to a recent security breach, our legal team requires you to check your most recent batch of business cards handed out this week. We've had numerous reports of misprints, so please make sure yours have your correct title on them and email me if they do not.

On an unrelated note, please be careful who you let inside King Sports properties, both in New York and the LA offices. Also be aware that Maddox O'Shay and Stacy King are no longer allowed to set foot on either premises.

Regards,

Damon King.

King Sports CEO.

The email is so random it's difficult to understand that it was Damon's partner and sister who were responsible for this.

Damon King is a fascinating man. He's so put together and runs a multimillion-dollar empire, yet he's surrounded by immaturity. How does he deal with it? I'm struggling hard.

"I'll take that apology whenever you're ready," Archer says.

I take my eyes off my phone to glare at him. "I don't understand though."

"Understand that a harmless prank could have been carried out by anyone but me?"

"No. I don't get *why?*" These people don't actually think Archer and I would make a good couple, do they?

"Why, what?"

"Why does mine say I should become your husband, but yours is work related?"

"Would you still have thought it was me if it was work related? Or only because it was practically a marriage proposal if it came from me? Think highly of yourself?"

"Yes! Wait, no. Yes, I still would've thought it was you if it was work related, but seeing as it wasn't you and it was the boss's partner, what have Camden and Xavier been telling Damon for Maddox to think you and I getting married would even be a remote possibility? It's offensive."

"It was a *joke*," he says. "It's probably because everyone knows how much you hate me for being better than you."

"Yes, that's the reason you drive me crazy. Absolutely has nothing to do with you sniping prospective clients right out from underneath me."

"Isn't that the same thing?"

This man is impossible.

"Either way, it's still offensive."

"Well, I take offense to your offense. I'm a catch. You'd be lucky to have me."

"And you would need a miracle to have me."

Archer leans back in his seat. "I'd take it as a compliment, if I were you."

"What, because you're so out of my league that—"

He puts up his hand to stop me from talking, and it's so fucking rude. "No. It's a compliment because they couldn't find anything wrong when it comes to your work ethic, so they had to make shit up."

I hesitate. Is ... is that true?

"Hence, compliment."

I'd hate to agree with Archer for once, but seeing it from that angle—

"Plus, they're probably playing into the whole bet thing."

Bet thing? "What bet?"

Archer's brow scrunches, but he quickly smooths it out. "You haven't heard?"

"Unlike others in this office, I try to stay away from gossip."

"Then maybe you should ask around."

Why is he like this? "I'm asking you."

"Sorry. I'm too busy sniping your clients to fill you in. Did you happen to see Asher Dalton's little bro is making waves in the AHL? Imagine getting the chance to rep both of them."

"But he's Damon's client along with Asher."

He shakes his head. "You didn't read the follow-up email to the card scandal, did you?"

Fucking hell. Lesson learned. No more losing my shit at Archer before I've checked all my emails. I look again only to find the announcement nearly everyone has been waiting for.

Damon King is only mid-fifties. Nowhere near retirement. But he's so successful we've all been wondering when he'd begin to step back and slow down.

Apparently, that time is now.

Subject: Client List

Dear valued employees

Shit. You know it's going to be big when he opens with that instead of his usual casual Hi.

As you're all aware, I closed off my roster for any new clients a while ago, and I've been taking active steps to reduce my workload. In the coming months, I will be moving into a purely administrative managing role for the company.

What this means:

The majority of athletes on my roster are at or nearing retirement, but there are a few legacy clients—those whose family members I have repped previously—who will be seeking new representation. I am leaving this up to the clients to decide who they want on their team.

If you are interested in any available clients, please make sure you represent King Sports with the same respect and decorum as I always expect. Treat each prospect like you would those coming from outside representation, while also being considerate of the other agents in the running. I don't want to see this turn into an intraoffice spectacle or rivalry between agents.

Why do I feel like that last part is mostly directed Archer's and my way?

The rest of the email has a list of those seeking new representation, and then he signs it off with his casual "thanks." Like he hasn't potentially set a live wire alight in the middle of everything he's built.

Archer's mention of whatever office bet he was talking about is long forgotten. I've got work to do if I'm going to beat him at scoring myself some of the biggest athletes at this firm.

Archer has had a head start, but I'm sure I can catch up.

Game on, Holloway.

Chapter 2
Archer

Fox leaves my office without so much as a goodbye. Am I offended Lincoln Fox thinks I'm the devil? Not even a little bit. Because in his defense, I am cutthroat when it comes to getting clients. I have to be.

The fact that he's one of the most attractive people I've ever met and his uptight nature makes me curious about what it would be like to watch him unravel doesn't factor into it.

When I first moved to LA, I had the biggest crush on the guy. That lingering attraction has fluctuated over the years, flaring up when he comes into the office looking disheveled like he'd spent the night before being thoroughly fucked to dying down when he does shit like this—accuse me of something I didn't do.

It doesn't matter how into the guy I am because it all boils down to business first.

With two younger brothers, an older sister, and then our dad being an Olympian, I was raised with that "must win" mentality. My siblings and I were forced into every water-based sport under the sun growing up, our father putting so much pressure on us to be the best. If we weren't, he'd put us in the next available specialty. He was determined for each of us to find our niche, where our natural talent was, and then pushed us to succeed.

My sister followed in Dad's footsteps, becoming an Olympic

gold medalist in the 400- and 800-meter freestyle. My younger brothers went a different route and are currently trying to make the US Olympic team for diving—single and pairs divisions.

Me? I was a naturally talented swimmer with my wide shoulders and big feet, but I lacked the drive. I became a water polo player in my college years, but there isn't money in that. Professional water polo players in Europe can earn a couple of hundred thousand a year, but the average is barely a livable wage.

I've always had my eye on doing this for a living: being a sports agent. I want to be the one to get those endorsement deals for my clients, especially those in the sports that don't get nearly enough of a wage without them.

That's why I do what I do. That's why I'm unapologetic if Fox gets pissed at me for signing a client he was chasing. Everyone is fair game, and I need to win. Not only to be successful and be the best, but to show my father that choosing not to pursue professional sports doesn't make me a quitter. If anything, I have more of a financially secure future than he ever did as a swimmer.

Especially if I can sign any or all of Damon's soon-to-be ex-clients. I don't exactly have the room for all of them on my roster, but if I can nab the important ones, I could be set for the next ten years.

Asher Dalton has a few years left in the NHL, but he's one of the greats. He will be a big payday, even if it's only short-lived. His little brother, on the other hand, he's young. Just started out in the AHL with the potential to be even better than Asher if he can stay away from injury and keep his head in check. I've been reading up on him since I saw that email this morning.

Emmett Dalton quit hockey after high school and made a comeback three years later, so whatever made him quit in the first place could be an obstacle in his future. I'm assuming the brothers come as a package deal, so while it's a risk signing Emmett, I have to if I want Asher on my roster.

Still, they're the big fish everyone is going to want, so I need to be smart about it. And to be smart, I need more coffee.

I stand from my desk and make my way into the break room,

where some associates are doing the same thing as me. "Refueling before going to woo Damon's clients?"

Beau Buckley—aka Buck—scoffs. "Between you and Fox, is there really any point trying?"

"Fair point. Should leave it all up to us."

Luca Smith cuts in. "I'll be taking my fair share, thanks, but I'm not dumb enough to waste my time on the bigger names. Have at them."

I pour a cup of coffee from the filtered stuff that tastes like mud, but it's too much effort to use the espresso machine for a good one. This does the trick. "Where's your sense of good ol' competition gone?"

"It's preoccupied with another ..." Luca glances at Buck. "Wager."

I grunt. "Not this bet about Fox and me. Did you see the business card fuckups? His implied we'll end up married, so he marched over to my office to tell me to my face how little chance there is of that happening."

Would marrying Lincoln Fox be the worst thing in the world? Aesthetically, no; he's extremely attractive in the conventional sense. He has golden highlights in his sandy-brown hair, styled in a perfect pompadour always, and he also has that permanent five-o'clock shadow that drives me crazy on a man. All of that paired with these striking pale green eyes that look gray in some light, and I would be weak in the knees if he were anyone but him. The problem isn't his looks.

Luca pulls something up on his phone. "Getting married actually has a payout of five hundred bucks. Worst odds of all the options, really. But if you think you can pull it off—"

"Wait, what? I thought it was a bet on if we would ever hook up. There are odds on us getting married?"

"There are odds on a lot of things. One-night stand has good odds but obviously a shit payout. One date has pretty good odds too. One-month relationship, two months, three—"

"How many people have actually bet money on us?"

"Bet is one hundred a pop. The pool is up to two thousand already," Buck says.

My first reaction is to be offended that they're betting on my life, but my competitive side knows that if they want to waste their time focusing on this instead of signing new clients, then all the more clients for me to poach.

"You two have fun with that while I go and do some real work."

Real work being ways I can put myself ahead of the game and get to the clients I want before anyone else has a chance.

On my way back to my office, I spot the top of Brady Talon's head in the bullpen. He's my junior agent that I'm supposed to mentor, but there's no doubt he will be running this place one day.

He's Damon King's honorary nephew, the son of some of Damon's most successful clients. They go way back, and I know for a fact that Brady will be connected to someone who can get me a meeting with Asher Dalton without going through the proper channels. Like company-wide scheduling programs that are visible to everyone.

Damon said no playing games, but if he didn't want us to ignore that, he would've assigned his clients to new agents based on merit and who he thinks the right fit would be.

"Talon," I call out and head for the bullpen.

He ducks his head, no doubt hopeful I haven't actually seen him yet, but no such luck. Sorry, dude.

Brady and Thad are as thick as thieves, and Thad is Fox's mentee. For some reason, they both flinch when they see either of us coming. What, like we're scary?

The thing is, I'm smart enough not to drag the CEO's nephew into our mess of a petty feud. If I did, he'd run off and tell my boss's boss. But both Thad and Brady act like Fox and I put them in the middle like we're divorced parents or some shit and are making the kids choose between Mommy and Daddy. I don't even acknowledge the behavior because it's always good to have subordinates a bit scared of you, right?

"Need to see you in my office."

He stands, his young features making him look more innocent

than he is. He's mid-twenties and in a throuple with two extremely attractive men. Jealous? Me? Maybe a little. But then I think of all those egos in the one bed and change my mind. I deal with enough egos in the office and with my clients. I don't need more at home.

Brady follows me to my office and closes the door behind him. "Need me to sit in on a client meeting?"

I take my seat at my desk, and he sits across from me. "Not today, but I might need your help getting a meeting with a client."

"If he's your client, shouldn't that be easy for you to do?"

I give him a half smile and try to look as innocent as he pretends to be.

Realization dawns. "Ah. You want one of Damon's clients."

Sure. One. Uh-huh.

"I need a meeting on the DL with Asher Dalton. You have some kind of six degrees of separation with him, don't you? He's a friend of one of your other uncles who was in the NHL a billion years ago?"

Brady frowns. "Asher? You want a meeting with Asher Dalton?"

"I know you probably want to rep him, seeing as he's a close friend of your family, but your plate is full already with your brother and Kelley. You don't need another superstar taking all your time. But if I sign him, I could put you on his case as a consulting junior agent."

"Oh, no, no. That's fine. You can have Asher all to yourself if you can land him. I promise. I'm good."

My eyes narrow. "Should I be worried that you're so against Asher as a client?"

He hesitates, as if trying to decide something. Then his lips hitch into a polite, professional smile. "It was a surprise, is all. You don't generally rep NHL players on multimillion-dollar contracts. You're more ... like, the sponsorship and endorsement guy. But hey, Uncle Damon always says it's good to spread your wings and all that. Or ... some other bullshit like it."

He's okay with me chasing Asher solo? Amazing.

"So do you think you can set up that meeting for me?"

He takes out his phone and stands. "Consider it done. I'll set it up and put it in your calendar."

Before he leaves, I stop him. "About that."

His brown eyes meet mine.

"Can you put it on the calendar as a scouting trip to Syracuse University instead of Buffalo?"

"Uh … sure. Can I ask why you want me to do that?"

"I want this first meeting to be off the books, so to speak."

Brady's shoulders slump. "So Lincoln Fox can't work out your strategy, you mean?"

I fake gasp. "I have no idea what you're talking about."

"Mmhmm." He taps away on his phone, making a note. "Syracuse it is."

Perfect.

Chapter 3

Fox

Okay, I have my game plan mapped out. I've organized priority of the available clients by looking at their career longevity, earning potential through wage and endorsements, and what I'd be able to provide them as their agent.

I'm not like some people in this office. I won't make empty promises to an athlete whose sport I have no knowledge of or interest in. Sure, I could research it, but I find that when I'm excited about a client and what they do, I actually like coming to work. Or doing the work, more specifically. Coming to the actual office is not too fun unless Archer is absent. I love when I check the office-wide calendar and see he's traveling.

But this time, when I do it and see an upcoming trip in two days, red flags dance in front of my eyes. He's going to Syracuse on a scouting trip while there are easy clients ripe for the picking? Nah, that's not a move he would make. Archer is up to something, and as I pull up the list of Damon's available clients and go over each name, my eyes stop on a pair of brothers.

Asher and Emmett Dalton. Asher, who's Buffalo's NHL star, and Emmett, Asher's promising little brother making waves in his first AHL season in Rochester, New York.

Archer's not going on some scouting trip. He's trying to snipe the Dalton brothers and sign them before anyone else gets a chance. Things like this are exactly why I don't trust him and never will.

The question now is, do I have it in me to fight for those clients, or do I let him have this and go for other names on the list?

The thing is, I've repped hockey before. I know that world. I rep a lot from the big five sports. Sure, not on Asher Dalton's scale. He's on a multimillion-dollar-a-year contract. The highest commission I've earned from any sport has been the low six figures. Even so, I have experience with NHL players.

Archer's client list has more of the type of athletes who rely on endorsements for their income. He's yet to negotiate a contract in any of the major leagues. He's repped some NHL prospects during their junior careers, but he chooses quantity over quality. He has a lot of little clients whose commission adds up to where he's outearning every other associate at our level.

I'm not sure if I can let him swoop in and take the Dalton brothers from me. They aren't even mine, but I'm the better option to rep them. I believe that wholeheartedly. They should be my clients.

A cynical voice in the back of my head asks, *Do you only want them because you know Archer wants them?* I tell that voice to shut up and try to convince myself that chasing after the Dalton brothers is a good idea when I wasn't initially interested in them. On my priority list, the brothers are under a rookie baseball player with career longevity on his side, a veteran baseball manager who's highly sought after in MLB, and a different hockey player who isn't as ... controversial as Asher Dalton.

Ever since before he joined the league, Asher Dalton has had the reputation of being a pain in the ass. Getting on a plane every time he tells a reporter to eat shit and die to do damage control isn't my idea of fun. Neither is doing overtime hours on the phone, telling his brands why he can't talk to the media to save his life. Even when he does say the right things on camera, you can tell he's clenching his teeth and hoping his snark doesn't fall out of his mouth.

On the flip side, Emmett Dalton is young. He has a bright

future in hockey and has been coached by some of the best players in the league, thanks to his connections with his older brothers. He only started in the AHL this season, but it wouldn't shock me if he was called up to the NHL next year. Year after that at the very latest. If he can keep his health up and avoid injuries.

That's a risk with every player though. These athletes sacrifice their bodies to do what they love, and they deserve to be paid the big bucks because of it. Not everyone has the talent to be an on-air commentator after they retire. Not everyone has the brains to go to college and get a degree when their sporting career is over. There are only so many coaching jobs available.

If these athletes have to earn enough to be set for life in what is usually a short career span, I need to make sure I get them the best deal on the table. They deserve it.

So even though Asher Dalton was not on my list of people I want to rep, if he and Emmett want to sign with the same agent, I'm going to have to chase them both. Though Emmett is probably my best way to get in with them. Knowing Archer the way I do, I'm sure he's going to pursue the older brother first. Logic dictates the older one would have a bigger influence on the younger brother. But if I can really sell myself to Emmett, there's a chance he might pick me regardless of what his brother is doing.

If there's one thing I've heard about the Dalton brothers—not only the ones in hockey but the other billion of them as well—it's that once they've made their mind up, there's no changing it.

They're all stubborn to a fault, and I could use that in my favor.

I check the Buffalo NHL team's schedule and then also Rochester's, who Emmett plays for, and my suspicions are confirmed. Emmett's team will be in Cleveland while Archer is in New York, so he is chasing the older Dalton first.

I guess it's decided. I'm going to Cleveland.

Apart from Archer, I get along with everyone in the office on a professional level. I find real friendships with coworkers are a recipe for disaster. Some people have a no-dating-a-coworker rule; mine is a no-being-friends rule. People may see that as me being uptight, but as long as they're professional with me, I'll be professional with them.

Edele, on the other hand, the sweet mid-fifties butch lesbian who is in charge of booking everyone's flights and travel arrangements, I will kiss her ass every day of the week.

I knock on her office door, always popping in to put in my travel requests instead of via email like most people. Kissing ass equals better flight times and higher-end accommodations. That's one of the first things Camden taught me when I came to work here. Though it was more of a warning of "Don't get on Edele's bad side. She looks sweet, but one time I forgot her wife's name, and the next hotel she booked for me was a no-name brand motel where I really hoped the stain in the bath was from rust and not blood. She claims it was the only one available, but her halo tilted when she said it. She is no angel."

The imagery was enough for me to always make sure I put in effort with her.

She smiles as she greets me. "If it isn't my favorite associate."

"I bet you say that to all the associates. How are you? How's Trish and the kids?"

"Can you believe she brought home another one? Like we don't have enough already."

"Another baby? You have to show me pics." In all honesty, even if my friendliness started out as wanting to get the daytime flights instead of red-eyes or a Hilton instead of a Motel 6, the truth is, I love her stories of her and her wife. And their three dogs ... sorry, four now.

She takes out her phone and shows me a sad-looking yellow Lab with three legs.

"In her defense, how could she have said no to that face?"

"She needs to stop volunteering at that shelter." Edele puts her phone back in her handbag at her feet and then leans forward, resting her elbows on her desk. "Would you know I came home the other night from work, and there was this delicious-smelling stew on the stove. I took a ladle and tried it. It had vegetables, chicken, a nice thick broth—"

"Sounds delicious."

"Yeah, it was, until she rounded the corner and said it was for the dogs. They eat better than I do!"

"She cooked it for the dogs, but you could've still eaten it."

"Maybe if she hadn't put their worming medication in it."

I bite my lip to stop from laughing. "At least you won't get a parasite?"

She grumbles, "You sound like her."

"I'm sorry. You're right. They do eat better than you. But you have to admit, you love those babies just as much as Trish does."

Her lips twitch. "Still doesn't mean it isn't true about her spoiling them."

"*So spoiled.*"

"What can I do for you?" she asks, our chat time abruptly over. It's probably what I like most about her. She keeps the small talk *small.*

"While Archer is off to Syracuse, I need to go to Cleveland, please." Throwing Archer under the bus? Don't mind if I do!

"Let me have a look." She moves her mouse and clicks some things and then squints at her screen. "It says he's going to Syracuse on the calendar, but when he emailed me ... hang on." She clicks on other things. "Hmm. His email says to Buffalo. He does realize there's a closer airport than that, doesn't he?"

"Maybe he's worried about the layover?"

"There are layovers to Buffalo too."

I know that, of course. "Huh. Weird."

"I'll have to fix this, but sorry, where are you off to?"

"Cleveland. Potential client meeting after an AHL game."

"Ooh, fun. I'll get that set up and send through your confirmation. Do you prefer red-eyes or—"

I give her a pleading look. "You know how much I hate to sleep on planes. I was thinking I could fly out tomorrow and stay for two nights. Save rushing around, and it will give me time to prepare for this pitch. I know we're not supposed to stay more than one night when we don't have an athlete to assign the overheads to, but—"

She smiles warmly at me. "Don't worry. I got you."

And this is why kissing her ass pays off.

She scribbles my requests on a Post-it before turning back to me. "Consider it done. Hope you enjoy the fight!"

"Don't you mean *flight*?"

"Nope. You know that old saying, I went to a fight and a hockey game broke out."

I laugh. "Right."

"Though you don't see many fights anymore. Not like there used to be. They used to fight until blood hit the ice. When did hockey get boring?"

She calls it boring, I call it looking out for player safety, but I play along and say, "No idea."

"Oh well. Have a good trip!"

"Thanks, I will." Especially while I picture Archer's face when he realizes he's been rerouted to Syracuse. Not that I think it'll actually happen. Edele will straighten it all out before he gets anywhere near the airport.

I wish I were an evil mastermind instead of a petty person who creates a minor headache for my nemesis, but it is what it is.

And hey, it's not my fault Syracuse is what was on the calendar. If he's not going to explain it to the entire office, he should at least have to explain his trickery to Edele. Maybe she'll put him in a murder hotel like she did that one time with Camden.

One could only hope.

Chapter 4
Archer

My alarm goes off after my one-hour power nap, seeing as Edele always seems to book me on fucking red-eyes. It would be all right if it was a long flight, but because there are rarely direct flights to most places in the East unless you're traveling to an airport hub, it means I have four hours to Chicago, three hours of waiting for my next flight, and then another two or whatever it is to Buffalo.

I checked in yesterday when the email saying it was open came through. The flight time had changed, but that wasn't anything new. Delays, cancellations, I'm used to them all.

It was only an hour later than the original scheduled flight, which ended up working out because I got to have this power nap.

A quick shower later, I'm in sweats with my suit in a garment bag and folded in my carry-on, but I told Edele to book me a place with a steamer so it at least won't be all wrinkled. Wearing it on an overnight flight would make it as wrinkly as packing it, and this way, I get to be comfortable.

I opt for a cab to take me to the airport, saving me from having to drive in LA traffic. I'm going to take as much time as possible to relax on this trip. It's a quick red-eye in, check in to a hotel, meet with Asher Dalton, and then get up at 3:00 a.m. to catch my early 5:00 a.m. flight home.

Maybe I don't want to rep the Daltons if regular visits to Buffalo are needed. Though a direct flight would be useful. I don't know if Edele doesn't like me or if everyone else gets stuck with the same old cheapest flight of the day like I do. I always ask so nicely in my emails with a list of my preferences and necessities, but I swear I only ever get one or two of them, and the rest she writes off and says, "As per company policy ..." ... *insert excuse here.*

Traffic is a nightmare, but I left with plenty of time to spare, and I don't have a checked bag, so I scan my boarding pass on my phone and breeze through security. It's not until I have to find out which gate I'm at that I actually look properly at my digital boarding pass. I've done this so many times, traveled all over the country, it's like second nature to skim the information on there. Like destination. Time and gate number is all I usually need.

Not this time.

My connecting flight was changed from Chicago to Detroit? Okay, not a big deal. But a change that big without me even acknowledging it wouldn't be something I would usually skim over. It would stand out to me. Surely.

To be sure, I check my next flight too, and my gut sinks.

Syracuse? Edele booked me to Buffalo. I saw the confirmation email.

I tap so many icons on my screen at once, trying to get my email app open, that even my phone can't process what I want.

After a quick glitch-out, I finally get into my work emails. There's a billion, so I search for Buffalo. And there it is, second result. My booking confirmation.

But then the unread one above it catches my eye. The one about a change of flight. I assumed it was the delay. I saw the new time in the preview part and didn't open the email. What is going on?

I delete my search and type in Edele's name, and when her emails pop up, I see one from yesterday. When we're traveling, she sends through a million confirmations, all saying the same thing. I used to open them, but just like not checking my boarding pass until I'm at the airport, I've become accustomed to ignoring most of her emails.

She sent three yesterday though. That should have tipped me off. The first one asks if I was supposed to book to Buffalo when the calendar has me going to Syracuse. Then there's another asking me what I want her to do. The final one says she has rebooked my flights for me because the office calendar has me going somewhere other than my requested destination, and as per company policy—

Oh look, there's that excuse again.

I know I can't be mad at her. It's my fault for not double-checking everything or reading her emails. I've become complacent about her competency. Turns out, she's too competent. I didn't think she actually looked at the calendar and cross-referenced the flights we'd booked.

This whole situation is my fault. I'm the one trying to keep it on the down-low. But fuck. What am I supposed to do now?

My flight is called, it's past ten at night, so I can't phone the office anyway, so I hustle to the gate and board my plane to the wrong city.

After not sleeping on either flight, trying to come up with a solution to my destination issue, I arrive in Syracuse at nine in the morning. New York time. Not LA. It's still six there, and Edele won't be in her office.

I could call the New York office and talk to their travel department, or I could take it upon myself to hire a car, drive the two or so hours to Buffalo, and keep this whole kerfuffle under wraps. Considering Damon was very specific about no funny business around trying to sign his clients, I think that's my best bet.

Sucky thing is having to get back to Syracuse for an early flight. Maybe I'll drive back tonight. Or maybe I'll call the airline myself to change my flight home. Okay, yeah. I'll get on that.

It means I'll be paying out of my own pocket, but if I can get this to go smoothly, I'll sign the Dalton brothers, and this trip will be a drop in the bucket compared to what they have the potential to earn me.

The car rental line is short, which I think is a good thing. Until the guy at the desk points outside. At a fucking blizzard.

"Roads are closed until the storm clears," he says.

It takes all of my effort not to bang my head on the service desk and cry. I'm tired, my plan is all going to shit, and if I can't get to Buffalo by this afternoon when I'm meeting with Dalton before his game, I can kiss his contract goodbye. It doesn't matter if there's a blizzard or my flights changed or any other excuse I could use. Agents move mountains for their clients. So that means I'm going to have to move a blizzard for Dalton.

"What if I do all the paperwork now, and when it clears, I can take the car?" I ask.

The guy, Benedict by his name tag, doesn't even dignify that with a response, only sends a derisive look my way as if reading between the lines.

Don't know what he's reading, but it can't be that I would take the car before the storm passes. No way. It's not like I was going to rush out and drive immediately. I'd at least wait until his shift was over so he couldn't see me.

"Surely, if we landed in a plane in this storm, it's drivable."

"You were one of the last planes to land. Everyone else is being redirected to Buffalo now."

Motherfucker.

I stare up at the ceiling. "Okay, I get it now, all right? I'll check my damn emails from now on. Every single one of them."

When I lower my gaze back to Benedict, he looks even more worried. What, like talking to imaginary deities isn't a regular occurrence in his life?

"What about trains?" I ask.

"If the road to the train station isn't closed. And the trains are still running." He shrugs.

"Okay. So, train station. Where is that?"

"It's about five miles. There's a taxi stand outside. Dunno if they're taking rides though."

I grit my teeth and smile as politely as I can. "Thanks for all your help."

After today, Upstate New York is definitely not my most favorite place in the world.

Chapter 5

Fox

Sometimes when watching a potential client do their thing, it's like an out-of-body experience. Not only is their potential palpable, but it's mesmerizing. It's as if you're right beside them, watching them from in the middle of the court, the field, or in this case, the ice.

Emmett Dalton is green, there's no doubt about that, but he hasn't taken the conventional route to get here.

Everyone was sure Emmett and his twin brother were going to go to a D1 college, play hockey, and get drafted freshman year. They had top ten picks written all over them. But shocking everyone, the brothers decided to end their hockey careers when they graduated from high school. They both went to college, but after their junior year, Emmett returned to the hockey scene. He might have gotten a spot in Rochester because of who his older brother is —Buffalo's, and arguably the NHL's, number one player of his generation—but he's out there proving himself to be worthy of his spot.

For an athlete to come back after a three-year break and be so good at what he does in his first professional year, yeah, Emmett Dalton is going to be huge.

Of course, he still has too many turnovers, too many wide shots on goal, and he takes stupid penalties, but these are skills that can be honed. The natural talent he has is going to take him far. Eventually.

And I want to rep him.

I was on the fence before, and if it weren't for Archer Holloway trying to sneakily meet up with Asher Dalton, I probably wouldn't have chased Emmett down. But now that I have and I've seen him in person, I really want to represent him. Even if it means signing Asher too. I'm still hopeful that Emmett will want to step out on his own, do his own thing, but at the same time, if I were in his shoes, I would follow everything my incredibly successful older brother says. It's one thing to ignore the opinion of someone who doesn't know what they're talking about, but ignoring someone who has lived the life you want wouldn't be the best business move.

I'm going to tackle this pitch as if Emmett were my only goal, though, because if I go into a meeting with him, talking about signing both of them, he's going to think I came to him to get to his brother.

When the game ends with Rochester kicking Cleveland's ass, it already gives me an advantage. Pitching to someone who's on a high from a win is so much easier than pitching to someone coming off a loss.

Emmett has agreed via a brief email exchange to come to dinner with me at the Marriott, where his team is staying.

I leave long before he'd be out of the showers to make sure I'm in the hotel restaurant before him. Being late and making a client wait is the worst thing to do in this type of situation.

It is possible, though, that I might rush to get there a little too fast because as I get seated at the table and wait, and then wait some more, the pressure of this going well starts to get to me.

Which is ridiculous because up until a few hours ago, I wasn't completely sure we would be a good fit or that the only reason I was interested at all was to beat Archer to signing a client for once. Now that I definitely want Emmett Dalton on my roster because of his talent and future prospects, I have to close this deal. Or, if he's not ready to make a decision yet, to at least make myself memorable. More memorable than Archer will be.

I don't know if I have that kind of charisma in me, but where I lack in charm, I excel in business talk.

The team isn't quiet as they arrive and make a beeline for the hotel bar on the other side of the lobby. Through some widely spaced slats that make up a feature wall in the restaurant, I see Emmett break away from the group and head toward me.

I stand when the host directs Emmett my way, and we shake hands when he reaches me.

"Thank you for meeting with me," I say.

We take our seats, and Emmett immediately opens the menu, perusing while he speaks to me. "Damon warned us all that we would be approached by his agents trying to sell themselves, but I didn't think I would be one of them. I assumed everyone would go through Asher."

Emmett is only twenty-two, but with the long, curly blond hair tied in a man bun at the nape of his neck, his bright blue eyes, and the way he stares at me over the top of his menu, he looks every bit the kid brother who never gets his own say.

"I believe some of my colleagues have already been in contact with your brother, yes." I lean forward. "But I came directly to you." Before he gets the chance to ask why, I answer the question written all over his face. "I think you have an amazing hockey career ahead of you, and I want to be part of your team because I believe I can sell your talent without the mention of your last name or hockey legacy."

Emmett shifts uncomfortably. Maybe the first call of business is building his confidence.

"I ..." He hesitates. "I think I'm probably going to sign with whoever Asher tells me to."

"Whoever he tells you to or whoever he is signing with?"

"Is there a difference between those two things?"

"Yup. If you're going to sign with whoever Asher signs with, then I'm going to have to set up a meeting with him too. But if you're purely going on what his opinion is, then I'll still have to set up a meeting with him, but it will be a very different conversation than if I were trying to sign you both."

"Wait." Emmett's menu drops to the table and hits his cutlery with a loud *thunk*. "You're not trying to sign Asher as well?"

"If I'm honest, anyone at the firm can represent your brother. He has had a good career. Long career. He only has one or two contracts left in him. Buffalo loves him, and he was a key part of the franchise's rebuild. Anyone could rep him because he could demand whatever he wanted at this point in his career. I want to represent you because you're fresh. You're only starting out, and because you had those three years off, future teams are going to use that to their advantage to say you aren't experienced enough and lowball you with their offers. I won't let anyone do that to you."

I can practically see my words ticking over in his head.

"What happens if I hit a slump I can't seem to get out of and I only ever make it this far?"

"Sans you having a career-ending injury, touch wood"—I knock the table twice because I know how superstitious hockey players can be—"I'm not the type of agent to abandon a client so easily. If you're in a slump, I'll find you the best sports psychologist in the world. I'll get you an endorsement deal for some energy drink so that when you are back on top of your game again—and you will get back up there because all slumps end at some point—your ad will run, and the brand will love you for selling their drink."

"And if I don't get my game back up?"

"You're still a professional hockey player, and you can't get to this level you're at now without that drink. You'll sell it even if you are still in a slump. We can go over hypotheticals all night if you want to, but the bottom line is, I'm the type of agent who only wants to sign clients I believe in, and after seeing you play tonight, I know you have what it takes to make it to the big leagues if you surround yourself with the right team."

He's contemplative as he takes it all on board and then picks up his menu again. "The steak here is good. I have it every time we stay here."

"Then we'll get two orders of that."

"You mean for me, right? Two orders for me? You're paying, aren't you?"

I laugh. "Exactly what I meant, and yes. Well, technically, the firm is paying."

"In that case, I really will get two servings, please."

"No problem. You deserve it after that game. You put your all into it. Just like I will if you put your career in my hands."

He smiles, and even though he hasn't given me a definitive answer, I think I got through to him.

Chapter 6
Archer

After my flight ordeal and the car rental issue, I thought my luck was changing when I was able to get a cab to the train station and the trains were still running.

I should've canceled this fucking meeting because now I sit somewhere between Syracuse and Buffalo on a stalled train due to too much snow on the tracks to move.

The voice-over assures us we'll get moving again soon, but for fucking fuck's sake ... Maybe this is a sign from the universe that I shouldn't be going after Damon's highest-earning client.

It's true I've never repped an athlete of Asher Dalton's caliber before, but this could be my in. Dalton is someone with an established career, so it would be really difficult to fuck it up.

Because of who my family is, I've spent my entire time as a sports agent repping those who rely on endorsements or sponsorships for income. I've been killing it. But it's time I do something for myself. Bigger contracts mean I won't have to take on so many clients to still be bringing in the same revenue to the company and to my paycheck.

Money isn't everything, but even though my dad was a big superstar Olympian, my childhood wasn't luxurious. We weren't poor by any means, but considering swimming is the most watched

Olympic sport, Dad's income was next to nothing. He earned most of his money from other championship meets, but as a swimmer, if you're not hitting that podium with every race, every competition, you're paid peanuts. Dad was talented enough to be great, but it's not like he was Michael Phelps level of great. So yeah, we got by and that's it. I want more than that for me.

By some miracle, the train starts moving again, but it's so fucking slow that I'm sure I'm going to have to cancel this meeting with Asher Dalton. I already don't have time to go to the hotel first, so I'm going to have to change into my suit on the train and go straight to the arena, where I said I'd meet him before his game.

It's not like I can ask to delay the meeting when he has to be on the ice.

I'm doing math Olympics all the way in to Buffalo, and I can probably make it so long as traffic isn't shit once we arrive.

The bathrooms on this train are absolutely disgusting, tiny, and there's no way I can get my suit out of my bag without getting dirty toilet water all over it. Or my sweats if I so much as take them off.

Okay, so plan B. I'll change quickly at the arena.

Time ticks over, and I get so anxious I feel like I'm about to yell at someone who doesn't deserve it. Like the attendants not driving the train have any power over how fast we can go. Or can control the weather.

Come on, come on, come on.

It takes so long to arrive that when we do, I almost can't believe it. It's like sitting on a fourteen-hour flight where you think it's never going to end, and then all of a sudden, you're landing and you forget the trauma of being in economy for that long. That is, until you stand up and your legs protest from being up next to your ears the whole flight. Stupid long legs. Why couldn't I have been a short king? Travel would be so much easier.

Now to rush my ass to the arena, change into a wrinkly suit which will fucking suck, but it's better than no suit at all.

Normally, while waiting for a cab, if there's a family or an elderly person behind me, I'll let them take the first one—I'm not a completely heartless jerk—but I can't tonight. Not even when the small child being carried by his overloaded mother, dragging bags and luggage, yawns and rests his head on his mother's shoulder, his bright gray eyes staring at me. His cheeks are rosy from the cold, and—

Damn it.

"You go ahead before me," I say.

"Are you sure?"

I nod. "It's snowing, and it looks like you've got your hands full."

The look of gratitude is enough to know I did the right thing, even if I don't have the time to do it. Who knows? Maybe I'll win some karma points back because I've obviously pissed off some higher power.

Like I said to myself on the train. Maybe this is a sign I shouldn't be chasing the Daltons, but I'm not the kind of person to back down from a challenge.

So I'm going to try my hardest, give Asher my best pitch, and hopefully win him over.

If only the next cab would hurry up and get here.

Will I be pissed if that mother and child cost me this contract? Probably. But not at them. This whole trip has been one cluster-fuck after the other, and it's not like I have anyone else to blame but myself.

A new taxi pulls up, and I jump in the back, praying the roads aren't a complete disaster, but apparently, my karma points are still in the negative. I send Asher a text saying traffic is bad and I'm going to be a little late according to Google Maps, but now I have to decide whether I make it a lot late so I'm in my suit or meet a client while wearing sweatpants.

My oversized, thick, long black coat will cover most of the casual parts of my attire, so maybe I can get away with it.

I'm still flip-flopping between getting changed or running in as I am when we arrive at the arena, but ultimately, I decide to go in as I am. I can explain if I need to.

Security lets me into the players' and employee entry after showing them my business card—my real one, not one Maddox O'Shay made—along with my King Sports ID. He hooks me up with a visitor pass and sends me on my way.

Asher told me to go to the locker room and ask for him—agents aren't allowed to step inside the actual locker room—but on my way down the hall, loud yelling and a thumping sound echo from another direction. It is the sound of chaos among camaraderie, and when I hear someone yell, "Dalton, stop gunning for me," I reroute and head down a different hall to my left, where I think the sound is coming from.

There's a door propped open with a brick, and that's where I find him, inside an empty room with concrete flooring and half of Buffalo's NHL team, playing some game with a soccer ball.

Someone kicks it to Asher as I appear, and everyone's attention drops from the ball and goes to me. All except Asher, who does some crazy spin kick and sends the ball flying into his teammate's nose.

"Ah, fuck," Zak Moses says and grabs his face.

I wince. "Oops. Sorry for the interruption." Great start, Holloway. Come on, you're so much better than this.

Asher Dalton turns to me, a murderous look in his green eyes.

I raise my hand and wave awkwardly. "Hi. I'm Archer Holloway. I'm here for our meeting." I really wish my voice didn't crack at the end of that.

Dalton's brow crumples. "You're late." He glances down at my legs. "And you're wearing sweats."

Wrong choice. I should've gotten changed. "I've basically been traveling for the last twenty-four hours. Apparently, blizzards are a pain in the ass to navigate, so I apologize for my tardiness."

"There's a blizzard?" Asher asks.

"There is. In Syracuse."

His frown deepens. "Aren't you from LA?"

"It's a really long story I won't bore you with now. Mainly because we don't have the time. Your game is going to start soon."

"It is. It's why we're playing sewer ball. It keeps us loose. Want to join us? You can play while we talk. You are dressed for it."

Hard to miss the dismissive tone. I'm blowing this, but if Asher Dalton wants to make me jump hoops to make up for screwing him around, I'll do it.

I take off my jacket and lay it on top of my carry-on bag and then join the circle. "I'm in. But first, uh, what is sewer ball?"

The whole group laughs.

"Strike two," Asher says with what I'm hoping is a joking tone. "Can't have an agent who doesn't know what sewer ball is." He tilts his head my way. "Have you ever repped hockey players before?"

"I, uh ..." I rub the back of my neck.

"Some people know it as two-touch," another one of Asher's teammates says. I don't know his name off the top of my head. He must be a rookie, judging by his baby face. "I asked the same thing a few months ago."

Yup. Rookie it is.

"Oh, two-touch. Totally know that game." It's definitely something I've never not heard of, and I know all the rules. Yup. One hundred percent.

The game starts, and I hope I can follow without making myself look like too much of an idiot. The first thing I notice, though, is that no one is using their hands. And as someone who is an ex-water polo player who's used to using their hands and not their feet to play, I can already tell this isn't going to go well.

As predicted, it doesn't, and it's obvious Asher Dalton is loving every second of my humiliation.

While we play, it's impossible to get any actual productive conversation going. Which means when the time comes for him to suit up for his game, he says I'll have to meet him afterward if I want to pitch my services to him.

While Asher Dalton isn't outright being obvious that he's tormenting me, he's also not being subtle about it. He's skirting that line between testing me and downright torturing me, and there's not a damn thing I can do about it if I want to sign him to my roster.

I'm starting to understand why Brady wasn't interested in being co-agents with me on this one. He's not a masochist like I am.

I regret all my life choices.

No, wait, no I don't. I love my life. I regret all the choices over the last few days that have led me here.

To a bar.

Babysitting a bunch of drunk hockey players.

When Dalton said his partner, Kole, was coming out after his shift at the hospital, I thought, "Amazing. Someone levelheaded to help me tame the beasts that are six-foot men drinking their weight in alcohol."

Boy, was I fucking wrong.

Kole and Dalton were made for each other because the second Kole showed up, he made it his mission to get as drunk as his partner and wasted no time catching up. To the point I fear for his liver. He's a doctor, for fuck's sake. Shouldn't he know his body can't metabolize that much alcohol so quickly?

This is fine. Everything is ... great.

I haven't slept in over twenty-four hours, I'm blowing this pitch, and nothing screams unprofessional more than literally trying to herd cats. I mean hockey players.

They might as well be cats. When I shove two glasses of water in front of Dalton and Kole, I'm half expecting them to swat them off the table. Dalton would totally look me in the eye as he did it too.

Surprising me, though, they take the water without complaint.

If they switch to water now, maybe they'll sober up enough in another hour for me to get them home.

If this is what repping Dalton is going to be like, I'm not sure I could handle his account. How did Damon do it for so long?

"I have a brilliant idea!" Dalton says, smacking the glass of water back down on the table.

"If it's drink more, I'm going to have to say no." I rub my temples.

"Yeah, that's something you probably should've done two hours ago. It's even better than drinking. Who misses poor old married Quinnie?" he asks his teammates, who all let out a cheer. "I think he needs a visit from his old team. How dare he retire at the perfectly respectable age of thirty-five? He should be here with us! Let's go drag him out of bed."

There are more cheers, and I realize my night is far, far from over.

We lose half the team somewhere along the way, but that's fine. Fewer cats to wrangle.

"Are we sure this is a good idea?" I ask as I force my way in front of Moses so I can get in the same cab as Dalton and Kole.

"Quinnie will love it." Dalton beams at me, which tells me one of two things. He's so drunk that he's physically incapable of doing his usual permanent scowl or—

"Why do I get the feeling that's a lie?"

Kole laughs as he climbs into the cab and shuffles over, and we follow behind him.

As I close the door, and Dalton rattles off an address, Kole leans around his partner and says to me, "Quinn won't care. Vance, on the other hand? The BAHs are going to hear about this, for sure."

"Bars? Like the one we just left?"

"Not bars. Baaaahs. B-A-H ssss. Boyfriends and husbands. If women can have the WAGs, we can have the BAHs."

Dalton makes a sound like a sheep.

I'm about ready to wave my white flag.

As we pull up in three cabs to a dark house in a fancy neighborhood, I don't even have the energy anymore to try to stop this.

I'm either overtired, or I'm hallucinating, but Dalton climbs the side of Quinn's house like Spider-Man and jumps onto the balcony on the second floor like it's the easiest thing he's ever done.

Then, leaning over the railing and looking back down on us, he says, "Aww, babe. Do you remember when we were in college and your dad was my coach, and he came home while we were fucking, and I had to climb out the window?"

"And then you broke the porch gutters and had to run to your car practically naked? It's the moment I knew I loved you."

That's ... weirdly sweet.

"This is like that! But in reverse!" Dalton yells, probably waking up the whole neighborhood.

Whether Dalton picks the lock or has a key, or maybe it was unlocked, he gets inside through the balcony sliding door and, a couple of minutes later, shows up at the front door to let us all in, and ... he's holding a toddler.

What the fuck?

Yet, instead of running away, I enter the house because I don't want the neighbors to see a group of men huddled outside in the middle of the night. I'm waiting for the police to show up at any moment.

Is it still considered breaking and entering if you know the person? Not that I know the person. Is a B and E a felony? I stare at the kid, who is sleeping on Dalton's shoulder. What about kidnapping?

"How about we put the baby back where you found him, leave a note for your friend Quinn to say hi, bye, whatever, and then we can get out of here and pretend this never happened."

Dalton screws up his face. "If we pretend it never happened, how would we explain the note?" He turns to Kole. "I don't think this agent is very smart. Maybe I shouldn't sign with him."

At this point, I'm almost ready to say, "Please don't."

Suddenly, the child wakes up and sees us. Even if he's met these other men before, it must be a shock to wake up to us all. So of course, he starts screaming his little head off.

"No, no, baby," Dalton coos. It is really fucking weird seeing a paternal side of this man who literally fights on the ice and glowers at anyone who comes near him. "I'm your funcle Fasher. I mean Dasher. *Asher*."

"Make it shut up," one of Dalton's teammates hisses. Honestly, he's probably louder than the baby.

I should've protested harder. I should have walked away when I was late to the meeting and knew Dalton wasn't going to make this easy on me. But no. I had to try to win him over. I had to do what he said. And for what? To get an account I don't even know if I want anymore?

Why must this stubborn streak of mine take over all logical thought when I want something?

The baby only screams louder, and Dalton looks at me, wide-eyed.

"I think I broke my godson. Here. You fix him." He hands *me* the fucking baby.

Me.

I don't know shit about kids.

The child continues to scream, and I awkwardly pat his back and glance from one drunk hockey player to the next and then land on the doctor.

"Can't you help?"

Kole sways on his feet. Guess not. I'm not handing a screaming baby over to someone who can barely stand.

From upstairs somewhere, footsteps louder than a herd of elephants come running.

Two men, both in only underwear, holding a hockey stick each, appear at the top of the curved stairs.

"What the fuck are you all doing here?" the older-looking one yells. "And who the fuck is that holding my child?"

That would be me. "Uh ... hi. I'm, uh—"

"We miss you, Quinnie."

The younger guy facepalms. "You do know Vance is going to tell Coach about this, right? Thank fuck I'm retired because I won't have to be there for the punishment."

Vance comes down the stairs, glare only scarier as he gets closer.

I hand over his child without a word.

It's only then I learn that Quinn's husband? Yeah, he's the

head trainer for Buffalo, and I've somehow walked into Dalton's trap. Not only will he and his teammates be punished for this tomorrow, but what are the chances he won't hold this over my head, being I'm the only sober one?

What am I doing here?

No, really. What the fuck am I doing?

Chapter 7
Fox

I usually hate flying into LAX, and wherever possible, I ask Edele to book me flights in or out of Burbank, but after what I think was a super-successful trip, I'm refreshed, dressed for the office, and excited to get back to work.

I'm in such a good mood that nothing will bring me down. Not even having to duck and weave my way through the clusterfuck of people at the arrivals hall.

There's a spring in my step as I swerve to miss a family with a billion screaming children, but because I'm too focused on not stepping on little feet, I miss the grown-ass person next to me and practically knock them into a wall.

"I'm so sor—" I'm cut off by an unusual sight. Not unusual because running into a coworker at an airport isn't a huge coincidence, but unusual because Archer Holloway has a giant scowl on his face. "Rough flight?"

"Don't even get me started." He has massive bags under his eyes, his suit is wrinkled, his breath is rank, and a teeny tiny part of me might feel bad for him.

The bigger part, however, is a little curious and excited that his work trip might not have been as positive as mine. Does that make me petty? Probably.

"Where are you coming from? Syracuse?" Is he going to keep up the lie?

"Why are you being chatty?" he grumbles. "You usually only yell at me."

True. "Even I won't kick a man when he's ..." My gaze rakes over him. Even as a total mess, he's still attractive. How is that fucking fair? "Down? Are you down? Tired?"

"Is that your way of saying I look like shit? Thanks."

"Not at all. You're usually just so perky. It's almost like we've body swapped."

"Wait, where are you coming from? I didn't see travel on your work schedule."

"Do you even look at the schedule?"

He relents. "Fair point."

I nod toward the exit. "You heading to the office and want to split a cab?"

"We really have body swapped if you're willing to share space with me."

"Either that or seeing you disheveled for once is kinda nice. Plus, it's an expensive ride all the way to the office. Gotta cut company costs wherever possible." Even if I'm coming from a two-night trip that was only supposed to be one. But hey, I have to make up that difference somewhere. Plus, I want to find out why Archer looks terrible.

It probably says something about me that I'm so giddy over it. Did he screw up his meeting with the older Dalton while mine with the younger one was amazing?

"Fine. But I don't want to talk about what happened."

"Oh, then I'm out. There's no fun in that."

Archer blinks at me, and a smile slowly spreads across my face.

"I don't think I like when you're in a good mood. Go back to being the uptight person I know. It's freaking me out."

"Sorry. I'll try." Yet, the happiness surrounds me like a cloak.

We head for the taxi stand and get in line, which is about a hundred people deep. Again, normally I'd be stressing about getting to work on time or people cutting the line, bumping into me, being rude, but today, it all slides off my back.

It is surprising to me, though, when Archer steps aside and lets the family behind us jump ahead.

I cock my head. "Are ... are you nice to ... children?"

"What? You under the impression I eat them for breakfast?"

"No. But you don't let anyone get in your way of what you want. I assumed that included children as well."

Finally, for the first time this morning, I see that cocky smile of his he usually likes to give me when he's doing something particularly evil. Like scheming behind my back.

"Kids are where I earn my karma points from walking all over everyone else."

"And what's the score?" We take a small step forward in the line.

"Score?"

"How many karma points do you think that earned you?" I gesture to the family in front of us. "And how many karma points did you lose by lying about going to Syracuse when you went to Buffalo instead?"

Archer's face drops.

I have to hold back a laugh. "Come on, Holloway. You didn't really think you were being subtle, did you?"

His gaze narrows. "Where were you really?"

I lift one shoulder. "Cleveland."

"Wait, Cleveland? Then how did you know I—I mean, what makes you think I was in Buffalo?"

"You mean other than it not being a secret that you will do anything to get as many clients as possible? A complete buffet of available clients was presented to us, and you put down 'scouting trip at SU.' The only logical conclusion was you picked somewhere close to where you were really going, which was Buffalo. Or Rochester. But Rochester wasn't playing in Rochester, which only left Buffalo, which meant you were going after Asher Dalton. It was all confirmed when I saw Edele had booked you to Buffalo instead of Syracuse. Don't worry. I set her straight."

Archer stumbles backward, his mouth agape. "You were the reason my flights got all mixed up? *You.*"

"Aww, someone jealous they didn't think of doing that to me first?"

He goes to talk, his mouth opening, but then he deflates. "A little. But what I hate more is that I got stranded in Syracuse because of a blizzard, I almost missed my meeting with Asher Dalton, and then he made me pay for it dearly in stupid games and a night of drunken antics where I had to babysit grown-ass men on no f—" He glances at the kids from the family in front of us. "—flipping sleep."

My smugness from having outsmarted the man for once dies with each word he says. "Y-you ended up going to Syracuse? Didn't Edele ask you to confirm your flights?"

He averts his gaze as he says, "I was kinda busy trying to get ahead of work, knowing I was going to be gone for a day and a half."

Okay, guilt is easing now. "You didn't check your flight details before you left? Have they studied you? Like, psychologically, I mean. Because that has to be sociopathic behavior. Surely."

"Are you saying with every single email Edele sends through to you, you read and take note of every little change? She emails through if the flight changes by five minutes."

I can't hold it in any longer. I start laughing. "So you ended up in Syracuse?"

He grits his teeth. "Yes. In a blizzard. Couldn't rent a car and had to get a train, which kept stopping because of too much snow. Then, when I was late to meet with Dalton, he sent me on a wild goose chase all night as punishment. I haven't slept in two days."

Yup. Definitely glad I chose Emmett Dalton.

"Sounds to me like your karma points are so far in the negative you're going to have to do a lot more than give up your spot in line."

"After what you did to me, you should look out for a karma bus while crossing the road."

If I believed in things like karma, he might be right, but I like to think I'm a decent person when it comes to everyone else.

"I thought the most that would happen is I'd give you a mild inconvenience of having to explain to Edele why the calendar didn't match your requested destination. How was I to know you don't check your flights? Which, again, sociopathic behavior. Did you sign Dalton, at least?"

"No. After dragging him, his partner, and a bunch of other Buffalo players home at dawn, he told me he'd think about it and get back to me. I haven't cried since my grandfather's funeral, but I came close in that moment."

"Do you think he ever made Damon follow him around like a puppy for an entire night?" I ask. Because there is no way. Agents don't need to be authority figures for their clients, but they do need to at least be respected.

"I'm not getting that contract, am I?"

I shrug. "You might not want it anyway."

"I was beginning to think that myself."

"If Dalton is testing you this early and you let him get away with it, what do you think a working relationship with him will be like?"

He gives a single nod. "Yeah, you're right."

I cup my ear. "I'm sorry. What? I can't have heard you correctly."

"Shut up."

"No, I'm serious." I'm almost speechless. Almost. "I think that's the first time you've ever said that to me."

"To be fair, it's the first time it's the truth."

For once, in the whole time I've known Archer Holloway, I laugh at one of his jokes.

We finally get to the front of the line, and the next taxi that pulls up is ours. The driver takes our carry-on bags and puts them in the trunk while we climb into the back seat.

My phone in my pocket rings, and I fish it out before getting into the car, but when I see Mom on the screen, I send it to voicemail. Not because I don't want to talk to her—I do, but not in front of Archer. And not when I have to tell her that I'm not going to be able to make it home. Again. It's been almost a year since I've been back to Arizona. I've been way too busy with work. Mom and Dad say they understand, but I still feel guilty anyway. I keep telling myself and them that once I'm in a completely established position with a stable client roster, I'll be able to make more time to go see them.

"Out of curiosity," Archer says as he clicks his seat belt in place, "who did you go to see in Cleveland?"

I grin. "Emmett Dalton. The sane Dalton brother."

Archer throws his head back in defeat.

It's the only time I've ever felt like I've won against him.

Chapter 8
Archer

I was outplayed by Lincoln Fox. The same Lincoln Fox who ridicules me for playing the same game. If the whole thing wasn't so absurd, I'd be pissed. Instead, I'm kind of ... impressed?

He's definitely impressed with himself if his smug expression is anything to go by. We crawl through traffic on the way to the office, and I can't help looking over at him. His silent gloating is written all over his face.

"You know, if the roles were reversed here and I'd sent you on some wild goose chase all over Upstate New York, you'd put in an official complaint about me. Welcome to my level. Hope you didn't have to stoop too far."

"Pfft. I have never once put in an official complaint about you. I'm playing by your rules here."

"Have you really never put in an official complaint against me? Every time you storm out of my office, I picture you going to HR. I've been waiting for them to come to me with a thick folder labeled *Lincoln Fox's list of grievances.*"

His exasperated sigh is one I'm used to hearing from him. "Sorry to burst your fantasy and obvious obsession over what I do or think, but you're under the false impression that once I leave your office, you're still under my skin."

There's the guy I'm used to. "Ouch. But fair enough. Here I was thinking I made your life a living hell."

"You wish you were that important."

He's got me there, but this is an interesting revelation. This whole time, I thought he held a grudge against me when I'm no more than a thorn in his side. That's more disappointing than I'd like to admit.

Do I want Lincoln Fox to hate me? No. But hate is better than indifference. Indifference means I don't affect him. He affects me. Always has. Only, it's not until this moment that I realize it might not be in a bad way.

Part of my drive comes from wanting to be better than the best. And there's no doubt Lincoln Fox is my biggest competitor at our associate level.

It almost makes me want to try harder to get his attention—negative or positive—but even I know there's a fine line between being charmingly annoying and pushing the boundaries too far. One day, he really will make an official complaint about me.

"You're in a really good mood today," I point out. "You get laid in Cleveland?" Hmm, is that pushing a boundary too far? By the way he glares at me, I'm going to go with yes.

"Okay, one, inappropriate. Two, none of your business. And three, maybe my good mood is because, unlike other people in this car, I had a productive work trip."

"Ooh, are you saying you landed Emmett Dalton?"

"I am so not giving you intel on that, and I'm not counting my chickens when nothing was signed. All I will say is that we had a good meeting."

"But nothing was signed. So you're saying there's still a chance for me to sign both Dalton brothers." Though the point he made about letting Asher walk all over me still stands.

I blame my lack of sleep on my poor judgment, thinking I was going above and beyond for a potential client. That is what it takes sometimes, but there's a big difference between professionalism and getting into personal territory. We barely got a chance to talk business strategy.

"Why do you even want to represent them?" Fox sounds like he's talking through gritted teeth or trying not to growl at me. Could be both. "They're not exactly your usual clientele."

"I've had hockey players on my roster before," I argue. Sure, they were draft hopefuls who quickly fell through the ranks in the juniors only to end up in the ECHL, earning less than twenty thousand a year, with ten percent of that going to me. It almost felt criminal to take money from them, but I still put in effort and deserve to be paid for it. My go-to move with the lower-ranked athletes is to get them some speaking gigs at high schools, community programs, and things like that. They didn't pay well either, but most of the ECHL guys are young and still have parental support. Plus, the ECHL houses them. Setting them up to be a content creator for their sport—I will cut a bitch who ever calls them influencers—is another I like to do, but going viral and building that following enough to get paid for it is tough. It's a matter of throwing everything at the wall and hoping something sticks.

"Do you think negotiating contracts for the ECHL is remotely of the same caliber as the AHL or NHL?" Fox asks.

"Of course not, but just because I haven't negotiated a contract as high as Asher's before, that doesn't mean I can't. I can do anything I set my mind to." And I have. Look at all I've already accomplished.

Fox mutters, "I actually don't doubt that one bit."

Whether it's a need to defend myself or maybe rationalize why I believe I'm good enough to rep the big leagues, my mouth keeps talking, even though he's not being completely transparent with me. I owe him nothing. "If you must know, I want more clients. Bigger names. If I'm going to make the same wage as someone like you, I need to step up my game."

"Like me? You earn a lot more than me in commissions. I've done the numbers."

"Yes, but did you do the math on how many clients you have compared to me versus income?"

He hesitates. "Not ... exactly, but I always figured you go for the low-hanging fruit. Quantity over quality."

"Damn. Elitist much?"

"No, it's not that. I mean that in the bigger leagues, you have more responsibility and need more time to focus on your clients. If you have athletes in the minors or on Olympic teams or a sport that doesn't pay well, your job is easier, meaning you can have more clients. That's what I mean."

"Yup. And I'm still calling you elitist. You think repping someone who barely makes a living wage is easier than repping the guys who make millions? Really? You want to know the real reason I'm going after someone like Asher Dalton? Because with his commission, I might be able to afford to dedicate more time to those who really need it. The ones who aren't famous enough to get multimillion-dollar endorsement deals and have to do mall appearances or go viral online to support themselves."

The crease in Fox's brow deepens, and he goes to say something, but no sound comes through his parted lips.

"No dig at me for that?"

He blinks away whatever he was concentrating so hard on. "How can I have a dig at you over a perspective I've never contemplated before?"

"You always seem to find a way to point out how I am morally bankrupt and have somehow screwed *you* over."

"In my defense, you go about getting clients the way you did with the Daltons, and it literally feels like you're trying to undermine me and every other agent in the office. I had on the calendar that I was meeting with Jeramiah Castleberry, only to get an email from you the day it was supposed to happen, saying you had already signed him."

"Why can't we pitch the same athlete and let them choose who they want to sign with? Either way, that commission is coming to the firm."

He grunts. "We can, but it's about common courtesy. Besides, you didn't let Jeremiah choose because you made him sign before he'd even met with me. If you really believed in the bullshit you spout, you would've let me have that meeting."

Even I have to admit that he has a point. Reluctantly. "Have you always been this smart? I'm not used to you coming to me with logic. Only yelling."

"It's so shocking that I yell at you when you are that complimentary about my smarts."

"I wish I could say I hate this whole side of you, Fox, but I can't. You should be logical and calm more often."

The cab pulls up to our office building, and Fox taps the business card to pay. But as we get out and pull our carry-on bags from the trunk, he shakes his head at me.

"You know the best way to make someone stay calm and level-headed? Maybe don't tell them they should be calm and logical." Fox stalks away, close to stomping but holding back as if trying to show that he's not as riled up as I think he is.

I can't help myself because I love when he's wrong. "Tell me that thing again how I don't get under your skin."

He doesn't respond and keeps on walking.

Why or how our back-and-forth fills me with energy, I'll probably never know, but I do know that our interaction will keep me going until the end of the day. Then I can go home and crash to sleep off the worst work trip I've ever had.

Chapter 9
Fox

Just when I think I'm getting through to Archer or that I might have the upper hand, he goes and pisses me off again.

Am I being a little too sensitive? Maybe. But he's exhausting.

Still, I'm determined not to let him get to me. Not after my meeting with Emmett Dalton went so well. I'm going to ride that high for as long as it lasts.

One point Archer made sticks out in my mind though, and I can't help the tiny amount of respect I gained for him because of it. The exceeding number of clients he has is because he wants to make extra money for those who can't rely on salary alone.

It makes sense the more I think about it. His father was an Olympian, his sister too. Apparently, his brothers are making waves in the diving pool—pun intended. And yes, I hate that I know all there is to know about his family, even though he doesn't talk about them much. He reps all three of his siblings, but I've never seen any of them step foot inside this office. Or maybe he does talk about them, just not with me. I can't say I blame him. I'm quick to judge, and that's perhaps a flaw of mine I could work on.

Unlike some people, I can admit I'm not perfect. If Archer were ever to do that, I'd be finding a bomb shelter as soon as possible to wait out the impending apocalypse.

I dump my stuff in my office and go to the break room to make myself a latte in the espresso machine. Some agents in the office only use it when they have clients coming in, but I prefer my coffee strong, and the instant drip stuff is neither strong nor tasty. I think the ones who drink that stuff only do it because they're too lazy to clean the machine after using it.

"I will pay you a thousand dollars to make me one too," comes a voice I know all too well. Usually, it makes me cringe, but after one shared cab ride, I might be cured from the ick. Total ick anyway. He's still a douchenozzle.

I turn to Archer. "Why don't you go down the block to the café if you don't want to make it yourself?"

"It's too far."

I roll my eyes. "Whatever. Sit. I'll make you one."

He hesitates. "I won't actually have to pay you a thousand dollars though, will I?"

"You? Full of empty promises? Never would've guessed that."

Luca gasps in the corner. "Did it actually happen? Did you two finally hook up?" He taps Buck's shoulder to get his attention. "Quick, look up who had February as the month they'd do it."

I frown. "What's happening?"

Archer takes a seat next to Luca and slaps him upside the head. "It's nothing. It's that stupid office bet I was telling you about."

"What exactly is the bet?" I get to work on our two coffees, pushing the button on the machine for it to grind the coffee beans into a powder.

Luca answers with something so ridiculous I know I had to have heard it wrong. It doesn't help that the loud whirring sound from the coffee grinder drowns half of it out, but it can't have been what I think I heard.

"I'm sorry, can you repeat that?"

"It's true," Archer says. "Everyone thinks we're going to end up having a one-night stand, date, or ..." He turns his head toward Luca. "You said marriage was even on the table, wasn't it?"

"Yeah, but no one's actually dumb enough to bet on that one. Brady and Thad have both split a bet on you two killing each other at one point."

While Archer laughs it off, the good mood surrounding my meeting with Emmett plummets to the floor, but I'm not going to give them the satisfaction of letting them know they're all fucking idiots. Except for Thad and Brady, of course. They're closest to what's more likely to happen between Archer and me. Though they, too, missed the mark.

"Please." I put on the best front I can. "Like going to prison for Holloway would be worth it." I turn my back to the three of them and focus on the coffee.

"Good point," Buck says. "We should add a new bet for physical assault. That's more likely than murder."

"I dunno," Archer says. "I have pretty good odds on me murdering you two right about now. Where can I put money on that?"

By the time I'm finished making the coffees and wipe down the machine, Luca and Buck have left, and I'm thankful I don't have to sit with them and make small talk. Come to think of it, I don't have to sit here and make small talk with Archer either.

"Thanks," he says as I hand over his mug.

"No problem. It's the least I can do, considering you haven't slept for two days because of me."

"The very least."

"Enjoy it." I turn to leave.

"You know the bet is only a joke, don't you? No one actually believes you and I would hook up. If they do, they need to see a psychologist. Or a psychiatrist. Which is the one that can prescribe drugs? I always get them mixed up."

"I know it's a joke." On my way out, I glance at him over my shoulder. "And it's a psychiatrist who can prescribe meds." I leave, even more agitated than before for the most irrational of reasons.

I can say there's no chance of us hooking up ever because, well, it's true, but when Archer says that same truth, it ... hurts? Like, what is it about me that's so damn unfuckable in his eyes? He'd be fucking lucky to have me.

Maybe I'm the one who needs a psychiatrist.

I get to my office and go to close the door behind me when

Archer steps through. "Are you lost? Your office is back the other way."

"Nope. Not lost. We weren't done with our conversation."

"We weren't? Do you have a word count you have to hit each day?" I leave the door open and head behind my desk.

"As annoying as you might see me, I need to be sure that you're okay with this whole bet thing. I had nothing to do with it, but the way you shut down back there ..."

"I didn't shut down." Ugh. Why do I have to sound so petulant? "I'm just not into entertaining the idea as much as you are."

"Because the bet is about me?" The slight tremble in his normally confident tone makes it occur to me that he might not be okay with me saying how ridiculous the idea of us is either. Even if it is ridiculous.

"No, because it's the same as the business card. Yes, it's a joke, but it also comes across like they don't take me seriously as an agent. Or as a human being."

"Do you remember what I said a few days ago about the business cards? If all they have to put on your card is that you should marry me, you have nothing to worry about when it comes to your work ethic. How do you think I feel being called out over my competitiveness?"

"I assume you don't care."

"Do I like that people might hold a grudge against me for whatever reason? Of course I don't. But do I lose sleep if I have to screw over other people to reach my goal? Generally, no. I *can* be heartless that way. Probably because of the way I was brought up. But the reason I do it almost guilt-free is because I also know how to compartmentalize and not take work stuff personally. It's just business."

"I *hate* that saying. It's basically the work equivalent of 'No offense, but I don't give a shit about you.' Oh, sure, no offense taken."

"That's not it." Archer runs a hand through his bleached blond hair. "I think I'm losing my point, but the gist of this whole bet thing is not to sweat it. It's not personal."

"And my point is I know that, but it doesn't make me any less self-conscious about it."

He stares blankly at me. "I wish I could help with that, but I don't have that problem, and other than telling you to let it go, which I know won't help at all, I've got nothing."

"Then why are you still in my office?"

There's a knock on the door behind Archer, but I can't see who it is because he's blocking them. When he steps aside, Thad still has his hand up from knocking, as if he's frozen from walking into this bizarre situation where Archer is in *my* office for once.

When we both turn our attention to him, Thad breaks out of his trance. "Sorry to interrupt. I was hoping to get a word in with Fox, but I can come back."

"It's okay, we're done here," I say.

Archer turns back to me. "Were we?"

"Yup. Bye."

He sarcastically says, "Such love," and forms a love heart with his hands over his chest as he backs out of the room.

"That was ..." Thad's gaze follows him. "Weird. There was no yelling or anything."

"I don't yell at him. Why does everyone keep saying that I do?"

Thad throws his hands up like a busted perp. "Just saying, that conversation *almost* sounded ... friendly?"

"'Almost' being the operative word in that sentence. I was kicking him out when you showed up. What do you need?"

He sits opposite me at my desk, but as soon as his butt is in that chair, his knee bounces so violently I'm worried he has an electrode stuck to his spine.

"Are you okay?"

"Yep. Good, good. All fine."

"Uh-huh. Then why are you so nervous?"

Being my mentee, he has access to all of my client files, contracts, and everything in between. I didn't have to give him all that access, but if he learns better seeing than being told, I wasn't going to deny him that. Now, I'm wondering if I should have. If he tells me he accidentally deleted all my files or corrupted some data, I might cry. Literally.

"What? I'm not nervous."

I nod toward his leg. "No?"

He shifts in his seat and stops the bouncing. "Okay, fine. Do you remember me telling you when I started here how I have a brother in LA?"

"Vaguely." My panic over my possibly deleted business files eases.

"It's a long story, but the short of it is, he stole a bunch of money from our parents so he could move out here and pursue an acting career. When I moved to LA, my mom asked to try to find Wylder because he'd cut off all contact."

"And you haven't found him yet? Do you need some time off to go looking?"

"No, it's not that. I ... I did find him. And ... he's not ... I mean, he's fine, but he ..."

"Whatever it is, you can tell me. I'll help in any way I can."

"Obviously, he didn't become this huge movie star, and he's run out of the money he took from our parents, and he needs a job, and I know he could apply through HR, but he isn't qualified for anything, but maybe he could be an office assistant or your personal assistant if you needed one or ..." He takes a deep breath. "Actually, you know what, never mind. I'd hate to put his name forward and then have him do something stupid like steal from the company or pawn your work laptop. You're right. It's not a good fit." He stands and goes to leave when I let out a laugh.

I don't mean to, but it slips out. "Thad, come back here. Sit."

He does as I say.

"You do realize you had that whole conversation on your own, right? I didn't even get a chance to tell you that I don't need a personal assistant."

"Oh look, now you have. It's no problem at all. I feel terrible for even asking and putting you in this position and—"

"That's not to say this office doesn't need someone extra. There are a lot of small things that could be done around the place, but we'd need justification for Cam and Xavier to put in the request for another employee." I lean back in my chair as an idea comes to me. "Holloway could use someone, even if it's only to check his emails every day." I smile as I recall him telling me the shit he had to go through all because he didn't open Edele's emails. "You should ask him."

Thad is hesitant, his eyes narrowing. "Is this ... some kind of torture plan you want played out on Holloway?"

I laugh again. "What?"

"I tell you that my thieving younger brother needs a job, and you send me in Holloway's direction."

"Hey, I'm trying to help you. If your brother is a thief like you say, he won't have a job for long, will he? And stealing from your boss is a little different than stealing from your parents. Doesn't every kid do that at some point?"

"Uh, maybe when they're a teen, not a twenty-one-year-old college dropout with parental issues and resentment of his older brother because he got everything handed to him growing up."

Damn. "Being an only child, I have no idea what that's like, but again, if his resentment comes from family issues, maybe he won't be like that with an employer. You know him better than I do, of course."

"That's just it. I don't really know him at all. We were never close growing up."

"Can I ask a personal question, then?"

He nods.

"Why are you trying to get him a job here?"

"I owe it to him?"

"Is that a question or a statement?"

His lips twitch. "Both? Growing up, my parents threw everything into giving me the baseball career I wanted, and then it didn't work out. Wylder has always resented me for taking our parents' time, their money for baseball coaches and private lessons and equipment. Because of me, I guess, he felt neglected by them, and I want to give him what our parents couldn't because they were too busy with my dreams and giving me money toward my future."

I lean back in my seat and sip from my mug of coffee that's quickly going cold. "And what's that? What did they give you that they didn't give him?"

"A leg up. No, I didn't end up making it to major league baseball, but because of them, I had the chance. I want to give him a chance."

"Okay."

He's more admirable than I am, but I also don't know what it's like to have a sibling. It's easy for me to say what I think I'd do in his situation.

"Talk to Holloway. See if he has something for him. Even if he doesn't, surely asking will win you some brownie points with your brother."

"I hope so."

Chapter 10
Archer

When Thad came to me yesterday after his talk with Fox, I thought for sure I was being set up. Hiring the brother of his junior agent? Total spy move. Then I remembered that Fox is nothing like me, and the only sabotage he's ever done was by accident.

So I said yes.

And that's why I'm now standing here with Camden and Xavier outside the elevators on our floor, waiting for this Wylder kid to show up for his interview.

The truth is, we could use an extra set of hands around the office, but not to check my emails, fuck you very much, Fox. Reception can get really busy between client meetings and fielding phone calls. Usually, an intern jumps in to cover Sandy when they can, but it would be better for them to be focused on clients than office grunt work.

The elevator dings, and as the doors open, Thad and who I hope is his brother are ... wrestling? Fighting? Trying to pull each other's hair?

I have no idea what I'm watching.

Thad pushes Wylder off him when he realizes they're no longer alone and shoves a hair tie into Wylder's hand, saying something under his breath that sounds like, "Tame your bird's nest."

I chortle while Cam and Xavier remain professional.

Looking at the brothers side by side as they approach, they couldn't be more different. Thad is muscular, with short, slicked-back hair and a chest tattoo barely hidden by his undershirt. Wylder is shorter, not by a lot but an inch or two, his hair is a wild mess of dark curls, but as he ties it back, underneath that bird's nest —as Thad put it—is a close shave. He's not only smaller in height but in physique as well. I can only guess that the suit Wylder is wearing is Thad's. He's swimming in the jacket, and the belt strangling his small frame bunches the waistband of his pants. Or maybe the oversized '80s suit is the look he's going for, and I'm so out of touch I didn't know that look was back in.

Wylder hasn't lifted his eyes yet, but when Thad says, "Camden, Xavier, and Archer, this is my brother, Wylder," and elbows him, Wylder finally looks up, and that's where the family resemblance lies: in their pale blue eyes.

They stand out more on Wylder with his darker hair, and while twenty-one-year-olds are not my thing, I can still acknowledge that those eyes are hauntingly beautiful.

Wylder clears his throat. "Nice to meet you all."

Thad turns to his brother with an expectant look, prompting him to say something else.

"Oh, and thank you for this opportunity."

I'm back on the idea that Fox suggested this as a form of sabotage because I'm not sure Wylder wants to be here, and he could be a pain in the ass more than any help.

"Welcome," Cam says. "Let's take this into the conference room."

Thad steps forward to go with us when Cam's hand lands softly on his shoulder to stop him.

"We won't need you for this. You can get to work."

The parting look Thad gives his brother is one of pleading for him not to fuck this up. It reminds me so much of how my father used to look at all four of us kids, so I'm quick to gain a soft spot for Wylder.

Once we're seated in the conference room, Wylder's stature

seems small sitting opposite the three of us at the table. He looks intimidated as hell, which is fair enough, considering we're the ones with the power to hire him.

"Why don't you tell us a little about yourself?" Xavier starts.

I hate that question in interviews. Be more specific. Do you want to know where he went to school, or are you asking if he likes to sacrifice goats on the weekend? Wylder doesn't look like the sacrificial ritual type, but you never know.

"Uh, I'm, umm, not sure how much Thad told you about me, but I moved out here in search of my big break, and ... it's not going well. Obviously." He turns his hand up, gesturing as to why he's sitting here with us.

"You a musician or an actor?" Xavier asks.

"Actor." His smile lights up his whole face. "I can't carry a tune to save my life."

"So no office karaoke for you, then," Cam jokes, and Wylder's shoulders visibly relax.

It's hard to get a read on the guy. I can't tell if he's nervous because he wants to be here or if it's because he doesn't.

"What about college?" Cam asks. "Did you do an arts degree, or—"

He dips his gaze as he says, "Dropped out."

Cam and Xavier share a look, and I can tell Wylder's losing them already.

I step in, hoping to help the poor guy. "Do you have office experience?"

"Uh, no."

Damn it, kid. Lie if you have to.

As if sensing the tension in the room about his qualifications, he perks up. "But I'm a techie person, so if I need to learn computer programs or whatever, it will be no problem. The rest ... I can figure it out. I didn't drop out of college because it was too diffi- cult. I dropped out because I realized a degree wasn't going to get me what I wanted."

"Which is to be famous?" Cam asks. "Are you still going to pursue that career while working here?"

"I-I hope to." Wylder's focus ping-pongs around the room. "I-I was under the impression this is an entry-level job. Is that not true?"

"It is," Cam says. "And the role we're filling has a lot of flexibility. While technically, you'll be hired under an administrative assistant for Archer here, it's essentially a floating position. You'll go where you're needed. But it's good to know up front if you're only going to be here for the paycheck or if you're going to want advancement to a more permanent position. Do you even know much about sports or the sporting industry?"

I don't think he needs to be passionate about sports to make sure everyone has their coffee in the morning.

"I know some from when my brother played baseball. All the hoops he had to jump through to try to get drafted. What happened when he was nowhere near good enough. The amount of effort athletes have to put in to get anywhere. The strain on their bodies. But if I'm completely honest with you, advancement in sports is not where I want to be. So if you're looking for someone who is—"

"It's not a prerequisite," Cam says, "and if you're only here for the paycheck, that's okay so long as you show up and do the work."

"It ... it is?"

"The company has programs for those interested in working their way up from positions like the one we're offering, but if you're not interested, then you simply won't go through that program," Cam explains. "We just like to know up front so we don't waste resources on someone who doesn't want it. Like I said, this is a floating position, and while we love employees who want to stick around for the long haul, in this kind of entry-level job, there's always going to be high turnover."

Wylder lets out a breath. "That's actually really cool of you. I wasn't sure if I should've come in here pretending to give a damn about sports or be brutally honest."

"Honesty is always appreciated. Do you have any questions for us before we wrap this up?"

He goes to open his mouth but refrains.

"Great." Cam stands and holds out his hand for Wylder to shake. "It was nice to meet you, and we'll be in touch."

Xavier shakes his hand next and then turns to me. "You all good to show him out?"

"Of course."

Cam and Xavier leave the conference room, and Wylder sighs.

"I so didn't get this job, did I?"

"What makes you say that?"

"It kind of ended abruptly after I said I don't care about sports. Maybe I should've done what Thad told me to do and lied through my teeth."

"Thad said to deceive his bosses? I'm gonna keep that in my back pocket for later." I'm not being serious, but maybe that isn't clear because Wylder's blue eyes widen.

"Please don't. If I don't get a job soon, Thad's going to kick me out, and then I'll have to move home and live with the parentals, who I stole from just to get out of that godforsaken town, and then I'll have to deal with the comments again. Ugh, the comments. 'Why can't you be more like your brother Thad?' 'Thad had a backup plan, what's yours?' Thad, Thad, Thad.'" He screws up his face. "And now I've gone and said all that to the person who would be my boss if that interview wasn't such a shitshow."

Okay, he needs to stop making me feel sorry for him. Though one part, I can't help but ask about. "You stole money from your parents?"

"Uh, I may or may not have done up a spreadsheet, showing Mom and Dad how much money they had spent on Thad's base-ball career to give him the best opportunities but refused to give me even half that to try my hand out here in LA. It drove me crazy that they put all this effort into Thad's potential but couldn't even see mine. So yeah, I did something stupid, and I had every intention of paying them back when I hit it big, but of course, that didn't fucking happen, and I ran out of money quicker than I thought, and I've been doing small jobs here and there but nowhere near enough to keep going the way I was. I need a job to pay my bills while I still fight for the career I want. And I know stealing is wrong, and I was a shithead, and that maybe they're right and I don't have the potential to make it big in Hollywood. Thad didn't end up making it in baseball, but they still invested in him. And I'm grateful my brother has given me a place to live after I got booted for not paying my rent, but at the same time ... Man, I resent that guy. Okay, not really, but a little." He hangs his head. "I'm a horrible person for even thinking that, aren't I?"

I hold up my hand. "Believe me. I probably know better than anyone how you're feeling. You know who my family is? You'd know my dad's name even if you weren't into sports. Dean Holloway."

He cocks his head. "The swimmer?"

"Yep. My sister—you've probably heard of her too—Leila Holloway, took after him. My little brothers are future Olympians. So yeah, I completely understand trying for a career that isn't approved by parents." And now, because I totally feel for the guy, I stare after Cam and Xavier. "Let me see where their heads are at. This job might not be your dream, and you might not care about athletes or sports, but it's not like we need you to."

"And it's not like I'm going to say that to any of their faces either. Thad might think I'm dumb and irresponsible, but that only seems to come out when I'm around him."

"Like there's no possible way you could live up to him, so you don't even try?"

He doesn't even need to answer for me to know I'm right.

"Ah. Living in someone's shadow. Can't say I miss it. Let me talk to them. If I have anything to say about it, you'll get this position."

"Thank you."

He sounds so genuine, but I have to only hope it is. Because if I push for him, and some of those red flags like stealing from his parents turn out to be the tip of the iceberg, it's not only his position that will be in danger but mine as well.

This better work out.

Chapter 11
Fox

AM I FREAKING OUT THAT IT'S BEEN A COUPLE OF DAYS AND I haven't heard from Emmett Dalton? Maybe a little. But I can't dwell on it. Not only would it drive me crazy, but I have other clients' problems to work into my schedule.

Time management and multitasking are necessary skills to be a sports agent. It's all good and well to have set aside time to work on each individual client's needs, but considering the uncertainty of the sporting industry and having to deal with trades, injuries, scandals, and whatever else tends to pop up, it's impossible to time these things.

I currently have a tennis player renegotiating with a sponsor, an up-and-coming hockey player in the AHL trying to get his shot in the big show, and a football coach hoping to get onto a pro team this upcoming season.

Knowing my luck, the phone is about to ring with one of my other clients getting a DUI or some other scandal I'm not prepared to deal with right now.

Damon has always let it be known—company-wide—that he wants his agents to have a good work-life balance, which is something he had personally always struggled with. He has praised his life partner for being his voice of reason when it comes to taking breaks from work, and as much as I want the same thing, I'm not sure there's another Maddox out there for the rest of us.

As it is, with the ten or so clients I have, I barely have time to hook up, let alone date.

There's always a revolving door of athletes on an agent's roster at any one time because of the amount of turnover in the industry. Careers are short. Injuries can take someone out of the game permanently. And when we lose a client, we have to replace them.

Realistically, unless I want to work myself to death, I only have maybe one or two spots at most that I could take on because I do want that balance between work and my social life.

Honestly, I don't know how Archer does it. The last time I checked, he had eighteen clients. That's almost double my load, and I struggle as it is. I thought it was easier for him because he has a lot of what we would call small clients—because their earning potential is small not because their sport is any less important—but as he shoved in my face the other day, he works even harder with them so they can earn a living wage.

It's hard to know what I dislike more: that I might be wrong about him or that I don't hate him so much anymore. He's a lot more human to me now, and that's making me reassess everything I've ever felt toward him. This whole time, I've been angry at him for signing those clients, for building his list, claiming he was taking away those opportunities from me, when the truth is ...

I don't want to admit this, even to myself. The truth is, I've been jealous of him this whole time. Jealous that he can sign anyone so easily, jealous that he has so many clients and doesn't drown in the amount of work that entails. Then again, he does skimp on reading his emails.

My office phone rings, and all this thinking about scheduling and workload makes me fear I've jinxed myself. Here comes the call saying one of my athletes has been arrested.

But when I look at the number on the little display, I realize it's an internal call. Not from any random office either. It's Archer's office.

Maybe he's psychic, and he can sense I'm thinking nice things about him for once, and he's calling to tell me to stop it. Or to prove those nice thoughts are wrong.

I pick up the handset and am proud of myself when I only say, "Hello," and not "What do you want?"

"Did you see Damon's email?" Is it just me, or does his voice sound even smoother over the phone? If he weren't so good at being an agent, I'd suggest he do something like phone sex work. Or audio narration or something.

I open my browser on my computer and navigate to my work emails. "You know, for someone who doesn't check his emails when he should, you sure stay on top of Damon's. What is it this time? More business cards with offensive suggestions on them? Our wedding invitations?"

The joke doesn't taste bitter in my mouth like it would have a few days ago, and I still can't work out if I'm okay with not being in a constant state of anger when it comes to Archer anymore. On the one hand, I'm growing as a person? Go me. On the other, could it be that I haven't actually hated him all this time, and the resentment had become a habit?

If I knew screwing him over half as much as he has screwed me would cure me of that useless emotion, I would've fucked him over years ago.

"Funny. But no. He has put in the calendar for us to have a meeting with him tomorrow though."

"Us? Like, you and me?"

"He's flying out to LA for it. Do you know what it's about?"

Have no fucking clue, but now I'm going to be stressing about it for the next twenty-four hours. "Maybe that stupid bet about us has gotten back to him, and he's coming to tell us that if we were together without disclosing it, he'd take it out on our asses." I realize what I've said a moment too late. "*Put.* Put us out on our asses."

Any hope of him not picking up on the mistake or letting it pass dies when he laughs. "Nah, he could do that via online team meeting. Fire us, I mean. Not take it out on our asses. You got a thing for the bossman?"

"Shut up, it was a slip of the tongue."

"Uh-huh. You want Damon to slip you the tongue while taking it out on your ass. That's hot. He is a bit of a silver fox."

I can't find it in me to fight about why this is wildly inappropriate. Though true. Damon is a silver fox, and if it weren't for not being attracted to people who are in committed relationships, I agree, the idea of hooking up with Damon would be hot. Though I think I'm more attracted to his brain than him, as someone who is basically twice my age.

"Nothing to say? Not even more about the bet about us? Are you warming up to me? Does this mean there's a chance of someone winning the bet?"

"Absolutely," I say dryly.

"Wait, really?" His surprised tone and the crack in his voice goes to show that he's messing with me. As usual.

Well, payback's a bitch. "Absolutely ... no fucking way." I can't help smiling, and when he laughs again, this time, it does something gross to my insides. Makes them all warm and fuzzy and—

No. No, no, no, no, no.

I can't start thinking of Archer in a positive way that makes me all mushy. That's a slippery slope I'm not willing to go down.

It's official. I've decided my stance on this not-hating-Archer-anymore thing.

I don't like it.

Thad barrels into my office. "Damon's on his way up."

I glance at the time on my screen and let out a curse. "He's early."

"Brady thinks it's because he secretly came to check up on him for his dads, but that's probably paranoia talking."

I hope that's why he's one hour early for our meeting. I've been scouring my accounts, pulling data, and putting them in some kind of order for what I think he might need from this visit. It's a pain in the ass that he didn't specify on the calendar like he's supposed to. As per his own damn rules.

Which makes me think this isn't about work at all, and it very well could be about the stupid bet that Archer and I have nothing to do with. Or maybe he found out about the fuck around with Archer and his Buffalo trip, and this falls under his "be respectful" instruction when he put all his clients up for grabs.

Fuck, what if I'm in trouble for sending Archer on a wild goose chase? Not that I meant to do it. Wait, would that also mean that he ratted me out? After all the shit I've let slide over the years?

"Fox?"

My gaze flies to Thad. "Right. On his way up. Here. Okay."

I'm only halfway through pulling data for my most recent client revenue, so I go with the last fiscal year's numbers. I throw them in a folder along with current contracts under negotiations and offers I've received for them. I don't know what he wants to see, if any of it, but it's better to be overprepared than under.

As I walk out into the main reception area, I see Archer has a folder under his arm too. Similar minds and all that. I would say great minds, but I'm still trying to convince myself that my initial gut reaction to him was right and that he doesn't deserve any praise from me.

He doesn't.

Just because he fills out a suit better than I can, has more clients than I do, more friends in the office, more ... fuck it, he has more everything than I do, but that doesn't mean he's superior to me. I can hold my own. I'm a damn hard worker, and I have an amazing, though still fledgling, career because of it.

Not only is Archer out here waiting, but so are Cam, Xavier, and Brady.

Thad is by my side, too, for fuck knows what reason, other than maybe wanting to get close to the gossip. If there is gossip.

Who am I kidding? When the CEO of the entire damn company wants a meeting with you and doesn't tell you why, there's going to be gossip.

The elevator doors open, and Damon waltzes on through, stopping short when he sees all of us standing here waiting for him.

His face drops. "Who died?"

We glance around at each other.

"Uh, no one?" Cam says.

"Was that an answer or a question?" Damon asks.

"An ... swer?"

"What's with the welcoming committee?"

"Admit it," Brady cuts in. "You're here to spy on me. Well, you can tell my fathers that I am well fed and well fu—fussed over by my loving partners."

Damon gives him an up-nod. "Nice save. I'll catch up with you later, and no, I was not sent here by your dads to spy on you."

Brady narrows his eyes as if he doesn't believe him.

"Maddox sent me to make sure your SEAL boyfriends haven't lost their SEAL physique now they're no longer in the military."

"That checks out. Come find me later." Brady turns on his heel and leaves.

Then Damon's focus turns to Thad. "St. James? Do you need something?"

"No. I want to see what this is all about." He waves his hand over the rest of us.

Damon simply raises an eyebrow at him.

Thad hangs his head. "Fine, I'll get back to work."

"Good man. And then there were four." He faces us.

"We're ready for our meeting," I say, unintentionally speaking for Archer.

Damon checks his expensive Rolex watch. "You're early."

I don't want to point out that he's the one who's early.

"I was going to check on things around here, try to get a hold of Lane while I'm in town, and then sit down for our meeting, but if you two want to get it out of the way first, we can do that."

Lane Pierce was the old PR manager for LA before Xavier took over. Lane still works for the firm and pops in every now and then, but most of his work is remote, and it's more of a consultant position now. He's who the firm brings in if there's a real PR fuckup.

Okay, so Damon's not in a rush to sit down with me and Archer, but he does want to catch up with Lane first. This doesn't help me decipher what our meeting is about. All I want to know is if my world is about to implode or not.

"Do you need either of us?" Cam asks.

"I'll meet you in the conference room in five minutes," Damon says to us. "I need to get a quick rundown from Cam and Xavier."

Yup, that doesn't ease my worries at all. If anything, I'm on the verge of having some kind of panic attack. I'm not an overly anxious person in general, but when something as important as my career is on the line, yeah, I tend to freak out.

Which is probably why I've dwelled on Archer's long client list for way too many days. Months. Years, even. It's why I've resented him for landing the clients I wanted, like Jeremiah Castleberry, even if I can admit that Archer is more than likely a better fit for a NASCAR driver than I am.

I wanted that account because NASCAR is one of the sports I've yet to tap into. It's also one of the most toxic sports in the entire industry, so I wanted to do my part to protect a gay man from any shit that might've got thrown his way. But Archer is just as capable of doing that.

I'm realizing that all my resentment toward Archer came from my perceived failure because I could never catch up to him, which made me feel not good enough.

It has nothing to do with him as a person. And as we head for the conference room, I watch him walk ahead of me.

He holds his head high. He's always so confident.

I hate that I'm in awe of him. I want to go back to where I was under the impression I actually hate him.

Because I can't deny that confidence and competency are a turn-on for me, and the last thing I fucking want is to see Archer in that way.

I'm a stubborn man, and I'll deny it for-fucking-ever. If not only so it doesn't go to his big head but to prove all those coworkers wrong about us.

I had planned to come into the conference room early and have glasses of water for each of us and a coffee for Damon waiting, but I don't have time for that now. It's not often Damon comes all this way or I have much interaction with him. Archer did his internship in the New York office, so he knows Damon well, and I don't. I wanted to show him personally how I would act if he were any of my clients coming in to meet with me.

I put my folder on the table and then duck back out and head into the break room to grab a fancy glass bottle of water from the fridge, palm three highball glasses, and then spin to go back to the conference room.

Only, I'm not watching where I'm fucking going, and someone is right there. I try my best to juggle everything in my hands, but the condensation on the bottle is slippery, and I have to choose between dropping it and getting water everywhere or dropping the glasses and having them smash.

So what does my body do? Drops fucking everything.

Luckily for me, the guy I run into has quick reflexes and at least saves the glasses from sending shards all over the place. The water isn't as lucky, the flimsy cap falling off as it hits the ground, but on the bright side, not much spills by the time I can pick it up again.

"Sorry. I was in a rush." I finally look at the person I've never met before and come face-to-face with a really pretty man. Like, supermodel pretty. His wild, curly hair hangs by his shoulders, his shirt isn't buttoned up all the way, and his suit pants are so tight he can't even tuck his shirt in. I'm assuming that's why it's haphazardly hanging off him.

He doesn't look like an athlete.

"All good." He gives a lazy smile, and something in it pings familiarity.

"Wylder," Thad barks from the doorway, and I flinch. "Aren't you supposed to be working?"

Wylder. Thad's brother. This is who I recommended for Archer to hire? An early twenties guy who's one part disaster and six parts gorgeous?

He turns to Thad. "I am. I have a spill to clean up."

"I've got it," I say. "It was my fault."

"Nope. This is what I was hired for. Doing all the work no one else wants to do. Besides, don't you have a meeting to get to? You are Lincoln Fox, aren't you?"

I swallow hard. "I am. Why? What have you heard?"

Wylder smiles wider. "All good things. I promise."

How? "Aren't you working for Holloway?"

"I am. He speaks very highly of you."

I doubt that very much. "I think you have the wrong person. I ... I need to go. Thanks for cleaning up my mess."

"It's what I'm here for."

I step past him, confusion still running rampant, but he says something as I get to his brother.

"If you need anything else, anything at all, let me know."

I wave him off. "Will do."

I don't know what to make of the new office assistant. Seems nice enough. Charming. Accommodating.

But he's obviously on drugs if he thinks Archer has had anything nice to say about me. I've been nothing but a dick to him ever since he started here after his internship.

When I get back to the conference room, Damon's already there, but my gaze goes straight to Archer. Where his light facial hair and killer smile make my gut swoop.

Jeez. I get told the man said nice things about me, and my body reads into it. *Calm down, loser. That's Archer you're looking at.*

Shit.

What the fuck is happening?

Damon notices me. "Oh, good, you're here. Let's take a seat. We have a problem."

That snaps me out of the weirdness that's trying to take over and allows panic to claw its way back into pole position.

So much so, I can't help blurting, "How much trouble are we in?"

Chapter 12
Archer

"Trouble? Why would you be in trouble?" Damon asks.

Fox looks like he's going to be sick, but I'm certain whatever this little problem is will be easy to clear up. I have to believe that, or I might turn green like him.

"What's the problem?" I ask because I think both Fox and I know he's not going to answer Damon.

With the way Fox is pouring water into those glasses, with a shaky hand and heavy exhale, I'm guessing he probably can't even speak at the moment.

When he got back from the break room, he was already frazzled, and he's refusing to look me in the eye. Though that part isn't exactly new.

Once he takes his seat, Damon sips his water, says, "Thank you," and then gets down to business.

"You both recently met with some of my current clients."

Oh, shit. Maybe this is about going out with Asher Dalton, watching him as he, his partner, and teammates downed eleventy-billion shots, and doing nothing to stop them, not even while breaking into someone's house.

"Is this about the Dalton brothers?" Fox not only finds his voice but a confident tone as well. "Or is it about *how* we met with the Dalton brothers?" He sends a suspicious eye my way.

Please. Like I care about what he did. He schemed the schemer. He deserves props for that, not punishment. I didn't rat him out.

"You mean separately?" Damon clarifies. "This is where the dilemma lies. They both liked you."

"And?" Fox asks.

"And they want to come as a package deal," I say. It's not a question. It's what I've always assumed about the brothers.

"Exactly," Damon says. "Can I ask you, Fox, why you went to Emmett Dalton instead of Asher?"

"Was I not supposed to?" There's his insecurity back again. "If I have to rep both of them, then fine, but I went to Emmett because I don't exactly have the time to add someone as high ... profile as Asher. Not without my other clients suffering."

Damon leans back in his chair. "What if Emmett Dalton is as successful as his brother?"

Fox smothers a smile. "With all due respect to Asher Dalton's hockey career, it's not his success I was worried about. It was his penchant to get in his own way when it comes to said success."

After going out with him, I can see what he means. I knew he had a bit of a reputation, but I wasn't aware of the extent until afterward. Having said that, had I known, I still would've gone for it. I try not to pass judgment on people I don't know. What he did the other night could have been seen as bad PR, which could make his agent's job a nightmare, especially during contract negotiations.

If I do sign Asher, I'm going to have my work cut out for me.

Damon tries to hold back a snicker. "You've done your homework, then."

"I always do," Fox says.

Why do I feel like that's directed at me?

"I, on the other hand," I cut in, "am not afraid of a challenge." I smirk over at him.

Damon glances between us, back and forth. "And this is where the problem lies. Here. With you two."

Here it comes.

Only what I'm expecting—something about the bet that we both have nothing to do with—doesn't come out of his mouth.

"It's no secret you two don't get along."

Fox's mouth drops. "It-it's not?"

Damon chuckles. "Did you think you were being subtle? Even Maddox knows. Why else would he have joked about it on your business card?"

Fox shifts in his seat. "I thought we were at least being professional about it."

"You know," Damon says, "when I assigned you two to Cam and Xavier as their junior agents, I would get emails asking if I was punishing them. Almost daily. I'm actually surprised no formal complaint has come across my desk."

I laugh, but Fox looks even more distraught.

"We've worked it all out now," I say. "We've been practically besties since Fox realized I'm not a client hog but a hard worker."

Before Fox can say anything to that, Damon brings his hands together and says, "Great. So you won't have any issues working together, then."

I want to point out that we already work together, you know, in separate offices far away from each other, and it works well, but I get the sinking feeling that isn't what he means.

"Together?" Fox asks.

"Emmett was really impressed with you, and"—he turns to me —"Asher told me what he put you through, and all I can say is you earned his account. If you want it. But that's the catch here. Asher wants to protect his brother, and he's adamant that they have the same agent. He's asked me what to do, and I want to propose something to him, but I can't do it unless you're both on board."

"Should we be scared?" I quip, but I get the impression we really should be.

"I want you to represent both of them. Together."

"Together ..." Fox purses his lips.

"That way, Asher can have input on his brother's career, you can share information with each other, but ultimately, you'll get to represent the clients you want to represent."

It's all good and well in theory, but how would it work? "What would that look like? Commission and workload-wise."

Fox pins me with a look I know all too well, coming from him. It's his *you can't be serious* look. "You can't be seriously considering this."

See?

"This would be a true joint collaboration," Damon says. "Meaning, hours and commission would be split fifty-fifty. How you go about your clients is up to you. If you wanted to set it up so that Fox mainly deals with Emmett, and Archer sticks with mostly Asher, that's okay by me, but you do need to be aware that both Dalton brothers' commissions will be shared evenly, and you need to be okay with that."

That hardly seems fair, especially if I'm doing all the work with Asher and running around Buffalo with him trying to prevent him from committing another B & E.

"I don't think it's a good ide—"

I cut Fox off before he can reject it again without thinking it through. If we don't accept this, Damon might say neither of us can have them as clients. "I'm interested in hearing more. Aren't you?"

He hesitates, and I can practically see the thoughts running through his head as he's trying to choose his words carefully.

I conjure my most charming smile. "Come on. I thought we got past everything after the Buffalo incident."

Mild threat of tattling on him so I can get my client any way I can get him? *Give me things that will piss Fox off for five hundred!*

"What was the Buffalo incident?" Damon asks.

I stare at Fox, silently asking, *Do you want to tell him, or should I?* When he doesn't say anything and the silence spreads a little bit too long to be comfortable, I wave Damon off. "I had some miscommunication over my flight schedule. Made me late. That's all. Fox caught me after having been awake for almost two days straight and gave me some sympathy. We bonded. We're good now." I cock my head at Fox. "Right?"

Fox's gaze ping-pongs around the room and everywhere but at

me. "We're good, but enough to work together on the same account? We'll kill each other. Why push it?"

"That was my concern too," Damon says.

"Whoa, no matter what is going on personally, I'd like to think we can be professional when it comes to our clients' needs."

"That's the hope." Damon turns to Fox. "But if you don't think you can leave your personal beef aside, then maybe this isn't what's best for the clients. Perhaps I should suggest a different agent to rep the Dalton brothers."

That's exactly what I thought would happen. I can't lose the chance at having Asher as a client. I try to come up with a solution, something I can bullshit my way through and run with, but other than saying I'll take them both on, which, let's face it, would also piss Fox off, I've got nothing.

"Archer can sign them," Fox says, and I want to smack him upside the head. Right after I pick my jaw up off the floor.

Do I want the Dalton brothers on my roster? Fuck yes. But he's seriously going to throw this away because of our issues, which aren't really issues?

"It's what you wanted from the beginning. You were smart enough to go to the older brother, who you knew had sway with Emmett's decision."

I want to scream at him. Like, what the fuck is he doing? He says he resents me because I supposedly steal clients from him, and now he's handing me one? One that he actually earned?

I don't think that in the whole time I've worked here and Fox has avoided me, yelled at me, and accused me of sabotage, I've ever once gotten mad at him. I've been frustrated, sure. But angry? Nope. In this moment, I'm starting to see how restrained he was with the yelling. He was tame compared to how I want to rip him apart with my words and talk some sense into him.

"Can we have a moment to discuss it between us?" I ask Damon.

Damon's slow to nod. "Sure." He stands, and upon exiting, he mumbles something about, "I only own the place, but sure, kick me out of my own conference room."

We both give a small smile, but Fox's dies first.

"What are you doing?" I ask.

"Sorry if I'm reluctant to collaborate with you when I only started to find you tolerable recently. As in the last week."

I fist pump the air. "Woohoo, tolerable. That's one step before likeable."

He doesn't react to that. No half-turned-up lips. No pressing his lips together, trying to contain his amusement. Nothing. "I didn't think you'd take offense to me wanting to protect my mental health."

"I'm a detriment to your mental health now?" Just how much did he resent me before, and why am I hurt by it? Sure, I've always known he hasn't liked me, but I thought it was purely in a business sense. "Are you saying I've actually done damage to your psyche?"

He makes an undignified "Pfft" sound.

"Why do I get to you so much, other than the misconception that I try to steal clients from you that were never yours to begin with?"

"Don't give yourself so much credit. You don't get to me." Yet, he can't look at me as he says it.

Either something else is going on here, or he must really hate me. Like deep down despise me.

"I'm not being conceited here; you're thinking of giving up a potential client who would be a great fit for you all because of me, and I can't understand how or why you would do that if I didn't get under your skin. Tell me how to fix it because here I am trying to convince you to take the client you wanted."

Fox runs his hand over his sandy-colored hair, messing up his usually perfect pompadour style. "I think working together in close quarters isn't a good idea. The same way I think it's a recipe for disaster to live with friends or to date someone at work. When you're forced to spend time together, things are going to get explosive, and when it all goes to shit, we'd go back to snarking at each other. Only this time, we'd have to find a way to get along for the clients' sake, and I can tell you now, squashing frustrations will only make it more damaging when you do explode."

"It's not like we're moving in together or dating or—wait, is this about the stupid bet? You think if we're partnered together, the rumor mill will get worse? They've already got us getting married. How much worse can it get?"

There's something in the way he levels me with his pale green eyes that makes something click.

"Ooh, are you worried that if we do work together, you might begin to like me too much, and then we'll lose the bet? Not that we're in it to begin with, but after one shared cab ride, you're already tolerating me. First comes hate, then comes love—"

"Tell me that thing again how you're not being conceited."

I grin. Hey, that wasn't a denial. "Look, I don't want you to give up this opportunity and hold it over my head forever like you did with Jeremiah. I think if we can put aside our differences and become a team, we could actually be an awesome asset to the Daltons and to this company. So if you don't take it, I won't take it." I'm bluffing because I'm me, and striving to be the best is in my nature. Or is it my nurture? Either way, he has to see how self-sabotaging he's being, and I don't want to be responsible for that.

Finding out his mental health could have possibly taken a dip because of me gets to me more than it should. It's always been pure business to me, but I have been told I'm better at compartmentalizing than others. While it's not my intention to hurt people, I can acknowledge that my business practices can be cutthroat. I've never cared too much about it.

Until right now.

Fox's gaze narrows. "Are you saying you'd give up Asher Dalton that easily?"

When I'd said it, I didn't think I meant it, but now I'm not so sure. "It wouldn't be easy, but I'm trying to show you that you're wrong about me. That I can be part of a team. And hey, look at it this way. If we share clients, I can't steal them from you."

Finally, I get a smile from him, but it drops, along with a slump of his shoulders. "Wait, you're not offering this because you're planning to push all of Asher Dalton's PR issues on me, are you?"

I rub my chin. "Damn. I hadn't thought that far ahead yet, but that's a good idea."

"And I'm out."

"I'm kidding. I handled him fine the other night on my own."

"Didn't I hear something in the hockey-verse about the rookies playing a prank on a retired Buffalo player by breaking into their house?"

"Nope. No arrest record, no crime. You must have dreamed that."

"Uh-huh." Fox still pretends he's not entertained by me, but he's coming around. Slowly. He just needs that last push.

"What if we keep it simple. You rep Emmett, I rep Asher, but if there's ever a meeting with one or both of them, we'll attend together."

"I couldn't do that."

"Why?"

"Because you heard Damon. We'd get fifty percent commission from each, and Asher outearns his brother by, oh, a couple of mil per year. It wouldn't be fair."

I lean forward, resting my elbows on the table. "And since when do I ever play fair?"

"That's true, but it's usually skewed in your favor, not someone else's."

"What can I say? I guess I have a soft spot for you." Always have, really. Even when he's been yelling at me. It's possible that's why his provocations never made me snap back.

"We can give it a try," he relents.

I slap the table, making a louder banging sound than I'd intended. "Yes!"

"Don't get too excited. We can start simple in the beginning, but I'm also willing to pitch in with Asher if you need me. Eventually, if things go well, we can have a fifty-fifty split on the workload, but if it turns out I'm right and we can't work together, then you can represent both of the Dalton brothers. We'd also have to figure out what happens once Asher retires. Do we both keep Emmett on as a client and only get fifty percent of the commissions?"

Damon, along with Cam and Xavier, comes rushing in with Brady and Thad trailing.

"What happened, who punched who, what was that loud bang?" Damon asks.

"So dramatic," Brady says under his breath.

I stand. "Sorry. I got too excited. We came to an agreement. We're in. We'll collaborate on the Daltons together."

Cam slaps Damon's back playfully. "I hope the company's liability insurance is up to date."

"I'm not sure it'll cover murder," Brady snarks.

"It's not set in stone yet," Fox says. "Technically, we're still negotiating." And even though he looks nauseous at the idea, and our coworkers and bosses have worried expressions on their faces, I'm actually looking forward to it.

Especially if Fox really is worried we'll lose this stupid bet the office made about us.

He is right that hooking up with a coworker is a dumb idea. But when it comes to Lincoln Fox? I'd pay anything to see that man unravel. I'm not sure he's even capable.

I'm going to do everything in my power to prove him wrong about me, and maybe if I can do that, he'll want to prove me wrong about him.

Chapter 13
Fox

I'M NOT GOING TO REGRET THIS. I'M NOT GOING TO REGRET this.

"Hey, partner," Archer says with a knock on my office door.

I'm already regretting this. "No. That's not becoming a thing."

"I have the contracts for the Daltons so their account can be reassigned over to us. You're the last one to sign it." He waves the folder in front of my face.

I can still back out. I can still back out.

Only, I can't really because my name is all over the papers he's holding, and I am not going to be the one to commit to something in front of my boss and then back out of it later.

I promised I would try, and I really will. The contract stipulates we will both represent the brothers for a three-month trial period, after which either one of us or the Daltons can choose to bow out. In the event that this does blow up in our faces like I'm predicting it will, the Daltons will choose who they want to represent them. Whether it be Archer or me or someone else in the firm.

"Are you going to sign them?" he asks, shaking the folder at me again.

I take it out of his hand. "Yes, geez. Impatient much?"

"Excited to get started."

Even though I've read through this document already, I skim

read it again to make sure nothing has been added without my approval. Trust issues? Me? Can't fathom it. "Your excitement unsettles me," I say, not taking my eyes off the pages.

"Mean, but fair, I guess. I did kind of steamroll you into this, and what can I say? I'm a hard man to resist."

I glance upward toward his smug face. The scruff on his face, darker than the bleached hair on his head, is extra thick. His blue eyes shine. I really do hate how good-looking he is.

"I still haven't signed on the dotted line yet," I say.

He mimes locking his mouth shut and throwing away the key. "Got it. Keep it zipped until you're contractually obligated to listen to me tell you how good I am."

What the hell have I done?

For fuck's sake, those types of comments used to drive me crazy. Now that my resentment has been replaced with the realization I've merely been jealous of him this whole time, I'm starting to see how everyone else could like his … charm.

He surprised me by refusing to take the contract if I wasn't in it with him.

My biggest issue with agreeing to work together isn't about getting along like I'd implied. I'm scared about giving an inch and him taking a mile. I'm worried that I'm starting to let down my defenses around him and that he'll play me.

Most of all, it's terrifying how I'm beginning to feel toward him. If one conversation can make all that hate and annoyance go away, one look can make my stomach flip, what's going to happen after two conversations? Three? What will happen when we have to travel together, plan strategies together, and work in close quarters? Late nights in the office, forced proximity, and all that crap.

I was hoping that his cocky and conceited attitude would continue to turn me off, but here I am, entertaining his so-called charm and having to force myself not to give in to it.

"Come onnnnn," he complains. "Signing a new client is like Christmas morning."

His attitude might not turn me off, but his impatience might do it.

"That's only going to make me read slower," I singsong. "Also, I worry about your childhood if contract law is like Christmas."

He ignores my sad childhood comment. "Are you seriously checking that I didn't add anything to it after we had agreed to the wording?"

"Yup."

"You know, one day, you're going to trust me, and when that happens, I'm going to dance and sing in your face."

"As long as you film it so I can put it on the internet to embarrass you." I finish with my read-through and put it on my desk. Reaching for the pen, I take it and roll it between my fingers. "Last chance to back out of this."

Archer puts his hands on my desk and leans in, his leathery cologne filling my senses. My stomach does that annoying backflip thing again. Maybe I'm coming down with the stomach flu. Correlation doesn't mean causation. Just because the two times it has happened have been in his vicinity, it doesn't mean he's the one making it happen.

Archer's blue eyes stare deep into my soul as if he can see right through me. His voice, raspy, sends shivers down my spine. "I'm not the one who has doubts. That's all you. So, what's it going to be?"

Definitely the stomach flu.

Reluctantly, but with a smidge of anticipation, I put pen to paper and sign my name.

It's done now. Archer and I are a team. And maybe one day, I'll be able to think that without flinching.

I push it all to the back of my mind and focus on all the work I have piling up. I'm almost done with my list of things I needed to get done by end of week when Archer knocks on my doorjamb and then leans against it.

I leave my door open because the bustling of interns and staff out in the bullpen is like white noise to me. It helps me concentrate, but I forget how much of an invitation it is.

Like earlier, I don't take my eyes off my work while I talk to him. "If this is going to become a habit, I'm going to start shutting and locking my door."

I'm trying to avoid eye contact as much as possible because I'm scared if I do meet his gaze, my gut will do that topsy-turvy thing it's been doing recently, and I'm still trying to convince myself it's because of a stomach flu and not because of him.

Out of the corner of my eye, I see him touch his heart with both hands. "It's like we're besties already! Come on, it's five o'clock and Friday, which means it's also bar o'clock."

Knocking off at five? What a novel idea. It does, however, break my concentration, and I look over at him. And damn it, the second we lock eyes, it happens again.

Stomach flu, stomach flu, stomach flu.

"You want to go to a bar. With me."

"The team is going out for celebratory drinks about the Daltons. You're part of the team. Ergo, let's get out of here."

"Do ... you go out drinking every time you sign a new client? Have you had your liver function checked recently?"

"Are you saying you never celebrate a milestone at work? This is a big deal. Asher Dalton will be my biggest client. Damon's semi-retiring."

"You really think that man will retire anytime soon? He's merely clearing his roster so he can focus on the bigger picture when it comes to his empire." But then I realize something. "Wait, so Damon's going too?"

"Everyone is going. And okay, Damon said he might stop by in that kind of dismissive way you tell someone that you definitely want to catch up soon when you actually don't, so then you never call, but he did say he'll try. So if your crush on the big boss will get you to come out with us, then yes. He will definitely be there."

Any face-to-face time with my idol is worth having to be in Archer's presence for a few hours. I want to pick Damon's brain, hear about what it was like to pave the way for queer athletes, and see if I can absorb his awesomeness by osmosis.

And maybe if I spend more time with Archer, I'll get over whatever the fuck this reaction toward him is.

I save my work, shut my computer down, and stand. "Okay, I'm in."

"Ooh, so you really do have a crush on Damon? You know he's a taken man, don't you?"

I sigh. "I didn't think that part of the conversation actually needed clarification, but no, no crush. Just admiration. And unlike someone else in this office, I didn't get a year of interning with him, so if there's a chance to catch any insight or words of wisdom from the most successful sports agent in the country, I'm going to take it."

I grab my suit jacket from where it hangs on the back of my chair, ready to head out, but Archer mutters to himself as we leave.

"Not a crush, my ass."

It's not a crush on Damon I'm worried about. It's this. Going out with people from work. Being in a social setting while keeping a professional distance. It breaks my rules. Then again, cosigning clients with Archer Holloway has thrown all kinds of professional rules out the window.

This is only the beginning too. Going from only seeing him or talking to him when I absolutely have to, to now having to collaborate cohesively is going to be a big enough adjustment. Now I'm going to a bar with him?

As long as I see this as a work event and I refrain from overdrinking, it'll be fine. I'll stay for a drink, talk to Damon if he does show up, and after an hour, if he's not there, I'll make an excuse and go home.

"Where are we going?" I ask as we walk toward the reception area and elevators.

"Where everyone always goes."

"If you've never noticed, I don't really go to these things. Like, ever."

Archer stops walking, his hand flying out to grab my forearm.

"Never?" He stares up at the ceiling with a concentration line in his forehead. He looks like he's trying to do math. "Huh. I always assumed you only didn't go to the ones I went to."

I shake off his grip. "There you go giving yourself way too much credit again. Has anyone ever told you that not everything is about you?"

"Never. I'm the light of everyone's life. Except yours, apparently."

"I really hate to break it to you, but everyone else is lying."

Archer laughs deep and loud, getting the attention of Thad, Brady, and Wylder, who are waiting by the elevators.

They turn to us, and Wylder's eyes shine in Archer's direction. That's ... an interesting development. Thad and Brady don't seem to notice though. They're too busy staring wide-eyed at us.

"Is ... is this actually happening?" Thad asks, talking out the side of his mouth to Brady. "Holloway is ... laughing? At ... Fox?"

"Fox said the funniest joke," Archer says. "Get this. He says I'm not the light of everyone's life, and anyone who says so is lying." He shakes his head.

Brady and Thad look at each other and then back to us, and both look like they're trying to bite their tongue.

We're technically not their bosses; we're their mentors, but I understand how they feel about talking back. I wouldn't dream of it. Though my mentor was my actual boss.

Apparently, Wylder doesn't have the same issue. "You know what they say, jokes that are the funniest are the ones that are true."

Thad hangs his head, Brady laughs, and I stand a little stunned, but Archer smiles.

"Just for that, you're buying me my first drink." He steps forward and clasps Wylder's shoulder as they step onto the elevator that has arrived.

For whatever reason, their comfortable yet mildly inappropriate banter gets to me.

Archer is Wylder's supervisor. Should they be ... that close? Where they can banter and go drinking together ...

It shouldn't get to me because if Archer crosses those lines and sleeps with a subordinate, he'd be fired, and then I'd get the Dalton brothers all to myself. But as ideal as that sounds, it still doesn't take away the ick feeling I get when I think of them being overly friendly. Too friendly.

Then again, I think going to a bar with a coworker is too friendly, so there's that.

I get on the elevator, but instead of hitting the button for the basement parking garage, Archer hits ground level. The bar is within walking distance then.

The office is on the south end of Downtown LA, where there are a few bars and clubs, but I've never been to any of them. Actually, I can't even remember the last time I went out anywhere.

I trail behind the group, following wherever they lead, but with every step, I get stuck in my head about how I became this person.

I stand by my rule that fraternizing with coworkers is a bad idea. Hanging out could lead to more, or drama, or really, anything that could derail my career. This career is everything to me, so I wouldn't want to fuck that up. But when did I become this person who only thinks about work?

Where did all my friends go? What about my friends from college? I went to UCLA, for fuck's sake. My friends from my hometown in Arizona don't keep in contact, but why would they when I haven't gone home in a long time? My parents are semi-retired, so they always come to see me because their work schedules allow for it. Though that hasn't even happened in the last year because I've always told them I need to work.

Mom's been begging me to come home for a visit, always finding some excuse for it. It started as it was Dad's birthday or their anniversary. Then it was to make sure I wasn't burning out, and now she's getting so desperate to see me, she's saying I need to make time for them because they need proof of life.

I've been so obsessed with trying to keep up with Archer that I've totally forgotten that work-life balance thing Damon is always emphasizing. I don't have a life outside of my work. Seriously, when did that happen? It all got away from me so easily.

I take my phone out of my pocket and open my contacts, scrolling through the countless names of people I once called friends.

"Whatcha doing?"

I jump at Archer's voice right next to me. Not only have I lost track of my life, but also my current surroundings.

"Thinking of calling a hookup? You won't have to with where we're going. It's a sea of ample potential."

"Do I want to know what that means?"

We've stopped walking.

"Literally." He points behind me.

When I turn toward the neon sign that's barely glowing in the late-afternoon light, I can't help wondering if that's what S. O. A. P really stands for.

"Been here before?" Archer asks.

"Nope."

Archer smiles. "Have you been to any bars before?"

"Not lately," I admit.

"Let's fix that."

The others are already making their way inside, so we're the last ones through the entrance. It's practically empty because it's so early, but we're not the first in suits to arrive. I'm guessing this is where a lot of LA business-type people go to drink on a Friday night.

You know, normal people who have friends.

"What's your celebratory drink?" Archer asks. "My treat."

I glance around, searching to see if Damon, Cam, or Xavier are here. They're not, and like Archer said, they probably won't be coming. Buck and Luca are though, along with a few interns. They all look comfortable with each other. Like they do this a lot. Without me.

I've never experienced FOMO before, but this would have to be the closest I've been. And it's not so much that I'm sad they're not friends with me; it's more that I've been holding myself back from forming any kind of friendships in the office outside of Edele.

So, fuck it. I've let work and professionalism dictate everything up to this point, and where has that gotten me? Rules are made to be broken.

Let's make some friends. "Rum. Spiced."

"Double?"

My reflex is to say no, but realizing that I have wasted so much of my energy in the last couple of years obsessing over comparing myself to Archer, I think I deserve to let loose. I still won't get drunk, but one drink isn't gonna cut it.

It's time I stop competing against Archer and start living for myself. "Sure. Why not."

Chapter 14
Archer

Buck raises his drink in the air. "To the new dynamic duo. May it end in marriage and not murder."

We all cheers to the new partnership—which may or may not include more snickering from everyone than usual—and I am genuinely happy about signing that contract today. There's something about having Fox on the Dalton account with me that's comforting. Like I have that lifeline in case my first major contract goes pear-shaped.

I'm not going to abuse it though. I'm not going to dump all the hard shit on him like he thinks I will. He has more experience with the big four leagues, so as much as it pains my ego to admit it, I could learn from him. As long as Fox can still tolerate me, I think we could work well together.

Cam and Xavier make an amazing team, even if you wouldn't think it to look at them. They're competitive and snark at each other. Yet, deep down, even though they disagree, they find a way to compromise.

Fox and I could be the next them. Uh, without the sex. Although that might be why they make a good team. After they have an argument, they can forget about it with orgasms.

It wouldn't be the worst arrangement in the world, but to bring that up with Fox? I'd worry about getting my dick cut off for the mere suggestion.

"You know," I say to him, my voice low so no one else can hear, "we could totally put money in on this bet thing and take the whole pot." Yet, I say shit like this anyway. Goodbye, dick.

Instead of the eye roll or getting shut down like I'm expecting, he laughs again. I'm starting to worry he's had a brain transplant at some point today. That contract we signed earlier must have been a deal with the devil, except he didn't take Fox's soul; he gave him a more fun one.

"There's one significantly big problem with that." Fox turns to me. "The only thing on that list I'm willing to actually do with you is murder, and I don't think a couple of hundred bucks is worth going to prison for."

"We could do the date one. It would work out to be a free dinner. Or for more of the pot, we could lie and say we had a one-night stand. Ooh, we could come up with a good story about how we slept together years ago, and that's why you've hated me all this time. Because I was so good in bed that I ruined you for all other men, and you can't stand that I couldn't give you more than one night."

"Yeah, I'm going to stop you there. None of that is happening."

"You're right. Not big enough. If we really want to take it all, we'd need to hop a flight to Vegas and have a quickie wedding and even quicker divorce."

He rubs his chin as if he's actually contemplating it. I'm about to ask if he's okay when he says, "Do you think they actually believe we'd be good together?"

And there he goes again, reading into it way too hard and not even trying to hold back the offense from seeping into his tone.

"You could do a lot worse than me. Just saying." Maybe I don't have control over my own tone because while I aim for my usual lightheartedness, it's missing. Hell, even I hear the disappointment in my statement.

"That's not what I mean. It's hard to understand why they see two people who don't get along and immediately think, 'They're going to end up together.'"

Ah, so it's not being so disgustingly turned off by me because he thinks he's better than I am but that he doesn't understand what ribbing and banter is. Does he not have any true friends?

"Trying to understand why people think the way they do is a waste of energy, but my guess would be that anyone who finds someone as amazing as I am so off-putting, it has to be because they're secretly in love with them. Only logical explanation."

"Totally logical. Because hate equals love and love equals ... What, exactly?"

Fucked if I know. "In all seriousness, they're probably mistaking the uncomfortableness between us for sexual tension." Can't say I don't understand it because I swear sometimes I feel it too. That draw. That crackle in the air around us. Usually right before he tells me I'm impossible and storms out of my office.

I must be like that annoying kid on the playground who picks on the person he likes because any attention from them is good attention. Or like a puppy. Oh, God. I'm an oversized puppy of a man when it comes to Fox.

The fox and hound. Isn't there a book or movie about that?

Though it's not like I follow him around anywhere. He always comes to me, and I can't help myself. Teasing is in my nature. Especially toward him. For whatever reason.

Fox hasn't responded, so when I glance in his direction again, I figure he's gotten distracted by something else. Instead, I see him contemplative as he stares into the dark liquid in his glass. "Yeah, I'm going to need more of these." He throws it back.

It's possible he's actually considering the idea of him and me. And there's a chance he could like it. I'm choosing to ignore the question of why that would make him want to drink.

"You want another one?" he asks.

I lift my almost full glass. "Thanks. Let me just ..." I down the rest and put it on the cocktail bar we're gathered around.

"What are you drinking?" he asks.

"Same as you. Look at that, we're already finding things in common. This is going to be a great relationship."

"*Working relationship*. And I get the feeling I'm going to need a lot of spiced rum to get through it."

I do my signature love heart over my chest with my hands. It's my go-to when he says something full of so much admiration.

He smothers another smile. It's like he doesn't want anyone to know he has the ability to be playful and have fun.

When he walks away to the bar, I can't help myself. I follow his ass with my gaze. It's a really nice ass.

"I need to call my boyfriends and tell them that if I don't make it home, it's because the world has ended," Brady says.

I drag my eyes away from Fox. "What are you yammering on about?"

Thad and Brady are right in front of me with their ridiculous and shocked expressions still on their stupid faces.

"I need to let Kelley know too." Thad takes out his phone. "I've never seen them have a civil conversation before. At least, not one that ended civilly."

We're not *that bad*.

"Smartasses," I mutter.

But maybe they do have a small point. Not that we've never had a civil interaction, but that it doesn't happen often. I don't want to push my luck too much with Fox, so I make a note to not spend too much time drinking next to him when he gets back. Quit while I'm ahead and all that.

The days of taunting him need to be over because we actually have something on the line now. I need the Dalton contract, and no one wants a black mark on their career by being dropped by a client. I need to stop doing ... whatever Fox finds annoying: being me, I guess.

So, when he brings me my glass and hands it over, I thank him and then nod in Corrie's direction. She's sitting at a booth in the corner with Wylder, and it has to suck for her being the only female in the intern program. Women are scarce around the office, but King Sports still hires more people who identify as women than any other sports agency on the West Coast. The issue comes from the sporting industry itself. With the exception of gay porn, it has more peen than any other workplace, so I always try to look out for anyone who isn't a cis white guy and take them under my wing.

"I'll be back in a bit. I need to check on something."

"O ... kay." Fox's voice trails after me as I make my way over to the booth and slide in next to Wylder and across from Corrie.

"What's happening?"

"Your new assistant was telling me how watching sports is boring," Corrie says with a wide smile on her face. "Especially baseball."

I press my lips together because that's not the right angle to take with anyone in the office, let alone Corrie. "That's interesting. And how do you feel about that, being an ex-professional fast-pitch player?"

Wylder begins to stutter, "Uh, I ... ah," and both Corrie and I laugh.

I lean in closer to Wylder and say, "Quick tip. A lot of people who work for a sports agency are generally ex-athletes."

"They're at a minimum interested in sports," Corrie adds.

"You catch more flies with honey," I say. "You don't need to like sports to work here, but those are inside thoughts."

Wylder looks sincere as he says, "Sorry. Didn't mean anything by it. I spent my whole childhood being dragged to watch Thad's games. It was painful."

"Sounds the worst," Corrie says. "Did you call Child Protective Services on your parents?"

Wylder laughs. "Maybe I should have, but I get your point. I'll stop complaining. I actually like working at King Sports. So far, anyway. And it keeps me in LA."

I grip his shoulder. "It's been good having you. I didn't realize how much I needed an extra set of hands until you came along."

I remind myself to thank Fox for suggesting it. But another time. Maybe the next time he's mad at me. I'm sure it won't take long.

Chapter 15
Fox

When Archer abandons me for Wylder, it only feeds the suspicion I have that they're fucking. Or at least being inappropriate. But I'm not going to let it get to me because it has nothing to do with me.

It is a little fucking rude though. He invited me here to celebrate our milestone, and now, I'm sitting at the bar by myself, drowning in rum. I've ended up alone because everyone has their own little cliques, and I don't belong to any of them. Because I've never let myself join in.

The contacts on my screen are a hell of a lot blurrier than they were an hour ago, and as I try to hit my cousin Dion's name, I miss and hit the name above it. Damon.

My reflexes are slow, and my panic is quick and debilitating.

I was trying to call my cousin—the closest person I have to a brother. We grew up together, but he stayed in Arizona while I moved out here to go to college. We used to catch up, used to keep in contact, and now I realize the only reason I know what's going on in his life is because I see it on his socials or Mom updates me when I speak to her.

I want my contacts back. My friends. I need to make more of an effort.

And that's when I realize I still haven't hit the big red button to end the call to my boss. "Shit, fuck. Why can't I fucking hit it? Stop. End. *End!*"

Finally, my phone screen goes black, and I'm confident I managed to do it before Damon picked up. I think.

I signal for the bartender to get me another one, and he does with a wink.

Why am I even still here if they're going to ignore me? And yes, I realize I'm ignoring them, too, by choosing to sit here by myself, but after Archer went and sat with Wylder, Thad had to leave because he wanted to get home to his boyfriend, and then everyone was talking amongst themselves, and it was as if I was on the very edge of the circle, barely being let in at all.

After I drink down my ... lost count of how many I'm up to, it really begins to hit me. I've probably had half a dozen in less than an hour, and now, the bar is spinny. Those drinks disappeared way too easily.

The second my empty glass hits the bar top, the bartender makes his way back to me.

"Should I be letting you have another?"

I meet his gaze and his sexy smirk. He seems super duperly more attractive than he did five drinks ago.

"Your eyes are looking a little glassy," he says.

I smile at him. "Your eyes are looking a lot pretty."

He laughs. "Yep. Definitely a sign you've had too many." He takes my old glass and pulls a clean one, filling it with a clear liquid. "Maybe switch to water."

My mouth is kinda dry and tastes gross. "Thanks."

The water is gone in the blink of an eye too. See, I'm not sad and pathetic, drinking alone. I'm *thirsty*.

"Ah. Here you are," a deep voice says, firm grip landing on my shoulder.

At first, I think it's Archer, and I'm about to snark something along the lines of, "Oh, pull yourself away from your assistant long enough to realize I've been sitting by myself for the five million drinks I've downed? Did he assist you with all the assistance and assisting?" But I'm saved from that rambly mess when I turn to find the bright green eyes of Damon King at my side.

Damon.

King.

The King of Damons. Like diamonds but Damons.

His silver hair is smooth as silk, and his salt-and-peppery beard hot as fuck. Maybe Archer was right and I do have some sort of crush on the big boss. Or maybe I'm drunk and lonely and everyone appears hot to me. Even the bartender.

"I thought you might have needed something urgently. Your, uh, voicemail was ... interesting."

My eyes widen. "Voicemail? I left a ... a voicemail?"

"Something about not being able to hit someone. I missed half of it due to the slurring. I got worried and thought you might have needed to be talked down from punching your new partner, but ..." He glances over at someone, and I follow his gaze to see Archer has moved on with Buck now, while Wylder and Corrie are still at their booth. "Things seem under control."

Sure. Under control. That's the exact word to describe the ball of drunken disaster I am.

"Slorry," I say. "Uh, I mean, sorry. Sooory." That last one came out Canadian for reasons I can't explain. "I was trying to call my cousin Dion and accidentally hit your name, and then my fingers were wet or something, and I was trying to hit End on the call. Not hit someone. I'm more professional than that."

His lips turn up as if he's trying to smother a smile. "Good to know." He pulls up the stool next to me and orders a Macallan.

Even his drinks are grown-up and sophisticated.

"So, how's your night been other than drunk dialing your boss."

"Drunk?" I make a pfft noise that comes out more of a grunt. "I'm not drunk."

Cutie McRumGoggles puts Damon's drink in front of him. "He is. I cut him off. Here. Have another water." He hands over another glass.

"Thanks." I sip it this time.

Damon's gaze burns into me.

"I didn't think you would show up, okay?" I say, feeling para-noid. "I wouldn't have drunk so much if I'd known."

Damon cocks his head. "Why not? You're off the clock. It's Friday night. Weekends are for having fun. It's why I was late. I had to pick up someone from the airport." He waves over his partner husband person, and Maddox appears, looking fifteen years younger than Damon when I happen to know there's only two years' difference. Yet another hot man I'm finding hot. Maybe I'm horny, and that's my issue. Everyone is suckable. Uh, fuckable. Actually, no, the first one works too.

"Maddox is the reason I have any fun," Damon says. "Because he's there to remind me to."

"But this is still a work event. Or it should be treated as such. I don't want to show up to work on Monday and have everyone laugh at how the usually professional and uptight Fox became loosey-goosey at a bar."

"Sounds like a Dr. Seuss book," Maddox says.

"I told the bartender he has pretty eyes, drunk dialed my boss, and fell off my stool."

"You fell off your seat?" Maddox asks.

"No. Not yet. Though I'm anticipating it. Is the bar on a tilt?"

"I have an idea," Maddox says. "I could catch up to your level of drunkeness, so then you don't seem as bad—"

"No." Damon shuts down that idea. "Lincoln is going to sober up, slink on home, and then think about doing something fun on the weekend." He leans in closer to me. "Because this job will eat you alive if you let it. You need to make time for the fun things outside of work."

I rub my temples. Is it possible for two glasses of water to sober me up enough for a hangover to kick in? My head throbs. "Are you a mind reader?"

"How so?"

"The reason I was calling my cousin is because I realize that I've lost touch with family. With friends. I think I've spent my entire last year trying to one-up Archer that I let everything else slip away from me."

"Eww," Maddox says to Damon. "He's a mini you. Maybe you should have hired me at your company after all. I could be the fun police. No, the opposite. Fun ..."

"Criminal," I supply helpfully.

"What?" they both ask.

"He wanted to know the opposite for police." Duh.

"You need an agent that's in charge of fun," Maddox says. "Ooh, Super Soaker Saturdays should be a thing. If you have to work on Saturdays, you have to come in trunks and arm yourself with water guns."

Damon says, "And this is why Maddox is not employed by the agency."

"It does sound fun though," I say. "But I'd worry about all the computers and paper files in the office."

"Speaking of fun," Maddox says. "Apparently, I owe you an apology because of the business card debacle."

Damon nudges the love of his life. "You know, when you put 'apparently' in front of an apology, it diminishes the effect."

"Well, Damon comes home and complains about you all so much—"

"Lies," Damon says.

"I knew what to put on everyone else's business cards." Maddox points around the bar. "Brady is a given. He's shacked up with two SEALs."

"Wait, what was on his card?" I ask.

"Seal Trainer."

I burst out laughing. "Okay, that one is funny."

"Even more proof that you are drunk," Damon says.

"That tall, tatted-up dude is Archer, isn't it? I remember when he was in New York, and Damon would whine about all the complaints over him stealing clients from others."

I pull back so quickly I almost do fall off my stool. See, I knew it was coming.

I manage to grab onto the bar, and Maddox is there behind me for support too. "People actually complained about that? What he does isn't actually stealing. It's him being annoyingly more charming or getting to the client first. Sure, there was that one time he canceled my meeting with—"

"Either way, I knew he was a competitive pain in the ass," Maddox keeps going. "But when it came to you, the only thing I'd been told about you is that you hate how competitive Archer is. So I went with the easiest, low-hanging fruit. The reason you must hate him is because you secretly want to do him. For that, I'm sorry. It's the only card I do regret making. It was to get Damon's attention, not to call you all out."

I groan because even though I appreciate the apology, I'm realizing that Archer was right about the cards. I hate when Archer's right. Still, I say, "Apology accepted."

"In all honesty though, you should want to do him. He is gorg—"

Damon puts his hand over Maddox's mouth. "For the last time, I am running a sports agency, not a matchmaking service. I already have way too many agents hooking up with other agents and clients and God knows who else. I hope that's it."

When he removes his hand, Maddox says, "You know, you'd be a lot less gray if you embraced the chaos that is your matchmaking agency."

Watching them interact, seeing the love they have between them, it's inspiring. It also makes me even more sad. "I wish I could find a relationship like yours."

It's official. The alcohol has swallowed my brain because I can't believe I said that to my boss.

"You might be able to find it one day if you remember to actually focus on something other than work," Damon says.

I glance over where Archer is living his best life, laughing at whatever Buck is saying. He's one of the hardest workers I know, yet today, when it hit knock-off time, it's like he switched it all off. I don't know how to do that.

Though the liquor is helping.

"You're right. I need something to change."

Chapter 16
Archer

I SEE THEM. IT MIGHT BE OUT OF THE CORNER OF MY EYE, BUT I notice. The way Fox, Damon, and Maddox are constantly looking this way, I know they're talking about me.

Is Damon asking Fox to watch over me? To help me because I'm in way over my head? Or is he asking if Fox can work with me without it ending in murder, like everyone else has asked?

The joke is getting old. Valid, but old.

I'm determined to win Fox over. We really will be besties after this. Sure, it might be the kind of besties where one side reluctantly admits to it or lies to everyone and says we're not, but I'll know. Deep down. He won't be able to live without me.

They finish up their talk, finally taking their eyes off me so I can watch them properly, but I'm too premature. As Fox stands and wobbles with Damon helping him, Maddox locks eyes with me. The smile that spreads along his face is one I can only describe as scheming or knowing. This isn't paranoia; they were definitely talking about me. And seeing as Fox is obviously drunk, maybe he'll even tell me what it was about.

The three of them join the dwindling group around the cocktail table, but with the way Fox sways, it's obvious he's been having a lot of fun on his own. Exactly how much did he drink? I wasn't keeping watch, but if every time the bartender was in front of him is any indication, I'd say a lot.

It looked like Fox might even have game. I had to keep averting my eyes because I'd never seen him flirt with anyone before. It was almost like watching a wildlife documentary.

See how the intoxicated peacock of a man makes the other homosexual laugh. This is the beginning of their mating ritual, and it's looking promising.

It made me feel ... things. Things I don't want to acknowledge.

Then Damon came in, and suddenly, their attention was on me.

Damon talks to some of the guys, but Maddox inches closer to me on the other side of the table.

"I know you. You used to work in the New York office."

"Yep."

"So listen. I came to LA to spend time with my partner, but he's worried that Lincoln has had too much alcohol and is insisting on us looking out for him. Would you be an absolute godsend and make sure he gets home all right so I can take Damon out?"

"Me?" Is that what they were talking about? Finding a ride for him? "Why me?"

"You're partners now, aren't you? In business, I mean. Not like Damon and I are partners. Lovers. Husbands in every sense of the word except on paper. Not like that. No."

He's being ... weird.

"Sure. No problem," I say. "I'll make sure he gets home safe."

"Great." Maddox walks back over to Damon and speaks over everyone and says, "Sorry, I'm going to have to steal him away. We have dinner plans to get to." He practically drags him out while Damon shouts to us all that he'll be in town for a few days and will see us all on Monday at the office.

Fox watches them leave with these big, sad puppy eyes, as if silently asking them to take him with them, but once they disappear through the doors, he wobbles himself over to the cocktail table and holds on to the edge like a lifeline.

He really is drunk.

Maybe he doesn't have game at all, and every time I caught the bartender talking to him, it was because he was actually ordering another drink.

"Where have you been?" Luca yells, also a little tipsy. He plants his hands on Fox's shoulders, and Fox winces.

"Dlinkin'." He frowns. "But with an *R* in there."

Luca laughs. "Ooh, this could be fun. Has anyone here actually gone out drinking with Fox before?"

Everyone strains to think about it, but I already know what each of their answers will be. No. Because I found out tonight that Fox doesn't do anything with anyone from the office outside of work.

"What's up with that, man?" Buck asks. "We're amazing people."

Fox snorts. "Incredibly amazing. So amazing that you have a bet on Holloway and me hooking up. What did I ever do to you?"

I'm suddenly regretting agreeing to help him get home. I raise my hand. "I'm right here."

He waves me off. "We're friends now. We're cool."

Luca takes out his phone. "Wait, was becoming friends on the bet list?"

Buck takes his out too, both of them scrolling.

"Ah-ha!" Luca says. "Lincoln Fox admits that he and Archer Holloway are actually friends. Payout ... Whoa."

"How much is it?" I ask, pressing my lips together to stop from smiling.

"Four hundred bucks. That's not as much as the getting married one, but it's still good."

"Who the hell bet that?" Fox asks.

Luca and Buck glance over at the booth where Corrie and Wylder are. "He did," Luca says.

"Wylder?" Fox asks, screwing up his nose. "Does it count if I'm drunk? I told the bartender he had pretty eyes. I wouldn't trust the words coming out my mouf."

"No backsies," I say. "We're friiiiiends."

"Ugh. The judgment I usually reserve for you is solely directed at me now." Fox's head wobbles.

I thought I was going to be the messy one, but between talking with Wylder and Corrie, and then focusing on Fox and Damon at the bar, I haven't been up to order a drink in over an hour.

"I'm choosing to ignore your self-pity over being friends with the most amazing person in the office, and I'm going to drive you home. Maddox made me promise, seeing as you are legless."

"I'm legless? My legs have gone?" He gasps.

"No," Luca says. "He said you're Legolas. That dude from *The Lord of the Rings*."

"That makes even less sense," Fox says.

I approach him and gently take his arm. "Let's get you out of here and get some dinner so you can sober up a bit."

"Fine," he grumbles and steps toward me. "But this doesn't count as a date, and it can't go toward that stupid bet everyone's got going on."

Everyone finds this amusing, and I have to say that it is nice to see a more laid-back side to Fox. I only worry he's going to be embarrassed come Monday morning because this isn't like the guy everyone knows.

"Not a date," I agree. "Never was and never will be a date. Sorry to all of you who bet on that one. Have a good night!"

"I have a feeling the betting odds for them sleeping together just got a lot higher," Buck says.

Fox either doesn't hear him or ignores him like I do. Because we're not going to hook up. Fox has made it clear he can barely be in the same room as me without getting frustrated, and I'm pretty sure you have to at least be in close proximity to have sex. Unless he has a giant dick that can reach from one room to the other.

We hit outside, and there's no breeze or that sense of fresh air. It's one thing I hate about living in LA. Not that New York was much better when I was there.

A silence falls between Fox and me. I think it's safe to say that has never happened before, so I try to break the tension.

"Are you sure you don't want to go back and give the bartender with pretty eyes your number first?"

Fox's footsteps toward the office are slow and deliberate, so I walk close to him in case he needs help along the way.

"Nah. I think I had beer goggles on. But without the beer. Rum goggles doesn't have the same ring to it. I was finding everyone in there hot. Then again, it might have nothing to do with the alcohol and everything to do with it being so long since I hooked up." His rambling is sort of cute, but it also confuses the fuck out of me.

"You haven't? How long has it been? A couple of months?"

A crease appears between his brows in his otherwise flawless skin. "Shit. Almost a year?"

It's my turn to stumble, and I'm not even drunk. "What? How? I mean, why? Maybe you really should go back and get that guy's number."

Do I want him to? Not particularly, but suggesting I throw him a bone—pun intended—won't go over well.

He shakes his head and almost loses balance. "Nope, let's not talk about this anymore. I'm turning a new leaf, making priorities a … well, priority."

"And hooking up is a priority?"

"What? No. Well, yes, but it's not the most important. I need to get back in contact with all my friends again. I've been working nonstop, and it's only been today that I realize I've shut everyone I love out of my life because I've been too busy worrying about my career and how I can become better than you."

"You've had a big year. I've seen your numbers."

"Not as big as you."

"Yes, but not everyone can be as good as me."

"I think it's time to accept that," he says softly.

"Comparison is self-sabotage 101. The only person you should be in competition with is yourself."

"Says the person who thinks everything is a competition."

That's what he might think, but it's nowhere near the truth. I am a competitive pain in the ass, and I am cutthroat, but I've never once blamed losing a client or not getting a contract on anyone else.

I've never begrudged anyone for being better than me. Because it just means I have to put in more work next time to get what I want.

"Really think about that though," I say. "Have I ever said you don't deserve certain clients? Did I get pissed you were also chasing the Dalton brothers? All's fair in love and business. Or whatever that saying is. The only person I ever compare myself to is past me."

Fox's concentration line in his forehead deepens, but I can't tell if he's focusing on my words or on where he's stepping.

"If we're going to work together, we're going to need some ground rules."

"Ground rules?" This should be interesting.

"Yes. Like, no spouting philosophical life lessons. It's a lot easier to dislike you when I think your motivation comes from being evil instead of being ... logical."

"All I'm hearing is you do like me. You just don't want to." I'm joking, obviously, but it's hard not to notice the way he ignores what I've said.

"Oh! And no fucking your assistant."

"Okay, that came out of fucking nowhere." I swear I'm imagining things because it sounded like he growled while saying it. "Where did you get the idea that was even remotely close to happening?"

"I see it. The flirting. The touching. All the touching." He puts both hands up in front of him and moves them around like a mime.

"Is this touching happening right now?" I mock.

He shoves me. Hard. But when I almost run into a light post, Fox gasps and covers his mouth with his hand. "Oops."

"I'm good. Luckily, I'm not as drunk as you are. There's nothing going on between Wylder and me, but even if there was, why do you even care?"

"It's unprofessional, and now I'm tied to you ... professionally."

I get the sense there's more to it than that, but his ramblings and accusations don't make sense. Drunk people are fun like that.

Chapter 17

Fox

It's been so long since I've drunk this much that I'm confused about what's happening to me. I could've sworn a hangover was already kicking in back at the bar, but with every step I take, I'm certain I'm getting more drunk.

That's the only possible reason I'm bonding with Archer and feeding off his words like a starved man.

We make it back to the King Sports building, and Archer uses his employee card to swipe in.

"You need anything from your office?" he asks as we arrive at the elevator banks.

I left my laptop up there, but I'm going to follow what Damon said and not work this weekend, so I'd better leave it where it is. Then I won't be tempted to use it. "Nope."

Archer hits the Down button.

"Are you okay to drive?" I ask.

Archer smiles, and it's official. I'm way too horny to be drunk. Drunken is bad. "Unlike you, I only had two."

"But they were doubles. So that's, like, six."

"Wow. How are you this bad at math? Is that why you earn less than me? You think fifteen percent of a million is one hundred thousand?"

That sounds right. Doesn't it? My face must give up my confusion because Archer laughs.

"You're fun when you're drunk."

"I used to be fun all the time." I sigh.

We get on the elevator, and he presses B for basement.

"What happened?" he asks.

"What do you mean, what happened? Life happened. Work. There comes a time where you get so busy that you forget to return your friend's call. You can't make their wedding or baby shower because you're out of town, scouting or meeting with a client."

"I hear that."

"Ugh. You make it look so easy though."

"Make what look easy?"

"Juggling a million clients and still having a social life. Having friends in the office without crossing boundaries."

The elevator spits us out in the basement, and I follow Archer on unsteady feet.

"It can be easy if you let it," Archer says.

"Oh, and I'm sure it's as easy as saying 'I want more friends,' and then a wave of a wand, a puff of smoke later, bam. I'm surrounded by loved ones."

"Okay, no. You need to work at it. Whatever effort you put into something will determine how much you get out of it."

"There you go being all wise and shit again. I thought I said you weren't allowed to do that? You're doing the worst thing imaginable to my brain. My poor, drunk, fuzzy brain."

"What am I doing to it?" He sounds way too smug.

"You're making me respect you."

His smile is evil. "Uh-oh."

"Uh-oh, what?"

We reach his car, and he unlocks it as he guides me to the passenger side, opening the door for me. I want to pull away from the hold on my arm, but at the same time, it does kind of help me balance.

"Well ..." he says. "Respect is a huge step up from tolerable, so we really are moving in the right direction."

We're standing so close to each other I can feel his breath on my face. I hate that it smells like Coke because it makes me want to drink him up.

Gah. No more alcohol. Ever. It makes my thinkies inappropriate. "In. A. Propriate," I say to myself.

Archer thinks I'm talking to him. "Respecting me is inappropriate?"

"Yes." Wait, no. "No." Hang on. "What was the question again?"

Archer laughs and says, "Get in the car."

I do as he says, sitting happily buzzed while he closes my door and gets in his side. The car rumbles to life—some beefed-up muscle engine under the small hood of whatever sports car it is— but when he pulls out of the parking garage, he pauses before turning onto the road.

I figure he's waiting for a break in the traffic, but when I glance over at him, he's staring right at me.

"I sorta need to know where you live."

"Oh. Right. That would be helpful. It's on South Broadway."

"So I get on Broadway until we hit ..."

"Basically, the Santa Monica Freeway. It's only a couple of miles away."

"How long does it take you to drive to work from there?"

"Forever."

He lets out a whistle. "Would be faster to walk."

"Faster, yes, but in a suit? Driving is a lot less sweaty. When I was looking for somewhere, I could afford a two-bedroom where I am without breaking the bank or move into one of the high-rises in Downtown and pay the same amount for a studio."

"Why do you need two bedrooms? Do you make hookups sleep in another bed?"

"Yes. That's exactly it," I say dryly. "I'm so uptight I can't even share a bed with someone." My insides long for being pressed against someone again. It's as if I realized how long it's been, and now I'm desperate. I went from not even realizing to I fucking need it now.

"Then why?"

"Huh?" I swivel my head in his direction.

"The two bedrooms. You have a roommate we don't know about?"

"Nah. Sometimes my parents come visit for the weekend. It's a five-hour drive on a good day, so it makes sense to get a bigger place so they can stay with me instead of getting a hotel or whatever."

"Aww, are you a momma's boy?"

"What's wrong with actually liking your parents?" Defensive much? Yes. But seriously. My parents did everything for me, and sure, as a teenager, I hated their guts, but I'm a grown-ass adult now who can see that everything they did, they did out of love.

"It's not normal. You're supposed to have a seed of resentment that's buried deep down."

And I thought I was being dramatic. "Resentment?"

"Yes. Because I quit swimming in high school and didn't want to pursue it, my father called me a quitter every day for an entire year."

"What the fu—"

"Okay, I'm exaggerating. It probably wasn't an entire year. It was most likely a few months, but he still brings it up at least once a year when I see my family for Thanksgiving or Christmas."

"That's so sad," I say, and there's only genuine softness in my tone.

"Thanks for the condescension, but I'm okay with it, really. That little seed of resentment drives me to be the best sports agent there is."

"What happened to your mom?"

He shrugs. "It was her job to drag us to Dad's swim meets, to lessons, to all the things Dad made us do growing up. She asked us to do it with as little complaint as possible because we weren't going to get out of it. I thought she was on his side, but as soon as we became grown-ups, she left him. She tells us to be our own people so we don't get tied to anyone or anything to the point we lose ourselves. I sorta wish she had gotten to that point earlier, but the important part is she's supportive now."

I reach out and touch the upper part of his arm, my hand wrapping around his bicep, and damn, that's a nice bicep. Only the touch must throw him because the car swerves.

I swear my life flashes before my eyes, but all I see is the time wasted focusing on work and not much else.

"What the fuck was that?" I yell, my heart hammering like crazy.

"You touched me. I thought you were about to strangle me."

"I was consoling you because you had sucky parents! Next time, I'll know not to feel sorry for you."

His lips purse, and my heart finally starts to settle down.

"I have a question," he says.

"Mm?"

"Where on the scale of hatred to love does pity fall? You think it's above or below respect?"

Unlike every other time he's said something ridiculous, I can't hold in my laugh.

"It's okay. You don't have to tell me. I'm going to take it as a step forward and not back. At this rate, you might admit we're friends for real soon and that you actually like me."

I glance out the window and mutter, "It was a better idea for me to hate you." It didn't open me up to seeing past all the bullshit. I remained safely closed off. I didn't fall for his charming front.

Now? Ugh, right now, I've got my drunk on, and in this state, Archer Holloway might be every bit as irresistible as he thinks he is. "How in the fucking world did you manage to flip that switch?"

Oh right. Copious amounts of alcohol.

"What switch?"

Oops. Thinky thoughts go out loudy louds. "Uh, I said it's weird Wylder put money on that. You know, that I would admit we're friends. Maybe we should do your idea and rig it so we get all the money."

"It's not too late. If you let me put in a call, I can tell the guys that you're putty in my hands and I'm going to take you to bone town tonight."

I scoff. "Bone town. How do you get anyone to sleep with you when you call it that?"

"We won't actually sleep together. I wouldn't put you through that. We can lie and say we did."

"You that bad in bed, huh? Wouldn't subject me to that kind of pain. I understand. You might be good at some things, but making men come isn't one of them. It's okay. I'll take the win on this one."

Archer's knuckles turn white on the steering wheel. "You did not just challenge that you're better at sex than I am."

"You were the one who said you wouldn't subject me to sleeping with you! What was I supposed to assume?"

"That I know you're not interested in me like that."

"Oh. Right. Of course. Knew that."

"Well, you're not, are you?" He cocks a sexy eyebrow at me. No, his eyebrow isn't sexy. He's sexy when he does it.

Ugh, no he's not. Stop it!

First the stomach flu, and now the alcohol. The entire universe is conspiring against me to make me see Archer differently, and I don't want to. Even if he's really pretty to look at.

I tell my eyes to roll. They don't. They stare at Archer's lips.

It's only a brief second that he keeps his eyes on me because he's driving, but he notices. I'm not exactly being subtle in my alcohol-induced horniness.

"Fox ..."

I tear my gaze from his plump lips, which are only emphasized by the scruff on his jaw and chin. "Yeah?"

"You didn't answer me."

"I didn't?"

He shakes his head.

"What was the question again?"

His lips quirk. "You're not getting out of it that easily. Would you or would you not be interested in a hookup?"

"Of course I would—oh, wait, you mean with you?"

"Fucking smartass. Are we at your apartment yet or what?"

I glance out the window, and yes, we are getting close, but I want to keep teasing him. It feels like he's had four years of taunting me, and I've only achieved that power recently. "Soon."

"Okay, so then hypothetically, if I wasn't me and you weren't you, would you hook up with me?"

"No. Because you said you wouldn't be you and I wouldn't be me, so how would I know what the other me would do if you were the other you?"

"What?"

"Exactly!"

Archer takes one hand off the steering wheel to rub that scruffy chin. "You know, you trying to avoid the question makes me think the answer would be yes, and that's an interesting twist of events, I must say."

"What are the circumstances? Are you gagged? Because that could be a turn-on. Maybe if you lost your voice in a terrible accident and couldn't speak. That would be sexy too."

"Ah-ha! You admit that I'm sexy. Maybe I will put down money on the office bet after all."

"I also said you would only be sexy if you couldn't talk." And I can't believe I'm actually fucking admitting this. Oh shit. He's going to tell the whole damn firm. Come Monday morning, there's going to be a mass email sent out telling everyone.

"Hey, duct tape exists for a reason, and I'm keen if you are."

Blood rushes south so fiercely I get light-headed. I throw my head back on the headrest. "Don't fucking tempt me." I point to my building up ahead. "I'm up here."

We come to a stop outside, but there's no street parking, so we're in the shoulder lane, and he's double-parked.

"Thanks for the ride," I say. Even if I'm getting out of his car super hard and wishing I could invite him up.

I might be drunk, but I at least have the wherewithal to know that's a dumb idea. The dumbest. Dumber than spending my life savings on a fake signed basketball by Michael Jordan.

I open the door and jump out, but Archer leans over and puts the passenger window down.

"Damn. You really are drunk."

I check myself over, making sure I've got everything because he has to be talking about me leaving my phone or wallet in the car. "What am I forgetting?"

"You were forgetting who you were talking to for a second there. You said you were tempted to sleep with me."

I step forward and almost stumble into the side of his car. I put my head through the window, and even in my messy state, I know I shouldn't say this next part, but I no longer have control over my body. Drunk Fox is in the driver's seat, and this is the real reason drunk driving is so bad for you.

"The part I hate the most? Is that I know exactly who I'm talking to."

I straighten and turn, leaving him and his stunned expression. That's supposed to be it. He's supposed to drive off now so I can go sleep off this alcohol and forget I ever admitted that.

I only get to the courtyard of my building before he catches up to me.

He grabs my arm, I think to help me, but in my drunken state, I almost fling myself into the fountain. Luckily, he catches me.

"What are you doing?" I ask.

"You looked like you weren't going to make it to your apartment, so I found a parking spot so I can help you. Which way to your apartment?"

I turn toward him and poke at his chest with my finger. "You're trying to sleep with me."

He laughs. "You really must have a low opinion of me if you think I'd take advantage like that."

For some reason, him denying that's what he's trying to do makes me want him to do it. Fucked-up, much?

I pull out of his grip. "I can get there on my own." But now that I've stopped walking and turned us around by facing off with him ... that might not be true.

My building is actually one of two, both identical, and in an L shape. So if I turn back the way I was walking ...

"Are you sure about that?" Archer laughs again. "What floor do you live on?"

I groan. "The second one. And there's no elevator."

"You going to let me help you now?"

"Fine," I relent. Because I really don't know how I'm going to tackle the stairs on my own. "But no funny business. I was only joking when I said I'd have sex with you if you were gagged." I glance at him to find that smug smile on his lips, and damn it. "Mostly joking."

Chapter 18
Archer

This is a bad idea. On a scale of one to the worst mistake in the history of mistakes, what I'm about to do sits somewhere between a required HR meeting and setting my entire career on fire.

I should have left Fox to find his own way to his apartment because it's like he suddenly has eight arms as I help him up the stairs. And they're all clinging to me.

I'm merely getting him into bed. Fuck. *Helping* him into bed. Helping. I didn't illegally park just so I could chase him down and ask him if he meant what he said or if he's drunk, horny, and I'm just ... here.

There's no way I'm going to act on it if he was telling the truth —I like my partners to be at full capacity to consent properly—but my morbid curiosity wouldn't let me drive away.

Even if I have to stay the night, *on the couch*, and ask him in the morning in the ugly light of soberness, I'll do it. My car will probably be towed, but that's future Archer's problem.

And this ... this is exactly why following—I mean helping—Fox to his apartment is the worst idea. Because one little truth bomb has thrown me back to when we first met and I immediately liked him.

Unfortunately, the feeling wasn't mutual, and that's how we

got here four years later: me chasing any scraps he's willing to give me, and him drunk off his ass where he didn't even want to admit that he could be mildly attracted to me.

I'm usually so confident, but when it comes to Fox, I feel like a teenager trying to ask someone way out of my league to prom.

His apartment building is upscale compared to my place, but I'm in a cheap studio in an older building in a crappier neighborhood. With the money we're on, I'm sure we could both afford something more extravagant, but I'm using the money I save on rent to get a nice down payment on a house. And if I want a nice house in LA, I need a chunk of a down payment.

We manage to stumble our way into his apartment, and when I ask, "Where's your bedroom?" he points at … the wall. Not helpful.

I put him in the first room I come across. He flops backward, half hanging off the bed, but his eyes are already closed, and his chest rises and falls evenly. He's so going to regret falling asleep like that come morning.

I should leave, but there's no way I'll let myself yet. I still need sober answers, and if I walk out that door, I'll probably decide to be the bigger person and pretend he never said anything. If I can stay here, in this moment, maybe when he wakes, I'll be able to ask him what I'm dying to know.

Did he mean what he said?

There have been moments of soberness from him mixed in with his drunken hilarity, so it's unclear if he's good at masking how drunk he is or playing it up so he could say things like "I know exactly who I'm talking to."

Though with the way he has passed out right away, I'm going to go with masking.

Which will suck, because I've had a simmering lust for him since the day I met him. That attraction might have faded and resurged over the years depending on Fox's attitude toward me at any given moment, but since we shared that cab coming home from our Dalton meetings, I swear something has changed. That was a turning point, and for the first time since that lustful crush, I get the sense he finally, really sees me. He no longer sees me as a two-dimensional villain in his story. I'm a multifaceted human being with real feelings and drive, but that doesn't mean I can't be genuine too.

I find his guest room, but upon reflection and noticing an en suite in here, I realize this is most likely his room, and he's asleep in his guest room.

Maybe I should take the couch after all. It would be weird, sleeping in Fox's bed ... wouldn't it?

His snore echoes through the apartment, and I realize I'm being dramatic, so I strip down to my underwear and climb into his bed. Annnd, this is the second mistake I've made because his sheets smell like him.

Now, I'm hard and wide-awake. Who needs sleep anyway?

Fuck me, what am I doing?

My mind races all night.

Does he remember what he said? Will he pretend he doesn't? Will he own up to it?

If I sneak out of here and wait to confront him, I can see it now —come Monday morning, if I so much as smile at him with others around, he'll accuse me of mocking him for being drunk or some other extreme reaction. He has always assumed the worst when it comes to me, and it's time I show him I'm not the guy he thinks I am.

I may have blurred lines in the past, and okay, canceling the meeting with Castleberry so Fox didn't get a chance to pitch to him was one of those times. In my defense, I know cars. Fox obviously doesn't because he mumbled something last night about my muscle engine. I'm pretty sure he didn't think it was out loud, so I pretended I didn't hear it. He was talking a lot of slurry nonsense.

Particularly the part where he said he would hook up with me.

Or heavily implied it. That whole conversation is blurry to me because I was in shock for most of it.

A groan comes from the other room. "Fucking hell." It's followed by a rustling noise and then footsteps.

I sit up, waiting for the inevitable—

"What the fuck are you doing here?" There it is. Fox is back to his usual grumpy self. Though, fair enough. I'm crabby when I'm hungover too.

Fox looks bleary-eyed, his hair's a mess, his skin pale, and there's a good chance this morning is not the right time to ask him the burning question on the tip of my tongue.

I know I promised I'd stop messing with him, but this is too hard to resist. "You don't remember? You asked me to come here and then begged me to stay."

He stares at me, blinking. "That doesn't sound like me."

"Hey, I was as shocked as you are, but here I am, proving I can be a team player."

"Why are you in my bed?"

"I started in the guest bed, but in the middle of the night, you climbed in next to me and begged me to hook up with you." Okay, now I'm pushing it.

His gaze narrows. "Lies."

I laugh. "You're right about that. You were pretty out of it when we got here, so I put you in the first bed I saw. You were snoring by the time I worked out it was the wrong room."

"Okay, well, I'm alive, you've done your duty. You can go now."

"I don't even get breakfast after taking such good care of you?" I climb out of bed and stretch, giving him a view of my almost naked form and my morning wood tenting my underwear. I'm hoping he'll show any glimmer of interest so I get the courage to bring up what he said last night, but he refuses to look at me at all.

"With the position I woke up in, I get the sense you literally dumped me in there with no finesse."

Guilty. I pick up my suit pants off the floor. "Does that sound like something I would do?"

"Yes!"

I laugh. "Fair enough. You got any good delivery places around here?" I fish out my phone and open my food app.

He blinks at me again. "You're serious about the breakfast?"

"Yep. You go shower. I'll order something for us."

I pick up my shirt and leave him to it, ignoring his words that follow me.

"I have no idea what is happening right now."

Neither do I. I don't know why I'm determined to stick around and possibly be humiliated. Why am I holding on so tightly to the notion that he might want to hypothetically hook up with me? If I were gagged.

I'm totally about to make a fool of myself, but I order food anyway and then sit on his couch while silently waiting for it to arrive.

Fox takes his time in the shower, and right before I'm about to go ask him if he's fallen over or passed out in there, the water stops.

My phone goes off with the notification that the driver is downstairs with our food, so I prop open Fox's door in case he decides to not let me back in and run down to get it.

When I get back, Fox is out of the shower, only in sweatpants, and it's possible I might drool. It's obvious he has never seen the inside of a gym in his life, but where he's slim, he's not skin and bones. He's tight, his arms are toned, and ... I'm looking way too hard at him.

"Did you go down there with your shirt undone like that?"

I glance down at my abs. "At least I'm wearing a shirt."

"It's laundry day."

"Saturday is your laundry day? You do nothing with your weekend but that? Why is that the saddest thing I've ever heard in my life?"

He crosses an arm over his chest, scratching his opposite shoulder as if that's why he's covering his skin and not his self-conscious way of hiding. "Because you've lived a sheltered life and don't know what real trauma is?"

I'd argue that generational expectations is a kind of trauma, one

I wouldn't wish on anyone else, but he was making a joke, so I'm not going to call him on it.

I hold out the bag of food and the drink tray with coffee. "Hangover food."

Fox averts his gaze as he takes it. "Plates?"

"Fuck plates. That'll mean dishes afterward. I'm good eating out of a wrapper. Unless that's too uncouth for you."

He screws up his face. "Shut up."

"You're so delightful in the mornings."

There are high stools at his kitchen counter, so I make myself at home and slide onto one while he passes over one of the four breakfast burritos in the bag. I take out my coffee from the tray, and he does the same with his.

Then we're in this kind of standoff where we lift the cardboard cups to our mouths while staring, yet trying not to stare at each other.

Fox lets out a sinful "Mmm" as the coffee goes down his throat. His eyes are closed, so I let myself appreciate him for just a moment. That's when his eyes fly open and pin me to where I am.

"This isn't poisoned, is it?"

"Yes. I carry poison around in my pants pocket at all times."

"Maybe it's one of your tricks for stealing clients. Put laxatives in your enemies' coffee so you have to take their meeting."

I cock my head. "Why do that when I can cancel their meetings?"

Fox glowers at me. "Too soon."

I lean my elbows on the counter. "If anything, I should be the one worried about being offed. Our contract is only void if one of us is dead."

"It is really good coffee," he says, staring at his cup. "Eh, death might be preferable at this point."

"Hungover that bad?"

"It's been a while since I drank anything, so it all went straight to my head. I have no idea what I said or did for most of last night. It's not like I blacked out. I remember things ... but it's all a bit ... fuzzy." He rubs his forehead. "Did I really ask you to stay?"

Confession time. "No. I stayed of my own accord."

Fox unwraps his breakfast burrito and takes a bite, groaning once again in a way that sends a wake-up to my cock. "Best hangover food ever." He chews around his food and then swallows. "So, why did you stay?"

Oh, you know, I wanted to see you and ask about all the crazy things you said last night about wanting to sleep with me. I can't exactly bring that up. Not yet. I could, but only if I want to be kicked out of here or embarrass him. "I ..."

He understands my hesitance without actually having said anything. "Shit. What embarrassing thing did I do last night?"

"Other than telling the bartender he has pretty eyes, not much. At least, I don't think it's embarrassing. It was ... enlightening."

"Ergh. I don't want to know what that means."

I get the feeling that if I were to ask him flat out, he'd deny it, and I find myself chickening out. My heart is beating so erratically, there's a chance I'll vomit if I actually say anything. "I knew you had a big night and a lot of drinks, is all. I was looking out for you."

He drinks more coffee and finishes his burrito in three bites. "This is the most thoughtful thing you've done for me yet. Not that you had a huge bar to meet."

I laugh. "You can't let me have a single compliment, can you?"

"It feels really weird complimenting you."

"Ouch."

"No, because if I ever did when we started working together, you'd smile and joke about me being in love with you or being obsessed with you. It's reflex to put a clarifier on the end so you don't think I'm hitting on you."

Maybe this is my opening to feel him out. If he balks, I can play along with how drunk he must have been and dismiss it. If he hesitates ... Shit, I don't know what I'll do if he hesitates because actually acting on it is not a good idea. Not with us now working together.

What are the chances that he's finally interested in me now that we're contractually obligated to get along? It would have to be some sort of man slut karma or something. Not that I'd call myself a man slut. I'll hook up when I go out—I'm too invested in my work for anything more than that—but it's not like numbers or promises are exchanged. Just blowjobs.

Damn, I could really go for a blowjob to make this buzzing in my veins go away.

"Funny you should say that." I take a bite of my own food and force a smug look.

He ignores me, though, and opens the paper bag once again. "Is another one of these mine, or do you get all of them?"

"Go for it. I didn't know how much you'd want to eat." To push or back off, it's hard to know. My past actions have always been to push, but ever since stopping that, I've gotten further with Fox in two weeks than I have in four years.

I watch him as he digs into his second burrito until words tumble out of me. "So apparently, you'd have sex with me if I was gagged."

Fox coughs and splutters, choking on his food. He bangs on his chest, swallows hard, and then coughs until his eyes water. "Apparently, I'd what?" Even his voice is raspy and coarse.

"Hey, that was my reaction too."

Fox puts his burrito down on the wrapper and walks to his sink to pour himself some water. After he downs the entire glass, he puts it on the counter and grips onto the edge with both hands. For a minute, I think he's going to possibly vomit, and if he does, then fine. I have my answer. The idea of me and him makes him puke.

But then he turns his head toward me while he's still holding on like a lifeline. "Did I really say that, or is this another 'you told me to stay' schtick?"

"You really said it. I thought we should clear the air so we didn't have to do it at work, where everyone will speculate."

"And place bets." He turns where he is in his tiny kitchen, now resting his lower back against the counter.

"Exactly."

"You don't need to worry about it getting weird or anything.

Didn't you say I also said the bartender's eyes were pretty or some bullshit?"

Okay, so he's playing it off. This is good. This is ... what we need. It's not exactly what I want, but it's better this way. Expected.

"You did. You said ... a lot of things. And I figured if you did remember, I didn't want you to be embarrassed or think I'd bring it up in front of everyone at work."

"Oh, don't get me wrong, I'm embarrassed."

"I'm not that bad a catch." I force a lighthearted laugh.

"No, not about that. I can't believe I actually said it. Out loud. To you."

That's the part he's embarrassed about? Why would it matter if it wasn't true?

Holy shit. It *is* true.

I stand. "I'm going to ask you up front. Did you mean it?"

"Of course not." Yet, the way he straightens and walks out of his kitchen and away from me says he's trying to get away from the truth.

I follow him down his short hallway, but he hears my footsteps behind him, so he stops and spins on me.

"Why are you following me? I'm going to my bedroom."

"And you say you don't want to sleep with me. Yet, here you are, practically dragging me all the way to your bedroom." Why am I like this? Why can't I tell him that I feel the same way instead of taunting him?

"I didn't say it. Or if I did, I didn't mean it. I was drunk."

"They say that people tell their truth more so when they're drunk because it lowers their inhibitions."

"They also say you shouldn't shit where you eat."

"That's less romantic than my sentiment."

"My point is, either way, even if I did want to sleep with you—which I don't—we work together, and it would be unpr—"

He tries to get past me to go back toward the kitchen, acting on flight mode, but unluckily for him, I'm in fight mode, and I'm fighting to know if he actually could be interested in me or not. I'm fighting for a chance.

Once I have it, I'm not sure I'll be able to stop myself from acting on it, but right here, as I stand in front of him and cut him off, I'm putting future Archer in charge of that mess.

Present Archer is dying to know.

"Do you know how many times you've said you don't do something because it's unprofessional? Like when you accused me of stealing your clients, you said you'd never stoop so low because it's so unprofessional. You never go out with the team because being social with the people you work with would be unprofessional."

"So?" Fox tries to slide past me, turning to his side and pressing himself against the wall, but I'm quick to turn in toward him. My hand flies next to his head. My left hip meets his right one.

"So ... Do you ever let yourself do anything fun?"

His hand goes to my chest as if he's going to shove me away from him, but then his fingers twist into my still-open shirt. "I'm not sure having fun with you would be worth risking my career for."

I tsk him. "There you go, underestimating me as usual." Even if he has a point. I doubt we'd really be ruining our careers. Sure, there's supposedly a rule about no fraternizing between other employees, but it's exaggerated. I know because I checked. Read the employee handbook cover to cover. Plus, our bosses are a couple, Thad is dating a client ... it would be hard for them to argue firing us over this.

"Tell me to leave, then," I say.

He doesn't. All he does is try to escape again, the other way this time.

My hand flies up to box him in on the other side. "Please tell me to leave before I do something we'll most definitely regret afterward."

"You ... I leave. Want."

"That was almost a sentence," I tease.

Fox's pale green eyes flutter closed as a shiver runs through his body. It's impossible to tell if it's in a good way or a bad way, so I give him another opportunity to tell me to fuck off.

"Are you going to tell me to leave, or are you going to let me kiss you?"

I'm glad I don't hold my breath waiting for him to answer. Otherwise, I'd pass out.

Chapter 19

Fox

Is this actually happening, or have I been sleepwalking with the most vivid dream I've ever had?

With Archer's body pressed against mine, his hands locking me in place beside my head, I'm in a daze of lust and confusion.

Do I want to kiss him? Weirdly, fucking yes. Should I kiss him? Fuck no.

"Why are you doing this?" And why am I so desperate for this to be real and not one of those meathead jock moments where I let it slip I'm attracted to him so he can make a mockery out of it?

"Isn't it obvious?"

"Do you want me to kiss you so you can go tell HR, get me fired, and take the Daltons for yourself?"

Archer's face falls. "Are we really back on not trusting me?"

"You have never shown any interest in me before, so why now? Why, when we're contractually partnered, do you think it's a good idea to do this?"

"Oh, this is possibly my worst idea ever, but—"

"Exactly. The only thing I can think of is that you want to fuck with me. If not to get me fired, then maybe it's to tell everyone you got me to hook up with you or kiss you so you can gloat." Which only reminds me of something else. "Or maybe you paid into this bet. You're only trying to win."

Archer's so close I can see when he grits his teeth, setting his square jaw that's usually hidden under scruff. "Or maybe it's because I've always thought about kissing you, but with your clear and often reiterated hatred for me, I didn't think it was even a possibility."

Why won't he admit this is all a farce? That I drunkenly said I'd hook up with him if he was gagged, and he's taking it way too far? That if I give in to him, it will fuck everything up? Why won't he stop fucking tempting me to give in?

"Just because we're attracted to each other doesn't mean we should act on it. We really fucking shouldn't. What happens at the office on Monday when we see each other? What happens when we have to work side by side with our shared clients?"

"Don't you think I fucking know it's a bad idea?" he growls. "You think I'm throwing myself at you on a whim?"

"Yes," I say. "Or you have ulterior motives."

"This would be fucking up my career as much as yours, yet I can't bring myself to walk out of here. Why do you think it's so impossible for me to actually be into you?"

Other than he's him and I'm me and the charismatic jock was never into the average gay guy that I am? "Because I've been horrible to you." A much more valid answer.

The croak in his tone goes right to my dick as he says, "But I have a confession to make. I kind of like it when you're horrible to me."

I think back to every time I've stormed into his office, pissed about something. "I mean this with sincere concern for you, but you might want to see a shrink about that." I hope to fuck he can't feel how much he's getting to me. He's wearing his suit pants, I'm in sweats, and I don't have any underwear on.

The longer we stand here, the more I ask myself why I haven't moved. Yes, he has me blocked in, pressed against the wall, but it's not like I can't duck under his arm. He's not keeping me hostage.

So why am I not running away? Why am I not kicking him out?

And why in the fucking hell can't I stop glancing at his lips?

Yes, I'm attracted to him, but I meant what I said. That doesn't mean we have to act on it. I'm a grown-up. He's a grown-up. Hooking up will throw everything off-kilter. It will make work unbearable. Especially if everyone else finds out. If Damon finds out.

Obviously, sleeping with a coworker or client isn't a fireable offense, or Thad, Cam, and Xavier wouldn't still be at King Sports. But that's not to say it's not frowned upon.

"I can't help it," Archer says. "When you get angry, your nostrils flare, and you look like a teeny tiny dragon. Or kitten. Have you seen those videos of kittens trying to be tough, and it's all fluffy cuteness?"

I hate that for me. "I'm so glad my serious work complaints are seen as cute and fluffy."

"It's not only that. I like that you come to me directly. You don't go tattle on me like we're in kindergarten. You face your problems, and even if that problem is me, I respect the hell out of you for it."

I suck in a sharp breath. Maybe I'm the one who needs a shrink. He calls me cute, I get offended. He says he respects me, and it brings me so fucking close to breaking.

"The more I get to know you, the more I respect you too," I admit. "But I'm not going to lie. I'm terrified if I give in to this, you're going to hold it over my head or do something to prove to me that my initial instincts about you were right."

There's a war inside me between the urge to take the risk and press forward or the strength to push him off me and shut this down. My entire body tingles, craving to be touched, but why does it have to be craving him? Up until a week ago, I wouldn't have even entertained the idea. Now, I'm fighting every instinct to sink to my knees for him.

To make him come.

Archer's frozen, his lips pressed together, and I hate that my instinct is to lift my hand to rub my thumb over them to pull his bottom lip out to make it its usual plumpness. I'm only thankful I can refrain from following through on it.

"I don't know what I can do to get you to trust that I have no ulterior motives here. And maybe I need to back off so you don't have to make the decision. But so you know, the only reason I'm doing this, the only reason I'm here and I stayed the night, is because last night while you were drunk, you gave me a glimmer of something I'd never had with you before: hope. Hope that you finally see me as someone worthy of you. That you could possibly see me as more."

He's saying all the right things, leaving this up to me, and I'm right on the edge of letting go. It would be so easy, so fucking easy, to say "Fuck it" and go for it, but I've been denying my awe of him for so many years—even to myself—that I'm wary of these new feelings. Of my desire to actually kiss him. Touch him. Think about what the tattoos under his clothes look like.

He huffs a laugh. "You say that you'd be the one embarrassed by this situation, but here I am, basically throwing myself at you, not asking for promises, vowing to never tell a soul, and you're still hesitating. If anything, I'm the one who should be embarrassed by wanting something so fiercely that I haven't removed myself from the guy who obviously wants nothing to do with me." He smiles, but it's not one of his cocky smiles. It's self-deprecating and almost defeated. "Maybe I shouldn't have stayed." He drops one hand from the wall, giving me a clear path. I don't move. "Drunken ramblings mean nothing. Obviously. But I thought if I have a chance, I'm not going to throw away my shot. Consequences be damned. So I'm sorry for putting you in this difficult position. I'm going to go." Yet, he doesn't move either. And it's not in a *I'm using this as a tactic to get you to give in* kind of way.

At least, I don't think it is. I hope it's not. Because it's fucking working.

The idea of him dropping his other hand, straightening up, and walking out of here is the thing that lets me bury my concerns about what will happen after this.

And as that second hand begins to leave the wall, every inch of my skin, every nerve, every molecule and atom inside me protests.

My fingers gripping his shirt tighten, and I pull him against me. "Wait."

"Wait?" Archer asks.

It's surreal that he's the one standing in front of me like this. That he's practically begging for *me* to kiss *him*.

I can't get my mouth to physically say "Yes" or "Okay" or any other affirmative words. They scream in my head, trying to break free, but I can't get them out. It's as if the stubborn part of me has metaphorically duct-taped my mouth shut.

Yet, there's no denying I want this. My heart hammers wildly, and my cock is so hard and aching that I can't let him walk away now.

There's a lot I can't do in this moment and only one thing I can.

I surge forward and press my lips to his.

It takes a few seconds for either of us to register it, but once he does and he moans into my mouth, everything is crystal clear.

I'm kissing Archer Holloway.

His tongue pushes past my lips and strokes against mine.

I'm kissing Archer Holloway.

His hands fly to my hips, and he squeezes them in his firm grasp.

I'm kissing Archer Holloway.

My own hands explore, running up his sculpted chest under the panes of his open periwinkle shirt.

I'm kissing Archer Holloway.

I still don't think it's sinking in, but there's no way I'm going to stop. All I can do is enjoy the ride and hope with every inch of my being that it's not a mistake.

Chapter 20
Archer

For something I never thought was a possibility and therefore had no expectations going into this, he's exceeding every single one of them. It really does pay to set the bar low.

It's probably because I've worked with him for so long, seen how uptight he can be, that maybe I thought he'd kiss like a dead fish.

But there's nothing dead or fishy about the way he meets each stroke of my tongue or the way he replies to my moans with a small one of his own. Unlike mine, where it's deep and long, the noise he makes is more like a short, needy whimper.

I think I'm still in shock that this is happening at all. I was prepared to walk away. I told myself not to push, but there's something in the way he was hesitating that made me hold my position. As soon as I dropped my hand, he was free to walk away.

I needed this to come from him, and not because I wanted to gloat to everyone like he thought, but because he's the one who distrusts me, so he has to be sure.

Maybe if I weren't so focused on being the best all the time, putting business over common courtesy, he never would've hated me. It wouldn't have taken four years to get to this point.

I've always thought he was an attractive man, but the way he grips my shirt with the material balled up in his fists, and the way his desperation vibrates from his body, it's sexier than I ever could have imagined.

I never let myself imagine because I knew it was a no go.

A never going to happen.

And now, here it is. Happening.

My skin feels too tight for my body. My clothes are too restrictive. Mostly my pants.

As much as I want to rip at them, to ditch every article of clothing on me, I also think that should come from him.

"Fuck," he croaks as he pulls back, breaking our mouths from one another. I'm almost certain he's about to put a stop to it, but before disappointment can set in too hard, he reaches for my undone shirt and slides it off my shoulders. "I need this gone."

Oh, thank fuck. We're still on the same page.

My shirt drops to the floor, and then Fox reaches for my pants and pops the top button.

"These need to go too." He might have hesitated to begin with, but since crossing that line and deciding to do this, he's all in.

He unceremoniously drops my pants and then brings our hips together, grinding his hard cock against mine.

There are still too many layers of clothing between us. I need to feel his skin on mine everywhere. But there's one thing I'm more desperate for, and that's his mouth again.

I cup his face and run my fingertips through the back of his hair. He looks so sexy with it unstyled. He usually has meticulously neat hair, but like this? The front falling in his face, the back a complete mess, he looks like he's been thoroughly fucked already.

His lips are shiny from our kiss, and as I bring our mouths back together, the chaos of trying to get each other naked slows right down. Fox becomes pliant, finally handing over some control to me.

It's quick though. A single moment of him melting into me. It's possibly even better than him taking charge, but then the control is back in his hands as he breaks his mouth from mine again.

"I need you naked. In my room." He tries to rid my pants with his foot from where they sit around my ankles, but they get stuck.

I'm quick to pull them free, and as soon as they're gone, Fox grips my ass and starts pulling me down his hallway toward his bedroom blindly while he goes back to kissing me.

He drags me all the way with his eyes closed—I know because I open mine to make sure we aren't going to run into anything. It gives me the impression that he has blindly found his bedroom time and time again with many different men. Or maybe one man. Either way, it's obvious he has experience with it, and while the idea of anyone I'm with having a past doesn't usually get to me, with Fox ... it's almost as if I never imagined he would fuck like this, so wrapping my head around it is not as easy as it should be.

I've thought about it for sure. Especially when he's come to work slightly unkempt because he's usually so flawless in appearance. But here, watching it for myself, it's almost like an out-of-body experience. Surreal.

Or maybe that's because it's Fox in general.

When we reach his bed, I prepare for him to fall backward and pull me on top of him. Instead, he spins us and pushes me down hard, breaking us apart.

My legs hang off the bed, and he stands in between them.

He's so fucking hot I can barely stand it. From his wide shoulders to narrow hips, he has a swimmer's body ... except with less muscle. I'm definitely not complaining about that.

I generally don't have a type when it comes to body shape, but there's something about the way Fox's slim but hard build moves that makes me think I've found my ultimate type.

He stares down at me, taking all of me in, and then he leans over me, keeping his feet on the ground and balancing on one hand on the bed while the other trails down my throat and over my chest tattoo.

"I've always wondered what ink was under your shirt."

"Now you know."

He traces the curving waves placed over my heart. It was the first tattoo I'd ever gotten. Dad had always told us that tattoos were tacky, and if we were going to be Olympians, we couldn't have any attention being drawn to us outside of swimming. So I found a place that accepted my fake ID, and the only thing I could think to get was something related to water. Being in the pool for what felt like more time than being dry, the calm water somehow felt like I was being constantly dumped on by wave after wave of disdain for the sport. So I got the waves.

Fox looks like he wants to ask me about them, but thankfully, he doesn't. I'm not going to get into my daddy issues with him so close to me. Touching me. His fingers move lower, down my torso until they brush the top of my underwear.

Fox is full of surprises because where I think he's going to tease me, maybe dip his fingertips under the waistband, he drops his hand to palm my cock. Damn the thin bit of material separating his skin from mine. His grip tightens, and he gives my dick a firm stroke. It's lucky I'm lying down or my legs might have buckled under me. The sensation sets me on fire.

"Damn," he whispers.

It's not in a sexy "Dammmn" kind of way where the word is drawn out. It almost sounds like actual disappointment. I don't have the biggest dick around, but I'd like to think it's not disappointment-worthy.

"Damn what?" I ask, though my ego doesn't want me to.

"I figured someone with so much big dick energy that you'd be packing something smaller."

I laugh, but it's more from relief. "You sound disappointed."

He releases my cock and stands straighter, digging his fingers into the sides of his sweats. "Eh, I've always found it's not the size that matters anyway. I was just hoping I was right about you, but it seems I keep being wrong at every turn."

I'm only half listening because my focus is solely on the bulge in his pants and his hands hesitating to pull them down his legs. "I'd be happy to prove you wrong in every single way if you hurry up and ditch your clothes."

He stares at me for a moment before subtly shaking his head and letting out a loud breath. "I still can't believe this is happening."

"Honestly, same. If you want to stop—"

"No. I don't. I should. But I don't."

"What do you want?" I ask.

His glance moves down toward my cock. "I ... I want to trust that whatever happens, it's not going to get out. You're not going to hold it over my head."

I try not to be offended, but when it comes to trust, well, yeah, of course we have issues. "Whatever you're willing to give me, I'll protect it. I know my sincerity might not mean much to you, but something I've never done is lie to you. You have my word. This doesn't leak to anyone outside of us."

His resolve disappears, as well as his sweats. His cock springs free, and my mouth waters at the sight. The mushroom tip is large and pink, and I lick my lips, wanting a taste.

"Fuck, I need that in my mouth," I say.

"Funny. I was thinking the same about yours. Same time?"

As hot as that could be, with his distrust of me, if we did that, he'd probably be so in his head about me saying something that he wouldn't be able to enjoy himself, and I don't want that.

"Nah. You first. Climb up here." I pat the top of my chest.

He hesitates again, but before I can doubt myself, he says, "At least let me get a good look first."

I lift my hips and pull off my briefs, chucking them on the floor.

Fox licks his lips again, but his eyes flutter closed. "Okay, that was a mistake. This is going to be over so fast." He climbs on top of me, knees going either side of my stomach, and then he starts inching his way up my chest. He leans over and reaches for his pillows to prop my head up, and when I lift my neck, the thick head of his cock is right near my lips.

He's so close I swear I can already taste him.

There's one more look of disbelief before he grips the base of his dick, his hips surge forward, and his cock brushes over my lips, leaving a wet trail of precum.

My tongue darts out to lick it off, and he lets out a shuddery breath.

"Fucking hell," he rasps.

"Give it to me." I sound like I'm begging. I am, but that's not the point. I don't beg. But I've also never wanted someone the way I want Fox right now.

I want him in my mouth. I want to suck him all the way to the back of my throat and hold him there.

This time when he pushes forward, I open my mouth and can't help moaning as I let him in. His tight, velvety skin feels hot on my tongue.

With how he's positioned, he's straddling me up near my shoulders so my arms are restricted from being able to stroke the rest of him my mouth can't take. I'm tempted to throw him off me so I can sink down and deep-throat him, but this is fine. For now.

It gives me the best view as I look up at him, up his smooth torso to the strained muscles in his throat and the look of bliss on his face.

I might not be able to reach the front of him, but my hands can grip his ass and guide him deeper.

Fox gives an experimental thrust, and I internally chant, "Yes, yes, yes." He does it again, and his breath catches. He keeps going, increasing his pace but shallowing his depth.

My abandoned cock leaks onto my stomach, and I can't wait for my turn. I want more, and I want it now, but I'm also enjoying this way too much to change positions.

I can see his rapid pulse on the side of his neck, hear the desperation in his small grunt, feel the swell of his cock in my mouth, and taste his pleasure on my tongue.

"Fuck, fuck, fuck," he says and pauses. He grips the base of his cock, but my mouth is still wrapped around the tip. "I knew this was going to be quick, but I'm probably one second away from it being over."

I sink back onto the pillow, letting him fall from my mouth. I'm torn because if he comes, that means I'm next, and I really want to fucking come, but at the same time, once that happens, this is over, and I have no fucking clue what will happen after that.

He strokes himself slowly, still staring at my wet lips, which are no doubt shiny with spit.

"Come in my mouth," I blurt. "I don't care if it's now or if you want to blow me first. I just ... Fuck, I want it so bad."

"Deal."

But instead of his cock back in my mouth, his whole body disappears as he slides off me and onto the floor. He kneels between my legs, dips his head, and before I realize what's happening, he deep-throats me all the fucking way until his nose hits my manscaped groin.

I suddenly have an intense understanding of what the fuck he means because I don't want this to be over, but it will be way too fast with his throat contracting around my cock.

The noise that leaves me sounds like I've been allowed reprieve after days of torture. It's feral and needy mixed with relief.

I want to lift my head and watch as he sucks his way back up my shaft and then swallows me down again. And again. But I can't bring myself to open my eyes. I know that once I do, this will be all over.

Yet, when he continues to work me over and the slurps echo around his room, I can't help myself. I give in to temptation to look, and it's even worse than I was expecting.

Because while I knew the idea of Fox's lips wrapped around my cock would be a salacious sight, it's nothing compared to the reality of it.

His mouth is stretched wide, his right hand working my base, but while his left hand is nowhere to be seen, I can tell he's jerking himself off with the way his shoulder shakes with the movement.

It's too much. I can't hold out much longer.

I only have enough time to run my hand through his hair and grit out, "I'm going to come," before my release floods his mouth.

Not that I was anywhere near being able to think straight enough to time that, but it had to have only been a few minutes. Tops.

I shudder through my orgasm, hips pushing up into his mouth as his tongue licks lazily around my head.

In the next second, he's on top of me again, still frantically jerking himself, and I've barely caught my breath when he says, "Open up."

He's already coming by the time I register what he says, and spurts of cum hit my cheek and chin, but that's all I let escape. I make sure I get every last drop of the rest of what he has to give, only releasing him when he slowly pulls out of my mouth himself.

He remains straddling me as we catch our breaths, and when he finally rolls off me, lying on his back, the silence in the room is deafening.

With the cloud of lust dimming with each minute we recover, a brewing storm of tension replaces it.

As I lie here, covered in sweat, I have to ask myself, do I regret it?

My dick must still be in charge because as I look at the spent lump that is Lincoln Fox, my gut reaction is no.

The only question left is, will he?

Chapter 21

Fox

Refusing to look at the person whose cum you've swallowed is an everyday hookup culture experience. Yup. That's what I'm going with.

Because as I stare up at my ceiling, I'm trying to convince myself I should be making excuses to get him out of here as quickly as possible or freaking out about what's going to happen at the office on Monday. While I do care about Monday, I'm not as worried as I probably should be.

I'm ... eerily okay with what's happened. It makes sense. When you're pulling on a rope so tightly, there's only so much tension it can withstand. Eventually, it will snap. Of course, when I anticipated the rope snapping between Archer and me, I figured it would be around his neck first. For it to go this way, I'm ... I can't say surprised, but it was definitely unexpected in an expected way.

That makes absolutely no sense, but it's impossible to think logically and clearly after blowing my load.

Archer shifts so he's no longer eye level with my dick and rolls over onto his side to face me, but I still refuse to glance his way. He doesn't dare touch me, and I can hear the smile in his voice as he says, "This is the part where you tell me to not let the door hit my ass on the way out."

I force myself to look at him and keep my face as passive as possible because I don't know how this is going to play out. "If that's how you want to play it, by all means."

I hold my breath, and he holds our stare. It's a battle of wills. He's waiting for me to kick him out, and I'm waiting for him to make the choice to leave without making it a big deal.

Ideally, we'd get up, clean ourselves off, he'd leave, and we'd never speak of this again, but I'm reluctant to put that kind of boundary on this. If I tell him to forget it ever happened, with the type of guy Archer is, it would be like telling him to never think of elephants. Then the only thing he'd do is think of elephants.

"What if I'm not ready to leave yet?" he asks.

This is why I'm not pushing any rules on him. Because he's like a child, and it's as if he has this inner need to be defiant. Or to have the last word.

If I truly want to keep this a secret from everyone at work, I have to play it off like it's not a big deal. Truthfully, in the big scheme of things, it's not. It has the potential to turn into something big, but only if we let it.

If it does happen to get out, the only concern I have is about what Damon will think. If my career will suffer because of it. There might not be official consequences to it, but that doesn't mean Damon won't lose respect for us.

I shrug and get myself up, ignoring the self-consciousness that takes over as he tries—very unsuccessfully—to not ogle my naked body. This is what my brain chooses to be insecure about? He heard my sex noises and saw my O-face, but this, being naked in front of him, is the thing that might break me.

I need therapy. I pick up my sweats and pull them up my legs. I'll probably burn them after this anyway because every time I look at them now, I'll think of Archer's lips. His cock. Somehow, I find a nonchalant tone. "Do what you want. I'm going to shower, throw on some clothes, and then go do something."

"Do what?"

"Anything. Nothing. Drive somewhere new. Not sure yet. Last

night might be fuzzy, but I do remember one thing." Sure, the memory is hazy around the edges, but I fully remember Damon telling me to take weekends for myself whenever I can. "Damon basically told me that any time I can forget about work, I should take full advantage. Otherwise, I'm going to work myself into the ground."

"He's a smart man. Though I recall saying something similar to you myself yesterday when I was trying to get you to come out for drinks." Archer leans up on his elbows, his muscular abs contracting, making that V more distinctive and drawing my attention toward his deflating cock resting against his manscaped pubes. He has absolutely no reservations about still being naked. "Why is his advice the one you're taking?"

I lick my lips, distracted from whatever he's saying. His small laugh pulls me out of my dick fog and his words finally register. "If you recall, I did take your advice. I went out. Got drunk. Called Damon by accident and left a voicemail rambling about not being able to hit the End button before he picked up, but of course, all he heard was me complaining about not being able to hit something, and he assumed I meant you. Which is why he made an appearance at all. His advice was to enjoy my weekends. Yours made me do some really stupid things."

"Stupid but entertaining, so we all win?"

"No. You win. Actually, if we're going by all the things I've done in the last twelve hours, it's not only you who's won. Whoever bet on us has too."

"You make that sound like the decisions you made weren't even fun for you, but that can't be right. Especially when I can still taste your ... fun." He's doing what he does best. Trying to get a reaction out of me.

"I never said it wasn't fun, but I'm almost certain it wasn't what Damon had in mind when he told me to forget about work for the weekend. Apparently, my brain decided that forgetting who I work with was also included in that."

"So this is you worrying about who at work will find out."

I throw my hands up by my sides, and they land on my hips. "What are you trying to pull from me here? Are you waiting for me to threaten you or tell you not to tell anyone or give you the kind of power you love to have where you hold something over my head?"

He frowns. "I want the complete opposite. I'm trying to gauge exactly how you feel about this and if it's going to blow back on me somehow. Like you'll blame me or tell HR or—"

"Okay, so we both don't want this getting out. Good. Glad we have that sorted."

Archer climbs out of bed, bypassing his underwear on the floor, and stands in front of me. Still completely fucking naked. He's playing unfair. "To be honest, I don't give a shit who finds out, but I'm not going to be the one to tell anyone. I do hope it means we can move forward and work together. Maybe you could even join the team again when we go out for after-work drinks. You can pretend this never happened if you want, but there's only one thing I hope for. I don't want us to go back to where you yell at me, I get mildly annoyed, and then I'm the one left feeling like an asshole. This"—he waggles a finger between us—"is separate to our working relationship."

We're on the same page, which is good, but separating work and personal issues will be more difficult now that we've slept together. This is yet another reason why I try not to get close to people I work with. Because stuff like this happens, and it adds more stress to an already stressful job.

"Think you can handle that?" Archer asks.

Not even a little bit. Still, keeping this as separate as possible is what I want too, albeit impossible for me. Probably. Who knows?

I nod once at him. "We're on the same page."

"Good." Finally, he puts me out of my misery and reaches for his underwear. "I'll let you shower and get on with your weekend."

"What have you got planned?" Maybe I can steal his idea and go do that. Uh, when he's not there though. I don't want to follow him, but I can't think of anything to do.

"Working." He grins.

"Why do you get to work? What happened to leaving work at work and going out, and—"

"I'm not the one who has issues with compartmentalizing. I can make time for fun and work."

"And switch in between that easily?"

"This might be shocking for you to hear, especially when you hold me in such high regard, but switching off parts of my brain is scarily easy. Maybe I hit my head one too many times as a child learning to do flip turns in the pool, so I can only have so many parts of my brain working at the one time."

As much as I appreciate him trying to make me feel better, it's only making me more envious of his ability to actually do it. "Or you might have your shit together and your priorities straight?"

"They might be the only straight thing about me."

I laugh.

"Go for a drive. See where you end up. Go to a roadside diner, gamble with food poisoning, and play the game Friend or Possible Murderer while you people watch."

"Do I want to know where you came up with that game?"

"The Olympics," he says like it makes total sense. "Watching my dad swim laps got boring really quickly. Me and my siblings had to come up with some way to entertain ourselves."

"So you'd pick random people in the crowd at the Olympics, of all places, and decide if they would be friendly or homicidal?"

"It wasn't always the Olympics. Any championship, swim meet, endorsement deal ... Basically anyone we didn't know. If it weren't for the expectation of us to be seen and not heard, we probably would've gone and talked to the strangers to see if we were right. We were that bored. Or perhaps we were resentful. Because I like watching swimming now that my sister is one of my clients."

"I'm sure the monetary value she brings to your life has nothing to do with that."

He rubs his jaw. "It's really not that much, but it's more than what I ever got from Dad, so maybe." Archer's still standing in my bedroom with nothing more than his underwear on and talking about his family.

He's giving mixed signals. First, he wants me to pretend this never happened, and then he goes and says something that's so real that it draws me to him even more.

I wonder if there's a self-help book that deals with compart-mentalization. I need it.

Chapter 22
Archer

Come Monday morning, I'm ready to put on a confident facade, a fake smile, and pretend like Lincoln Fox didn't blow my mind—and other parts—on the weekend.

Usually, Fox and I arrive at similar times, and the thought of having an awkward encounter in the elevator didn't sound appealing to me, so I've made sure to be a few minutes later than usual. Forty-five can still be considered "a few," right?

The thing is, I'm not scared of seeing him or nervous I'll lose my ability to speak around him—I can fake confidence better than anyone—it's *his* reaction I'm worried about. And not even for the reasons I should be.

We agreed to keep it quiet, and I trust him to do that, but I don't trust that this won't send us backward. I'm expecting him to be cold and distant like he has for the past four years.

But when I finally make my way onto that elevator and it opens on the King Sports floor, I steal a quick glance toward his office when I step off. My expectations are blown out of the water, but not in a good way.

His office is dark, his door wide open. He's not even in yet.

"Good morning, boss," Wylder says from behind the reception desk. He's literally spinning on the chair while pulling the lever to make the height go down, then standing and doing it all again.

"Productive morning you're having, I see." At least he's distracting me from staring at Fox's door like it could give me answers if I looked hard enough.

"Vi called in sick, so I'm on reception duty. How much does she get paid, by the way? Because I've been here for an hour, and not one call has come through. If she is so sick and dies, can I have her job?"

"Did you turn the messaging service off and redivert all calls to you?" I ask.

He finally stops spinning. "Did I do what with the what?"

Hoo boy. He has fucked his whole day. I step forward and lean over the reception desk, picking up the phone, hitting the divert button, and entering reception's extension. As soon as I hang the receiver up, the phone lights up like a Christmas tree, and ringing hits our ears.

"Have fun with that," I say. "You're lucky I caught up with a lot of work over the weekend, so I shouldn't need you today."

Wylder stares at the flashing phone and groans, but when he answers the call, his tone and greeting is professional. He might not like sports, and this certainly isn't his dream job, but he's pulling his weight. That's the main thing.

As I head for my office on the opposite side of the floor from Fox's, I can't help glancing back once more. Light is still off; door is still open. He hasn't magically appeared while I haven't been looking.

This is so much worse than I was expecting. There's nothing on the work calendar saying he's out of town or meeting with a client, so I try to tell myself that I arrived late and that it's possible he planned to do the same, but as the hours tick by and I use every excuse possible to leave my office—I think I'm up to my eighth cup of coffee before midday—that light in his office never turns on.

This morning, when I told Wylder I'm all caught up on my work, it was true, but now that I've spent all morning obsessing over why Fox isn't here, I'm behind schedule once again, so I block out the Fox drama and focus on work. It's more of a struggle than it usually would be to compartmentalize, and if this is how

Fox feels on a regular basis, no wonder he's so tightly wound at work.

Before I know it, it's past 5:00 p.m., and everyone is going home. With the day over and the realization that Fox never came into work, I go in and check the office calendar for the millionth time today. Though I haven't checked it in the last five hours. And there, in black and white, is the thing I feared most would happen. His schedule now says he'll be working out of office for the entire week.

I went so far past the line with him that we can't even see the line anymore. The line is in Canada. This needs to be fixed. Preferably before we have to have a joint meeting with one of the Daltons. We don't have one scheduled, but it's inevitable.

Instead of texting him, which he can ignore, or calling him from my phone, which he can also ignore, I play dirty and call his cell from the office number.

"Lincoln Fox," he answers, his voice distinct and professional and not at all sick-sounding like I was hoping.

"Oh, so you're not dying of the flu, then. Good to know."

"Flu? Why would I—wait ..." I can picture him pulling his phone away from his ear to check who has called. "Who said I had the flu?"

"No one, but I was sorta hoping for it."

"Thank ... you? I hope you feel like you're dying too."

I smile. "It was either that, or you're not in the office because you're avoiding me, and I'd prefer it if you were staying away because you're sick and not because of us." I wince and prepare to hear what he has to say to that, even if I already know I don't want to know.

Except, he surprises me by playfully making the tsk sound. "There you go again, thinking everything is about you."

"Okay, if it's not about me, why are you out this week?"

"Because I'm not even in LA."

"Oh. Where are you?"

"I don't want to say ..."

"You ran away to join a traveling circus." While I'm relieved his disappearance isn't about me, and he does seem to still be in high spirits when it comes to interacting with me, I'm not one hundred percent certain I don't have something to do with him not being in the office. He might have a genuine excuse for being wherever he is, but it's weird that two days ago, he didn't mention plans of going out of town.

"After you left my place on Saturday, I thought about what I could do. Where I could go. And the embarrassing thing is, the only place I could think of was home. As in Arizona home. It's been too long since I saw my parents, my cousins, my friends who never left that town after high school. So I called Damon, told him after we talked I realized I had been neglecting my family, and asked him if it would be okay to ask to work from home this week, and he cleared it with Cam and Xavier for me."

"You were too scared to ask Cam and Xave, but you felt confident enough to call the CEO?"

"It was Damon's idea," he says.

"Still. That's ballsy."

"After Friday, I figured I couldn't embarrass myself any more in front of him than I already have and had to shoot my shot. Maybe something happened on Saturday morning that gave me a false sense of confidence." The smile in his voice makes me wish I'd called him via video chat. I want to see that smile.

"False? Nah, you earned that confidence." I'm not getting that performance out of my head anytime soon.

"Whatever it was that made me ask, I'm glad I did. Damon invited me to that NFL anniversary thing in Phoenix this weekend, seeing as the firm has represented a lot of players over the years. Marcus Talon is getting some lifetime achievement award, so Brady will be there too."

"Who knew drunk dialing your boss could make you his favorite?"

"Aww, is someone jealous they're not every boss's favorite? Don't worry, you still have Cam."

I laugh hard. "You say that like he doesn't think I'm the biggest pain in the ass."

"You are a pain in the ass, but everyone still likes you."

"Everyone except you."

He mutters so quietly I barely hear him. "Nah. I don't think we can really say that anymore."

"Sorry, what was that? Could you please repeat the phrase that opens the bowels of hell to let the snow in so it can freeze over?"

Fox sighs. Loudly.

"Oh, never mind. All is right with the world." There's a pause, the longest silence in fucking history, and I figure I need to end the call. "I'm glad to know you're not in hiding because of me. That was all I was calling for. To make sure we're all good."

"We're good."

"In that case, I should get back to work. I'm behind after someone made me worry about him all day."

"You know, I'm starting to think you might be the one with a work-life balance problem. Didn't you work all weekend too?"

The only reason I've been behind lately is because I haven't been able to stop thinking about him, but it's not like I can say that out loud.

"Eh, I'll climb out of this hole soon enough."

"I'll let you go so you can get closer to it. I'm about to have dinner with my parents."

"Are you at least doing fun things while you're there?"

"Having dinner with my parents is fun. And delicious. Nothing beats a mom's home cooking."

"I'll have to take your word on that." Even when Mom and Dad were together, my mom wasn't a trad wife. She couldn't be with the rigid swim schedules Dad had us doing. We basically lived on protein shakes and takeout. Not the good takeout either, but the type where Mom had to ask for modifications to make our meals as bland and healthy as possible.

"Damn. I forgot about your sad childhood."

"It wasn't sad," I say, but let's face it, it sorta was.

"No traditional home-cooked meals? Child abuse."

"Eh, I'd say I turned out okay without them."

"Would others say that though?"

Fucking hell, this guy. I always found his barbs entertaining, but after sleeping with him, it's like they turn me on. It's foreplay, and now I'm sad I won't get to see him until next week.

We end up talking for over an hour, basically ribbing one another and talking about our different childhoods.

We only end the call when his mom's voice interrupts him mid-sentence to tell him dinner's ready.

"It's like I'm back in high school," he says in a low voice. "I have to go."

"All good. Talk to you later."

As soon as he's off the line, I immediately miss the conversation. I'm thankful there was no time to tell him to call me as soon as he's done eating so we can talk some more.

I'm in trouble when it comes to Fox, and it's something I never saw coming. I don't know how to handle it either.

Chapter 23

Fox

Dɪᴏɴ ʙᴏᴜɴᴄᴇs ᴏɴ ᴛʜᴇ ʙᴀʟʟs ᴏғ ʜɪs ғᴇᴇᴛ, ʟᴏᴏᴋɪɴɢ ᴀʟʟ suave and sophisticated but impatient as he watches me put finishing touches on my bow tie. "What if I shit myself when I meet Peyton Miller?"

If only my cousin's mouth were as sophisticated as his tux.

"Please don't. It's embarrassing enough that my plus-one is my cousin. I don't need you to lose control of your bodily functions in front of my bosses, clients, or any NFL legends."

Dion stops his nervous bouncing. "You're only taking me because I begged you to go. If you needed a date, you could've got one easily."

"It's sweet you think that, but no, you're doing me a huge favor."

"Are you ugly in gay circles? I think you're a good-looking man."

"Coming from my straight cousin, I'm not sure if I should trust your opinion. You're either kissing my ass because I'm taking you to this thing, or you really believe that and have thought about how good-looking I am, which is creepy."

"Actually, I was thinking people used to think we were brothers when we were growing up, so if you're ugly, that means I'm ugly, and I can't accept that."

"Can't argue with that logic. You ready to go?" I let go of my bow tie but keep my hands close in case it unravels faster than a ball of yarn.

I could've worn my work suit, but it's black-tie and a huge event, so I figured I'd step it up in the fashion department.

Coming home this week has been really good for me. Even though I've still been working remotely and doing the same amount of work I would be doing if I were in the office, having that reason to put my computer down at the end of the day has refreshed me to go back to the office next week.

It's made it obvious that my issue in LA is I don't have anyone I'm close to or a reason to stop working. In the last year or so, I'd convinced myself that being better than Archer was the only goal on my list, and I had to do everything to get there.

I need to find that someone or something outside of work that will remind me that being a sports agent is my job. It's not my life. And being here in Arizona with family has made me realize that. I might have lost sight of what's important, but I'm reminded now.

Dion races me out the hotel door, but he's like a little kid because I'm not actually participating. He just thinks I am.

We got a hotel in Phoenix because my family lives in Lake Havasu City, about three hours away. We drove in this morning and will head back tomorrow.

Dion's footsteps are heavy as he runs down the hall toward the elevators, and the sound echoes off the empty hallway. I really hope I don't regret bringing him with me to this work event.

Maybe I should've brought my mom. Though that would be more embarrassing than bringing my cousin. At least from the outside, it might look like I managed to score a date.

Despite what Dion says about us looking like brothers, we really don't. Maybe when we were younger, but certainly not now. He's a scruffy mechanic type, permanent five-o'clock shadow and a typical masculine man. When not in a tux, he's covered in grease and motor oil. I'm more smooth-skinned and ... shiny, for lack of a better word. My skin products probably cost more than his entire wardrobe.

Another good thing about having Dion with me is that I'm not alone. Yes, Damon and his partner will be there, and so will Brady, but considering Brady's dad is one of the award recipients, Brady will be with them, and I didn't feel comfortable asking Damon and Maddox to tag along with them to the venue.

There's a row of cabs out front of the hotel and no line, and even though the Phoenix Symphony Hall is within walking distance, I direct Dion to the cab. I don't want to be dripping with sweat before the night starts.

Dion gets in first and slides over, but as I get in and go to close the door, it gets stuck on someone's hand.

I glance up at the person trying to steal our cab, ready to yell there's a whole fucking line of available ones for them to take, when my words die on my lips. Because standing there with a smile on his face is the last person I'm expecting to see.

"Surprise. Slide over."

What the fuck is Archer Holloway doing here? I'm too stunned to move until he gives me a little shove. I shuffle into the middle, still too shocked for his presence to sink in properly.

"Symphony Hall, thanks," Archer says to the driver.

Okay, that confirms I am still in Arizona and this is real, but I'm still blinking at him.

"Think you're the only one who could score an invite?" He leans forward to see around me. "Hi, I'm Archer." He holds out his hand for Dion to shake.

"Dion."

"How did you ... I mean wha—" I close my mouth and take a deep breath, trying again. "What are you doing here?"

"Brady couldn't decide on who he should bring, boyfriend one or two, so I suggested he bring his favoritest mentor he's ever had."

"And he chose ... you?"

Dion nudges me, I assume for being rude. Archer always makes me forget my manners.

"Well, no. He made a joke that Damon was already coming to the event, but that if I wanted the ticket instead, it was mine. Though secretly, I think Brady was happy that neither of his boyfriends could come. I thought it sounded sketchy that he was trying to decide between which one he wanted to punish more by forcing them to go. Said something about his dads embarrassing him all the time. So even though he called it a pity ticket, I'm taking it to mean pity on him. Not me. No, definitely not me."

I pat his shoulder. "What I'm hearing is you were so desperate to come to this event that you begged your mentee to get you a ticket." Old me would've thought it was to try to poach potential clients from a room full of current and ex-athletes, and maybe that is why, but I can't help thinking he might be here because I wasn't in the office all week.

Sure, it's probably wishful thinking, but it's still in my head anyway.

The cab ride is short but still awkward as fuck, seeing as I haven't told my cousin anything about Archer, and I feel his inquisitive stare against the side of my head. It's squishy in the middle. The more Dion stares, the closer toward Archer I gravitate, but our thighs are already pressed against each other, so there's nowhere I can go far enough away from Dion. Sitting in Archer's lap is only going to make Dion ask more questions. So even though the ride is less than ten minutes, it feels like an eternity until we arrive out the front of the venue.

There's a red carpet lined with sports reporters, but with us being nobodies, we get to bypass all that. We head inside and give our names, where we're directed to one of their event ballrooms for the dinner portion of the night before we'll go inside the hall for the actual ceremony and awards and all the other stuff they have planned. It feels like we're at the Oscars of football.

Dion pulls on my jacket sleeve like a little child. "When can I meet Peyton?"

"Why don't you go try to find him?"

"And introduce myself? Are you forgetting what I'm worried about when I meet him? You have to be there with me."

"Fine, go get us drinks, and I'll be on the lookout for him." I wave my cousin away.

"Okay. Do you want anything, Archer?" Dion asks.

"Thanks. Whatever beer they have."

"You got it."

"We'll find our table while you're gone," I tell him.

As soon as he's out of earshot, Archer leans in close. "Is that how you treat all of your dates? Make them fetch you beer and find their own way around?"

I swear I can detect a hint of jealousy in his tone, and as much as I want to tell him the truth—that Dion is my cousin—I'm more tempted to test out how far his jealousy will go. "It's how I seduce men. It worked with you. Four years of being snappy, and I had you."

"Playing the long game. Smart."

"Obviously. Getting things easy is for simple thinkers."

"Why does that feel like a direct hit at me?"

"I have no idea what you mean. You're reading into what I said. Obviously. No direct hits here at all."

He chuckles. "Let's find this table so your date can meet Peyton Miller."

And there it is again. It's almost as if he can't say the word *date* without an edge to it. I'm not ashamed to say I want to hear that tone again and again. If I weren't so grossed out by playing it up with my cousin, I'd be tempted to.

Still, when we take our seats at our empty table—we're either the first ones here or the others are mingling—and then Dion brings us drinks only moments later, I make sure to say thank you and smile instead of treating him like the brother I see him as.

I even hold back asking if he spat in my Bud Light as a joke. Wouldn't be the first time he's pranked me like that. See? Just like brothers but even better. Because when we were kids, we didn't have to live in the same house.

"Dion, your name is here." Archer pats the spot beside him. Which is weird. Because I could've sworn it was on the other side of me.

I narrow my gaze at Archer. Did he move Dion's nameplate? And what does it say about me that I like it? Maybe if Dion were my real date, I'd be annoyed by the toxicity, but I'm nowhere near annoyed.

With that thought though, I become unsettled. Because if I'm finding it difficult to see the things Archer does as annoying now, how am I supposed to keep my distance? When every little thing he does should piss me off and instead turns me on and makes me like him more ...

Yeah, I'm fucked.

I don't regret having sex with him, but I do regret letting go of my petty feud with him. Even if it was mostly one-sided, it prevented me from actually liking the guy.

"So, Dion. What do you do for work?" Archer asks.

"Uh, mechanic."

"Interesting. How do you know Fox? Let me guess. High school?"

"We grew up together," I cut in.

Dion looks confused but doesn't add "We're family," so that's good.

I'm not ready for the illusion to drop yet.

"Really?" Archer drags out the word. "Do you have any embarrassing stories of him? Please tell me he wasn't always such a—"

"Choose your words carefully, Holloway," I warn but hide my smile by lifting my beer bottle to my lips.

"Such a ... stickler for rules." He turns his gaze on me. "You have to admit you're that."

"Maybe before last weekend," I say low enough for only him to hear.

Dion is none the wiser. "Sorry to say, he was always the good student. Drove me nuts. But he always said he was going to get himself out of our small town, and shit ... looking around this place, he really did it. He made something of himself."

"Hey, Hasavu Lake City needs mechanics, and you're good at what you do," I assure him. He'd contemplated trying to go to college to do something different than what his dad did, but he'd been working on cars since before he even started kindergarten. It's in his blood, and he's good at it. It doesn't make a lot of money, but I know he'd rather be happy than rich.

So would I, come to think of it.

The veil of my competitive streak has come off, and I'm able to see clearer now. For a while, besting Archer and his commission check was all I wanted. Now that's gone and I'm in a good financial position, it's time I find my happiness.

Preferably in someone healthier than my nemesis turned ... friend. Who I've seen naked. Because I couldn't control myself.

It's taken me way too long to realize that's what is unsettled about me. I have absolutely no control over my ever-changing feelings for Archer, and they're changing so fucking quickly.

A few weeks ago, the idea of hooking up with Archer would've made me want to punch something. Not, like, a person because I'm not a violent guy, but definitely something. Like a stuffed toy or a pillow. Something that wouldn't hurt my hand. I'm not above kicking a teddy bear's ass. I'm fierce like that.

That pull toward him, the same I had last week right before I caved in and gave my body what it wanted, is there again. Stronger than ever.

I wasn't lying when I said I'd come home to Arizona to catch up with my family, but it is possible that having sex with Archer was the thing that made me think it was a brilliant idea. I got some space, and I got to come home. Win-win.

But it obviously didn't work because now that I'm next to Archer, I'm right back where I was last Saturday: buzzing with the desire for him to touch me.

He continues to make small talk with Dion, and I can't tell if he's sizing Dion up or is suspicious already because Dion is nothing like Archer.

Hey, maybe I don't have a type. I definitely wouldn't have said Archer was my type a few months ago. Though I will admit if we were only going on the physical, I've been drawn to men who look more like Archer and Thad in the past than those who look like lumberjacks. More bad boy and less plaid.

Out of nowhere, in the middle of rambling about the different make of cars Dion would recommend, my cousin gasps.

That can only mean one thing.

The four men walking toward our table confirms it. The Talon-Millers are in the house. Marcus Talon, second greatest quarterback of all time—though everyone knows not to mention that he's runner up for that title—his husband, Shane Miller, son Peyton Miller, who is kicking ass in the NFL and might bump his dad into third place eventually, and their other son, Brady, who we see every day at work.

Archer and I stand to greet them, but Dion remains seated, too stunned to move.

Brady gives us an up-nod. "Dads, shithead, this is Lincoln Fox, Archer Holloway, and ..." He glances at Dion.

It's such a Brady thing to do though, calling his brother a shithead in a professional setting. He gets away with so much being who he is and having the last name he has, more than any other person in the office.

I know some agents hate the nepotism, but I don't even think it's that. I've seen Damon be hard on Brady before. Thad has told me how much pressure Brady has on his shoulders. I think people let him get away with being unprofessional because everyone loves him.

"D-d-d—" my cousin tries.

"That's Dion," I say for him. "He's really excited to meet you all."

"He's Fox's *date*," Archer says.

That breaks Dion out of his celebrity trance. "His what?"

"My plus-one," I interject. Like that's any better.

I didn't notice Damon behind the Talon-Millers until he pushes his way through.

"As in *Dion* Dion? The one you tried to drunk dial when you accidentally called me?"

Oh, good. My boss is going to bring that up every time we meet. If I answer vaguely, maybe he won't point out to everyone that he's my cousin. "The one and only."

Marcus Talon, all intimidating in his perfectly tailor-made suit, steps up next to me. "You drunk dialed Damon? You're my people. I'm going to sit next to you. I want to hear everything."

Please don't want that.

"It's really not that fun of a story," I try to assure him.

"I'll be the judge of that." Talon—as everyone calls him—sits on the other side of me to Archer, ignoring where the nameplate says Brady's name. "Who's Dion? What's the history between you that made you want to drunk dial him and accidentally hit Damon's name instead? Ooh, did you also not realize and then profess your undying love for your boss by accident, causing Maddox to threaten to kick your ass when he actually found the whole thing entertaining?"

That sounds a lot less embarrassing than the truth, which is I missed my family and wanted to talk to them.

"Not quite, but close." I sip my beer. "You might want to hold on to your story than hear the real one. It has more drama than the truth."

Talon leans forward to yell across me and Archer. "Yo, Dion. You Fox's high school sweetheart? The one who got away?"

I refrain from facepalming but barely.

"What?" Dion pulls back. "I'm his cousin. And I'm straight."

Archer's stare burns into the side of my face. There goes my cover and any jealous caveman behavior that I was enjoying.

Chapter 24

Archer

DION IS FOX'S COUSIN? THIS IS AN INTERESTING development.

When I'd first seen them together tonight, my gut sank the same way it did after we'd hooked up and Fox didn't come to work. Out of the two of us, I'm supposed to be the calm one, but with him running away and bringing a date—granted, not really a date but one in my eyes—I've been far from the calm one. And this revelation only intensifies the butterflies in my stomach and the urge to kiss Fox again.

Marcus Talon, losing all interest in the gossip that turned out not to be gossip, leaves and mingles with all the other NFL alum. Everyone talks amongst themselves. Dion has attached himself to Peyton Miller and Brady, and I have no idea where Damon and Maddox went.

"Cousin, huh?" Okay, there's no hiding my smug smile now. "Were you going to let me think he was your date all night? Or is he your actual date, and this is how it's done in Arizona?" Yep, definitely never going to let him live it down.

He casually shrugs. "You were the one who assumed he was my date."

"And you didn't think to tell me the truth? Why is that, I wonder." I rub my chin, pretending to think.

"Because I like seeing you make an ass of yourself?"

That's probably true, but— "Nah, that's not it." I lean in closer to his ear and lower my voice as I say, "You liked seeing that I was jealous."

"So you admit you were jealous."

Normally, admitting something so vulnerable wouldn't even cross my mind, but with Fox, there's something about him that makes me want to bare my entire soul. "I was so green with envy you could've called me Elphaba."

He snorts. "Nice musical reference."

"Don't mock musicals. They're amazing."

Fox can't tell if I'm being serious or not, his side-eye speaking for him.

"No sarcasm. When I lived in New York and I'd meet up with my sister, she insisted we see a show. It's sort of our thing. It's another little fact about me that you didn't know because you've always been too busy only seeing my competitive side." I'm not going to mention that before meeting with a potential client, I sing "My Shot" from *Hamilton* in my head.

"Maybe your competitiveness is the only side you've shown me for the last four years. How was I supposed to know you're a musical-loving nerd under your tattooed exterior if you were never willing to show it?"

"Uh, because you never gave me a chance to?"

Defeat fills his eyes. "Fair point."

"There's still a lot you don't know about me, but you could ... if you wanted to ... hang out."

Hang out, have sex again ... same thing.

Fox glances around, making sure no one hears as he leans in closer and says, "Last time we 'hung out'"—love his use of the air quotes—"mistakes were made."

"Are we calling it a mistake? Lines were crossed, but that doesn't mean that's a mistake. A mistake is an accident. I definitely didn't accidentally land on your bed."

Again, he does the glancing around thing. No one is listening to us though.

"It might not have been a mistake, but it will be if it gets out. Which is why we shouldn't hang out."

"Shouldn't but want to? You haven't learned my deepest darkest secrets yet, and how are we going to be able to work together if you don't know those?"

"I'm sure we can manage working as a team without having to know you watch dinosaur porn."

I mock gasp. "How did you know?"

"You seem like the type."

"The type into paleontology?"

"Yes. Exactly what I meant." His dry tone is not nearly as dismissive as it used to be.

"If you ever want to change your mind and learn more about me, the offer is always there. We've worked together for so long but really only know the surface stuff."

"Maybe that's a good thing."

"Aww, scared too much of me will be a good thing?"

Fox shakes his head. "Too much of you will be a bad thing ... for my career."

"Only if we let it."

"Says the professional compartmentalizer."

He makes a good point. Because if I keep letting him get under my skin, show my jealousy, and taunt him into a repeat and then another repeat, something is going to give. And it will most likely be our careers because of the scandal us hooking up will bring, along with the awkward business meetings with our new joint clients. Not to mention the tension and resentment if we were to end things on a bitter note. Which, let's face it, for Fox and me, is likely.

I've known this, knew it that night I stayed, knew it when we hooked up. Still know it now. Yet, I followed him to Arizona because I hadn't seen him in a week. Because I haven't stopped thinking about him.

I've never had this kind of pull before, and I wasn't aware of it until recently. He's always been attractive to me, but that's base-level attraction, where I could acknowledge that he's good-looking without it being any deeper than that.

But as soon as he opened that door to there being something between us, it's as if he reached into my brain and flipped a switch. No, not just one switch, a bunch of them. It used to be in constant work mode with my fun motor running at a slower pace. My relationship motor wasn't even turned on.

Now, everything inside me is awake, and I have no idea how to decide which one takes priority. It should be the job. It should be King Sports. And as much as I can lie and say this gala tonight was an opportunity to network, all I want to do is sit here at this table, teasing Fox some more.

Or better yet, skip the awards ceremony, throw him in a cab, and take him back to the hotel while everyone is still here and won't see him coming into my room and never leaving. Well, until checkout.

"What, no witty remark about me being obsessed with you or some other bullshit?"

"Why would I need to say that when you're already thinking it for me?"

Fox sighs. "You're insufferable, and that's why we shouldn't hang out again."

"I thought it was because it would be a mistake. You know, for someone who supposedly doesn't want to hang out with me, you keep bringing up reasons why we shouldn't. I haven't yet heard the one that says because you don't want to."

That reason used to be a given, but not anymore.

"We're hanging out right now," he points out.

"Yeah, when I *hang out* with someone, there's usually a lot less clothes. And other people. Usually somewhere a lot less ... public."

"That's definitely not happening." He finishes off his beer. "Again."

"It should. We've already made the mistake once. May as well take advantage of breaking the rules. We should break them as hard as we can."

"No flaws in that logic."

Even though he's being sarcastic and I need to back off, there's that part of me that wants to push so I can test how hard his line exactly is. So I stand from the table and stare down at him as I say, "Shall we, then?"

When he immediately stands, hope actually blooms deep in my gut. But then he says, "Sure. Why don't you go back to the hotel, I'll get myself another drink, and then after I've networked with potential future clients you can't steal from me because you were too busy waiting in a hotel room, I'll knock on your door."

"Maybe you're right, and we shouldn't hang out. I'm rubbing off on you, and not in the fun way. You're thinking like I would at an event like this."

He leaves me with a hearty laugh, heading for the open bar, and all I can do is watch him as he goes.

He's thinking like how I should be, and if it weren't for him, it's exactly how I would see this situation. Instead of pursuing potential clients, I'm chasing him. Why does he get to me so much?

After we're fed, I manage to make myself mingle with others, taking advantage of this work situation, but my eyes never stray too far away from Fox. I'm so distracted by him I don't think I'm making an impression on anyone. I miss half the stuff they say, nod in agreement to fuck knows what, and then when Fox moves on to someone else, I excuse myself and follow like a little puppy.

From the conversations I'm overhearing, and with the way Fox is conducting himself, I'm starting to think I don't rattle him at all anymore.

I'm really going to need to fix that. Rattling Lincoln Fox has always been the highlight of my day.

The lights start flashing, letting us know that it's time to make our way to our seats inside the hall where the televised event is taking place.

I try to make sure I stick close to Fox, planning on coincidentally finding the seat next to his, but with everyone trying to leave the banquet room, it's easy to lose him in the crowd of other tuxes.

There's a slow bottleneck of people entering the hall, so I step to the side and let them all go first. I've already lost Fox, so I'm in no rush to get in there now. Hey, maybe if I go in last, there'll be no seats left for King Sports guys, and I'll have to sit on his lap. That would be a terrible, horrible shame.

Not that others in the room will appreciate it. After all these years, decades after Matt Jackson, Marcus Talon, and Shane Miller were among the first out active players in the NFL, it's still a toxic industry. Granted, better than it ever has been before, but tolerance is not acceptance, and until true acceptance happens, I think it's important for queer athletes to have their queer support systems in place. Like King Sports.

I slowly inch forward, keeping my distance from the big crowd as much as possible, but as I get close to passing the bathrooms outside the entry to the hall, the men's room door opens, and I'm yanked inside.

The world is a blur until I'm shoved up against the wall and I'm looking into the eyes of a very pissed-off Fox. It's impossible to know what I've done this time, but there's something else in his glare—something that isn't usually there when he's about to yell at me.

Pure unadulterated lust.

He reaches over and flicks the lock to the entire restroom. The three stalls are empty, no one at the urinals, which is hard to believe, considering the stream of people passing by just on the other side of this wall.

Am I going to point out this is a terrible idea and an easy way to get caught? Not with him right in front of me, and definitely not when he presses himself against me, his hard cock digging into my groin.

I'm about to ask what he's doing—not that I will protest it, but fuck, I want to hear him tell me how much he wants me.

"You drive me so goddamn crazy," he growls.

Not quite the same sentiment, but close enough.

Also surprising considering how cool and collected he has been all night compared to me. It's as if I've been itching out of my skin, waiting for him to ease it. Now that he's against me, the frustration has stopped. My insides are vibrating, but it's not from being unsettled. It's from need.

Need for him.

"You're one to talk. I offered to take you back to the hotel, but no, you wanted to network instead. We've been here for hours, Fox, and you've been killing me slowly by trying to run away from me at every turn."

Fox grinds against me. "Me? You were the one who made sure you were always in my line of sight. Looking all hot and devilish with that evil fucking smile I used to hate."

Speak of the devil, and it will appear.

"Yes, exactly that smile you have on your face."

"I can't help it. You said you used to hate it. What does it do to you now?"

He rotates his hips, and a shudder runs through me as our cocks brush against one another. "This. This is what it fucking does to me." His voice is raspy and sounds like sex.

"We can still leave," I breathe.

"You think I have the patience for an entire cab ride?" Fox reaches between us and starts undoing my belt. "We don't have time for that. We're going to make each other come right here and now and then walk into that award ceremony as if it never happened."

My cock jerks behind my zipper. "And how do you propose we do that without making a mess of our suits?"

Instead of answering me, he gives me his own version of a devilish smile and sinks to his knees. The second he gets my cock free and his lips are on me, I melt against the wall.

Chapter 25

Fox

I'm sucking Archer Holloway's cock again, and just like the first time, I don't know how it happened.

One minute, I'm angry at the guy, and the next, I have my lips wrapped around the base of his dick. His tip is playing hockey with my tonsils, teasing my gag reflex, but I don't let it best me. Because even though I'm in a rush, I want to savor his heady flavor. I want to feel every pulse, run my tongue along the thick vein on the underside, and then swallow every drop of cum as he unloads in my mouth.

I thought I could walk away after last weekend and have him out of my system, but all I've been able to think about all week is doing this again. And again.

Fuck, if I had the time, I would make this last until my eyes watered and my jaw ached.

Archer grips my hair tight, my roots giving a nice sting. I leak into my underwear, my cock aching with need. The idea of sucking him off was so things didn't get messy, but there's a real possibility that if we don't get to swap positions soon, these tux pants will be ruined, and it's a goddamn rental. Explaining the weird stain on the inside of the pants upon return is not a game I want to play.

I fumble with my belt and top button, trying to get my pants open.

I'm stubborn enough to struggle with it if it means keeping my mouth exactly where it is. Sure, my rhythm has gotten sloppy and I've given him a chance to come down from teetering on the edge, but I refuse to let his cock slip from between my lips. It's only a small reprieve I give him, because the second I'm free, I deep-throat that motherfucker and don't plan on stopping. I run my hands up the back of his legs and grasp his ass cheeks, pushing him further down my throat.

"Holy shit," he whispers. "You're so fucking good at that."

The compliments aren't going to slow me down any.

Archer's breathing becomes heavy, his grip tightens in my hair, and when he starts grunting, I know he's close. My cock twitches, begging for me to pay attention to it. Knowing Archer's so close, I should be able to hold out. I should be able to resist touching myself and giving in. But the truth is, the sounds he's making break me.

Grunt.

Loud breath.

Moan.

A mix of all three.

I can't hold out for him to fall over the edge first. I have to touch myself.

My fingers wrap around my painfully hard length, and I jerk off fast, ignoring Archer's breathless protests about him doing that for me.

I want to come, and I want to come right fucking now.

"Seeing you on your knees like this..." He breathes heavily. "Not on my bingo card for this year, but it's the hottest thing I've ever seen."

I glance up at him through my lashes, and if he thinks I look hot down here, it's nothing compared to his flushed cheeks and parted lips. And when his blue eyes meet mine, my entire body tightens as waves of pleasure pump through me. My brain fogs over while my veins buzz.

A second later, Archer's head hits the wall behind him, and my mouth fills with the warmth of his cum and salty taste.

I moan long and loud, drinking him down while wringing out my own orgasm.

I turn to jelly; the only thing keeping me upright and not sprawled out on the floor is our location. While the facilities seem clean, it's still a restroom.

Archer's cock slips from my mouth as he catches his breath, and when I rise to my feet, he gives me a lopsided, satisfied smile.

I'm quick to wash my hands at the basin and fix my pants, tucking my shirt back in. Archer isn't in the same rush to fix himself up.

"Ready to get back out there?" I ask.

After he's tucked away, his shirt still askew, he steps forward and pulls me against him. "Your hair looks like you just got fucked in a bathroom." He runs his fingers over my hair, flattening out the parts that are spiked up all over the place.

All I can do is watch his face as he does it. There's an adorable concentration line between his brows. His lips look fuller and redder, and I can't help wondering if he bit down on his bottom lip as he came.

I wish I had been able to watch him then too, but I was too busy being lost in my own pleasure.

"Can I kiss you?" I blurt.

Archer's smile grows. "You never have to ask me that. My answer will always be yes."

I ignore the implications the word *always* has and take it to mean that if I ever want to hook up with him again, he's up for it.

I must take too long to follow through on it because in the next second, his hands are out of my hair and gripping the back of my neck as he pulls me forward and presses his lips to mine.

I push my tongue inside his mouth, and he moans, breaking away from the kiss.

"I can taste myself on you."

I'm about to ask him if he has a problem with that, but he beats me to it.

"So, so fucking hot," he rumbles and then kisses me again, deeper this time.

If I'd known how sexy Archer could be, how passionate, how fucking easy it would be to get lost in his mouth, maybe I would've been able to swallow my resentment years ago.

Somehow, the physical stuff makes up for the deep-seated insecurities he once brought out of me.

And if it weren't for someone knocking on the door forcing us apart, I could stay in this bathroom all night if it meant I could keep kissing him. Archer pulls away and unlocks the restroom door to let in whoever is impatient and annoyed on the other side.

Eh, it's only Keith Warner. All one hundred years of him. He was one of the great NFL coaches back in the day. Great as in he was able to produce a lot of wins for Kansas. Not great as in great person. I've heard he ran his locker rooms with all the homophobia of a Westboro Baptist church.

"Sorry about that," Archer says. "Got a shy bladder situation over here." He points to me.

"Sure, shy bladder." My tone is dry. "I definitely wasn't blowing you in here." I leave with a laugh. It's the only way to deal with those types. Flat out shock them into picturing two men having sex.

Archer glances behind us as we walk out. "Uh, did you know that guy?"

"Not personally, but know of him. Hates the gays."

"Ah. Okay, what you said makes sense, then. I thought you must have come your brain cells out and decided we were now telling people about our ..."

"Transgressions."

He cocks his head. "Is transgressions better or worse than calling it a mistake?"

"Like I said, a mistake is an accident. Twice now? Can no longer claim I slipped and fell or accidentally somehow thought your dick was a popsicle."

The crowd has thinned, though when we cross the threshold into the hall, people are still trying to find their seats.

Brady sees us and raises his hand, so we make our way down close to the front, where the King Sports dynasty has a row.

Dion has somehow wormed his way into sitting next to Peyton at the other side of the row, and there are two seats up this end left for Archer and me.

"Where did you guys go? Get lost?" Brady asks in a suspicious tone.

"There was a line to get into the bathroom," I say casually. "Someone apparently locked the door."

Brady leans forward and hisses at his dads next to him. "Did you two sneak off and have sex in a bathroom? You promised you'd behave."

I have to smother my amusement.

One good thing about Archer's and my reputation for hating each other is that no one would immediately suspect it was us.

"I swear it wasn't us," Marcus Talon says, but it comes across as too defensive to sound genuine, which only makes me more entertained.

Brady slumps in his seat. "They're so embarrassing."

"For you," I murmur. "I find them highly entertaining." You know, when their probing questions aren't directed my way.

This time, Brady leans around me so he can talk to Archer. "I see why you don't like Fox now."

A few weeks ago, that would've pissed me off. Now, I'm actually liking that we have this secret. Maybe Archer has been right this whole time, and all I needed was to get laid so I could relax more in work situations.

"I have nothing against Fox," Archer says. "He's the one who has a problem with me."

Yeah, that problem being I can't get him out of my head.

The award ceremony goes for so damn long I almost fall asleep at multiple points. The only recipient who doesn't ramble on about

God and has something profound to say is when Marcus Talon gets his lifetime achievement award.

Or maybe it's because his heartfelt speech is a full-on clapback at the others who have received awards tonight.

"First up, I want to say ..." He holds the trophy in his hand, staring down at it like he's letting the moment sink in. "This feels ... correct."

There's a round of snickers from the audience.

"There's been a lot of talk about God tonight, and I know football is an industry full of those with faith. I don't know if there's a God or not. I'd like to think that if there were, people like my husband and me would be more widely accepted. I don't judge those with faith, but as I stand here, holding an award that is long overdue—come on, guys, I retired twenty years ago—I only have one thing to say. God had absolutely nothing to do with my career achievements. Guys like me, like my husband Shane Miller, Matt Jackson, and countless others who have been out in the NFL, had to fight for everything we've achieved. I'm not going to attribute that to a higher deity I'm not one hundred percent sure exists. The only faith I have comes from the love I've received from my family, my friends, my agent, Damon King, and most importantly of all, my husband, Shane, and our sons, Peyton and Brady. Thank you."

"Damn," Archer says. "Nice speech."

"I wish I could've seen Keith Warner's face during that."

With the lifetime achievement award being the last of the night, the host wraps it up, and then we're free to leave.

Being on the end of the row, Archer and I are able to make a quick getaway, but because Dion is mixed in the crowd, we have to wait outside the hall anyway.

"Before everyone gets out here, are you going to find your way to my hotel room tonight?"

As much as my body is screaming yes, the smart thing to do here is say no. "This might sound weird coming from the guy who dragged you into a bathroom two hours ago where anyone could see, but ... it's probably too risky going to your room."

The smile he wears is tight-lipped. Forced. "You don't need to lie. A simple no wouldn't have broken my heart."

"I'm not lying. I'm staying in the same room as Dion, and who knows if Damon or the Talon-Millers are staying at the same hotel. Plus, Dion and I need to head back to Lake Havasu early."

"Will you be back in the office next week?"

"You think the office is a safer place than a hotel room three hundred miles away?"

He shoulder bumps me. "Not to hook up, doofus. I'm ... asking if I'll see you there."

Why does a simple question make my stomach do flips? "Unless one of my clients falls into a shitstorm of epic proportions, I'll be back in the office."

"Dude. Why would you go and jinx yourself like that?"

Ugh. Jocks and their superstitions.

Chapter 26
Archer

He had to go and motherfucking jinx it, didn't he. I rest my elbow on the armrest between our plane seats, my hand under my chin as I stare at Fox with a smug look on my face. We managed to get a direct flight to Buffalo, but we're only two hours into the almost five-hour flight. Fox still pretends he hasn't noticed, burying his head in the in-flight information booklet that is literally only two pages. He can't be staring at the menu for that long. He has a choice of terrible airplane food or terrible airplane food. Have no idea how he's going to choose.

He finally puts it down. "Stop looking at me like that."

"Why? It's my right to gloat as the person who told you so."

"And everyone knows how people who revel in that are universally loved for doing it too."

I laugh and go back to facing forward. "Maybe from now on, you'll take jinxes more seriously."

"Or maybe your client shouldn't have thrown a puck at an intern, given them a black eye, and then told the media about it."

Fucking Asher Dalton. I knew he was going to be trouble, and yet I was still so fucking eager to sign him anyway. When the news broke, I messaged Damon to see if he wanted to handle it, seeing as we're only new to Asher's contract. He literally sent the laughing face emoji. About twenty of them. The next text he sent through simply said: *Good luck.*

"In Asher's defense," I say, because I'm his agent and even if I'm angry at him, I still have to defend him, "he didn't leak it to the media. Someone else in the Buffalo team did. Probably someone with a grudge against Dalton, which means our list of suspects could be narrowed down to a short few hundred people. And he's not my client. He's *our* client."

"When he's fucking up my schedule, he's *your* client."

"Aww, it's like he's our child. Coparenting already. Cute."

Still, Fox doesn't smile. "Are you telling me you're not at all freaked-out that we signed Dalton less than two weeks ago, he already has a scandal, and there are rumors about trading him when he only has three years left on his contract? He's a Buffalo franchise baby. Trading him would be like ... Pittsburgh trading Sid. Washington trading Ovi. Boston trading Marchand!"

"Didn't that last one happen?"

"Yes. And their fans were pissed. Asher's fans will blame us if we can't defuse this Dalton situation."

"While I understand we need to do what's best for our client, if we can't fix his mistake, that mistake falls on his shoulders. Not ours. The fans will hate the franchise, not us. So no, I'm not freaking out. I'm still holding out hope that this whole situation is a misunderstanding and once we see Dalton face-to-face and talk to Buffalo management, everything will get straightened out."

"As long as it's hope you're holding on to and not your breath."

He might not have faith, but I do.

The first thing out of Dalton's mouth as we meet him in the reception area of Buffalo's head office is, "I swear I didn't do it."

I give Fox another smug smile. It must be so hard for him. Being wrong all the time.

"Well, okay, technically, I did, but ..."

Fuck.

"But what?" I ask, and it comes out a little harsher than I intend.

"We have an office to go into to talk about it." He glances around the main floor, where employees wander. "We don't know who we can trust around here anymore."

At least he appears to be taking this as seriously as we are. He even seems ... nervous? That can't be right though. This is Asher-fucking-Dalton.

He leads us to more of a meeting room than an office, but it works.

We all take our seats, and Fox gets out his tablet and stylus pen. "Tell us what happened. From the beginning."

"Did you see the game last night? We sucked. I don't mean we had a bad game; we had the worst game in the history of games. San Jose beat us seven to nothing. Nothing. At *home*. They got a fucking shutout. I'd expect that from the big teams in the league. But San Jose? That team has done nothing but go to shit ever since Oskar Voyjik left."

"What does a bad game have to do with anything?" I ask.

"We were all frustrated, and the puck that scored my thousandth point was on the shelf of my cubby. I figured throwing it at the wall would be better than punching someone or the wall and hurting my hand, so ... I did ... right as TJ, the equipment team intern, walked in the room."

Jesus H Christ.

"It's not like I meant to hurt him or even hit him, but then some fuck told the press that it was on purpose, and now management is telling me to fix this, or I'll be looking at being placed on waivers. It wouldn't surprise me if Jim Conroy released this bullshit himself. He's had it out for me ever since he became the GM last season."

Usually, when people say someone has it out for them and nothing is their fault, they're full-blown narcissists, but with Asher Dalton, I get the sense that he doesn't say something without cause.

"Had it out for you how?" Fox asks.

"He's always telling the team that this new style of hockey and entitled attitude wouldn't fly back when he was playing, blah blah blah. He wants to get rid of me, I just know it. And if this scandal is still fresh in everyone's mind, no other team is going to pick me up, and I don't want to sound elitist, but if I land my ass in the AHL with my little brother, there will be no coming back from that embarrassment."

"I wouldn't worry about the AHL," Fox says.

"Really?" Asher's eyes are hopeful.

"With this scandal, if they put you on waivers, it will most likely be with the intention to terminate your contract altogether."

I kick Fox under the table and send a glare his way. He flinches and mouths "ouch" to me. He deserves it though. This is his idea of being supportive?

"Wow. Makes me feel so much better," Dalton deadpans.

"But," Fox adds, "we won't let it get to that. It's obvious this was a huge misunderstanding. You let your frustration from losing get the better of you, and immaturely, you lashed out, but there was no intent behind it. We'll get the team to make a statement or even hold a press conference if they prefer, you'll make a public apology to TJ, we'll make sure that he's in the wings with makeup over his eye and a big smile on his face, and then it'll go away."

"You'd have to get management to agree to it," Dalton says. "And they've made it clear that they will trade me if they get a good enough offer or dump me if it doesn't go away."

"We're not going to let that happen," I say.

It's Fox's turn to kick me under the table. "But we can't make any promises. I know we're new to representing you, but I'm not going to sugarcoat the situation you're in. We'll do our best, and we will fight for you, but you know everything in this industry isn't a given."

Dalton swallows hard. "You know what's funny but kinda not? This team could have dumped me so many times with the shit I've done over the years."

"Like when you repeatedly told reporters to eat shit and die," Fox says.

"Broke into Ayri Quinn's house and scared the shit out of him, his child, and the head trainer for the team," I add.

Asher doesn't even dispute what I say. "Exactly. So many things I could've been let go for. So if it ends up being an accident that finally gets me kicked out of this place, that's going to fucking suck. Like, can't they wait until I actually assault someone on purpose? Maybe a prison donkey?"

"How about we put a pin in that," I suggest. "But also, what's a prison donkey?"

"A ref, duh," Dalton says.

It takes a second, but— "Oh, because ref, stripes, zebra, prison donkey. Got it. But yeah, no assaulting them either, please."

"No assaulting anyone," Fox adds.

I snap my fingers and point at him. "Yes. That. What he said."

Dalton's gaze ping-pongs between Fox and me, and then he visibly deflates. "I'm so fucking fired."

Fox stands. "Not if we can help it. Let's go to management."

Fox's take-charge attitude reminds me of how he is when it comes to sex. It shouldn't be this much of a turn-on to see him be professional.

When dealing with management, I've always taken the business negotiator role. I'm stern where I need to be, fold when a good deal is on the table, and always keep a level head.

But the minute we're called into the GM's office and Fox tells Dalton to wait outside, I can't say Fox has that same level head. Because as soon as we're seated across from Jim Conroy, Fox dives right in.

"Here's what's going to happen. We all know this incident is already spiraling out of control and has been blown out of proportion. Asher Dalton is the biggest asset you have. He leads the team in goals and points this season and skates circles around guys ten years younger than he is. So you're going to call a press conference. Asher Dalton will apologize for being so passionate about this team that the loss to San Jose was so devastating to him, he lashed out. It was immature, and he meant no harm, and he is deeply sorry that a valued Buffalo employee got hurt by a flying puck that was not aimed at him. It wasn't aimed at anyone, but unfortunately, it was one of those times where it was wrong place, wrong time. Still, he takes full responsibility and apologizes for letting the team down. You're going to be beside him the whole time, and when he's done being the most apologetic Asher Dalton has ever been in front of the press, you're going to announce that the rumors of a trade because of this altercation that wasn't really an altercation were fabricated and you absolutely support Asher Dalton and his career."

Buffalo's GM leans back in his seat. "Or we finally have a chance to let go one of the team's biggest pains in my ass."

"You're new to this position, aren't you? You were appointed last season. Want to know what happens to GMs who let lead scorers go? You think putting Asher Dalton—arguably the only reason this team has had a Stanley Cup trophy in the last fifteen years—on waivers will result in termination? Any other team in the league would be frothing at the mouth to have him. You'd be better off trying to trade him and get an amazing deal out of it, but even then, the fans will hate you, this club will suffer, and you will be out of a job by season's end. I guarantee it."

I'm super impressed and genuinely scared. Scared he's going to fuck this whole thing up while simultaneously scared I'm going to sit here and do nothing for my client because I'm speechless. Utterly in awe.

If I had signed Asher Dalton on my own, I have no doubt I could handle this situation, but the way Fox is doing it? I could learn a thing or two from him.

"Dealing with Damon King was so much easier," Conroy mutters. "Okay, I will agree to your terms. We say the whole thing was a misunderstanding and that he lashed out and didn't mean to hit anyone with that puck."

Did he just ... agree? This seems too easy.

"With one caveat," he adds.

Ah. There it is.

We wait, and it's as if he's pausing for dramatic effect.

"He's suspended for five games and goes into an anger management program."

Dalton is going to hate that. Like, throw another puck across the room kind of hate. I might not know him well still, but I know him enough to predict that. The thing I'm wondering is if this GM is predicting the same thing.

Dalton might have been right. This GM is out for his blood for whatever reason.

"Why the five games?" I ask. "The NHL can't sanction that over an in-team dispute."

"But it sets a precedent that violence of any kind is unacceptable."

"It was violence against a wall," I say. "Where someone happened to get in the way." I realize how that sounds as soon as the words leave my mouth.

"Think people will like that excuse? Why don't we use the good ol' he was *trying to catch the puck with his face* argument?

"We can agree to the anger management," Fox says. "But I'm also questioning the five-game suspension. How about one?"

"Three," Conroy counters.

"Two," Fox and I say in unison.

"Deal," Conroy says. "If you can get Asher Dalton to agree to two games and anger management, this organization will help squash all the rumors going around about trades, waivers, and any real or nonexistent fight that may or may not have happened in that locker room."

"We'll talk to our client and get back to you." Fox stands and turns to leave. I at least shake the man's hand.

Asher is waiting outside the office on a couch across from Conroy's assistant. He stands as soon as he sees us. "What happened?"

"Not here," Fox says. "We need to talk."

Something about this deal doesn't sit right with me, and with the way Fox wants to leave, I figure he's got a similar feeling.

Conroy has it out for Asher Dalton, and this deal might hand him the technical map to get rid of him without backlash on the team. And it's our job to fix it.

Why was I adamant about signing this client again?

Chapter 27
Fox

We take Dalton away from Buffalo headquarters and get him to drive us to our hotel for the night. We weren't sure if we would need to stay, but after that meeting, it's safe to say we're going to be here for a few days.

This whole situation is a shitstorm of red flags, but I can't pinpoint exactly what Conroy's plan is. Other than the obvious bias he has against Dalton. I'm worried if we agree to his terms that he's laying some kind of groundwork for termination with cause.

If Asher admits to having an anger problem—which is kind of a given; I've seen on the ice and how brutal he can be—then it's as if he admits to throwing that puck with intent to harm someone, giving the team causation.

Archer and I only have our carry-on luggage, and we can check in after we have this talk, so I lead them to the hotel restaurant and get a table for three.

Considering what I know of Asher Dalton being impatient as fuck, he's doing well to not hound us about what happened in that meeting. Dalton has been scared into actually worrying about his career.

Once we're served water and put in our order for food, I set my tablet on the table and open my notes app.

"Okay, so what is Conroy's deal with you?" I ask.

"You think he has an issue with me too, then." It's not a question.

"It's possible. Before we met with him, I would've said you were being paranoid or that he had a right, considering your ... colorful career full of media taunts and a reputation of being difficult to work with."

"Agreed," Archer says. It's still weird to be on the same page as him, but at least he saw it too. "The way he was talking about you, it was as if he was looking for an excuse to get rid of you."

"It's not just me either," Dalton says. "Ever since he came in, he has been determined to force Coach into a rebuild that we don't need. Coach has been shuffling our lines around, trying different defensive pairings, watching our deep goalie bench for our next superstar, but it's all in hope of stopping a rebuild from happening. Conroy wants to gut us, and granted, since Quinn retired, I haven't had that connection with a teammate on the ice, but throwing different dudes at me every other week isn't going to help us find our groove. The trade deadline is coming up, and my biggest worry is they're going to get rid of all the veterans for draft picks when we're still in a chance for a playoff run. Sure, it's going to be a fight, but we aren't out of it yet. We will be if they rip the team apart."

I write that down. "Sounds like it's not only you Conroy has an issue with, then."

"He hates us all. He wants new guys he can mold to what he thinks a player should be. Total narcissist."

"I've heard that word being thrown around about you a lot over the years," I point out.

"Exactly. Game recognizes game."

I laugh. "Nah, narcissists would never admit what they are. My guess is you act like one so people don't want to get close to you, and then you don't have to be vulnerable with them."

Dalton's mouth drops, and no sound comes out, but he shakes it off and turns to Archer. "I regret agreeing to having two agents now. Can we go back to where I tell you what to do and you do it?"

Archer smiles. "Sorry, I'm with Fox on this one. Besides, in this kind of situation, you're better off with him on your team."

Dalton hangs his head. "Maybe I would be better off to have you ask around about a trade. At least if we initiate it, I might be able to ask for teams I'd willingly go to. Only issue with that is little bro is still with Rochester, and we kinda had a plan where we'd play together one day. He's doing so well, I know it's only a matter of time before he gets called up. I wouldn't want to leave and then subject him to Conroy's shit without me to back him up. If Conroy has issues with me, then you know he's going to have issues with anyone else who has the same last name."

I rub my chin. "Leave it with us. We'll do some research on this guy, review your contract within an inch of the law, and come up with a solution. Hopefully one that will keep you happy and satisfy the team, but if we can't, you're going to need to send us through a list of teams you'd be willing to go to."

"This isn't another test, is it?" Archer asks.

Dalton's wide eyes make him look more innocent than he is. "Test? Whatever do you mean?"

"Like our meeting. You pushed me to see how far I was willing to go for you."

"Have no idea what you're talking about." His smirk says otherwise. "But no. This is not like that."

I hand over my tablet and pen to Dalton. "Write down the teams you're willing to go to and, if possible, all your teammates who have issues with the new GM. Also, if you can think of any other run-ins or incidents with him, put those situations down too."

For the first time since Archer and I landed in Buffalo, Dalton's shoulders lose some tension, and he gets to work.

Even while we eat, he'll continually stop to write down something else he remembers.

This is going to be an uphill battle, and it very well could be the workings of an overinflated ego of a generational hockey player, but it's our job as his agents to do everything we can to make sure he's getting the most out of his career.

Archer and I have a long night ahead of us.

It's two in the morning, my eyes are bleary, but I'm determined to find something in Dalton's contract to save his ass. Maybe I shouldn't be doing this on the hotel bed, using the headboard as a backrest. If I were to lie down, I'd be out like a light.

Archer's at the small desk next to the TV, talking to some of the West Coast agents who represent other players on the Buffalo team via video call. He started with the East Coast agents, but it's too late to be calling them now. It's true that agents need to be on call twenty-four hours a day, but if we're getting calls at 2:00 a.m., someone better be on fire. Considering this mostly involves Dalton's career, annoying other agents at this time of night will only get us firmly on their shit list if it doesn't directly affect their client.

We can call who we don't get through to tonight in the morning.

But from what I've overheard of Archer's conversations with other agents, a lot of Buffalo players aren't happy under the new management.

Archer ends yet another call and then stands, rubbing his tired eyes. "This Conroy guy is a piece of work. How did he get this job in the first place?"

"I looked it up earlier. He and the owner of the team go way back, and it appears he got the job on the merit of 'I did hockey once. I know things.' What he doesn't know is how to run a team as a business. He's willing to throw their season away to make it look like he knows what he's doing. After not making the playoffs last year, possibly not making it this year, he needs to do something to show his friend that he's being proactive."

"Instead of doing the actual thing that will help, which is telling Coach to do as he sees fit with the players?"

"Yup."

Archer walks around the other side of the bed and sits next to me.

Considering we've both been traveling half the day and working for the rest of it, he still smells good. Too good. Like leather-bound books and smoke, but the good kind of smoke, like from a bonfire.

"You have your own hotel room with a bed, you know," I say because I have to. If he thinks sitting next to me is going to make me put down this contract and jump him instead, well, he'd be right.

Hence, needing him to leave because I still have work to do.

"I do know. Even though I told you we could get one room with two beds, you insisted on your own room."

"Because of the optics. What would Edele think if we used the company card for one room? She's already way too invested in my love life to let it slide."

"She is? Are you two actually friends? I thought you didn't do that with people in the office."

"We're *friendly*. Which is smart, considering she's in charge of our travel budget."

The reality drops on him like an anvil. "That's why you get all the good flight times and hotels?"

"Why are you surprised by this? Cam told me on my first day that you catch more flies with honey than vinegar when it comes to Edele."

Archer still seems shocked. "You manipulate her situation to gain an advantage?"

"Are you, Archer Holloway, really accusing me of that?"

"Don't get me wrong, I'm not appalled by it. I'm impressed."

I snort. "Figures."

"But also, calm down. I didn't ask to share a room so we could have more mind-blowing orgasms. I knew we'd be working late and that I'd be in here anyway. Have you found anything?"

"Not yet, and I'm starting to think there won't be a magic loophole to fix it. Let's face it. Damon worked on this contract, so we both know it's going to be ironclad."

"It's getting late. We should probably get some sleep and relook at this in the morning."

My eyes sting, but I'm not going to pack it in yet. "You can. After I've scoured this contract, I'm going to look at the teams Dalton is willing to go to and look at their stats for the season to find out who needs a top six forward and who's most likely to keep him after his contract is up."

Archer stands, walking over to the minibar and pressing the On button for the in-room Keurig.

"What are you doing?" I ask.

"If you're going to keep working, then I'll keep working. Maybe I'll look into how to oust a general manager without going directly to the owner. If Conroy is friends with him, going above his head isn't going to do much."

I flip through all the hockey knowledge filed in my brain. "The only time I can think of that happening or almost happening was a few years ago. I think it was Carolina. They'd almost made it to the Stanley Cup finals the year prior, but the beginning of their season was so bad, management let go of their head coach after only seven regular-season games. Then the GM and new coach decided to trade their captain. It was a mess."

"What happened?" He brings over a coffee for me, and even if it tastes like drip coffee, the caffeine will help.

"The players got together to have an official player-only meeting. No one knows what was discussed in it, but there were talks of them refusing to skate until management got their shit together or at least paid attention. Who knows? Maybe all they did was sit in the locker room and talk about their wives or kids. Either way, them merely meeting behind closed doors turned everything around. Management paid attention. And while that scenario didn't end with the GM being fired, it must have been enough for him to pull his head in. They went on to make the playoffs again that season."

He picks up his own coffee next to the Keurig and turns, leaning against the wall cabinet. "We could do something like that."

"There's one huge problem with pulling off something like that."

"What's that?"

"If management get tipped off, find out who's organizing it, it'll only put Dalton in the firing line even more. Plus, what happens if management calls the team's bluff?"

"Who's to say they'd be bluffing?" Archer unleashes the kind of smile he usually reserves for when he messes with me.

I have to say, being on this side of it is a lot more fun.

Chapter 28
Archer

I NEVER MAKE IT BACK TO MY OWN HOTEL ROOM. WE WORK until my eyes refuse to stay open, and that's how I find myself waking up next to him. Or under him would be a more accurate description.

He's using me like his very own body pillow, one arm and leg thrown over the top of me, and his face buried in my shoulder. The soft snore coming out of him tells me he probably doesn't even know he's worked his way over to me at some time during the night.

His laptop is closed on the nightstand, so he was at least conscious enough to do that before falling asleep, but the question is whether or not he was conscious while he cuddled up to me.

I'd like to think he was, but I highly doubt that.

My arm is sweaty from where it's trapped between us, his body heat making it feel like it's in a furnace, but when I try to move it, it brushes against something hard. Really fucking hard.

I internally groan and have to use my free hand to bite my knuckles to stop the sound from coming out loud. I'm uncomfortably trapped but also don't want to move because it's sweet torture having him pressed against me with raging morning wood, and there's nothing I can do about it because the man is unconscious.

Do I continue to lie here as still as possible, drowning in the need to touch him? Or do I wake him up in the hope he's as up for it as his dick is?

The right thing to do would be to try to slip out of bed as quietly as possible, maybe go downstairs to get proper coffee for both of us, and get stuck back into work. We have a full day ahead of us. My argument that starting the day off with a bang instead of a caffeine infusion will make us more productive wouldn't fly. Probably. Maybe?

Whether he can sense my overthinking or he's naturally waking up, Fox stirs in my arms. I'm thankful I don't have to make the decision. Because even though I know I should get up, it's the very last thing I want to do.

Slowly, Fox opens his eyes. His brow furrows, and his whole body goes rigid as he stretches out, removing his leg and arm from across my body. He yawns, and it's as if that's when everything comes into focus.

Me, next to him. Him, on my side of the bed. Sure, this is his hotel room, but crashing out means there's a "my side" and "his side," and he's well and truly across my line. I'm obviously not complaining, but he better not blame me for him being stuck to me like glue.

"We fell asleep."

"Well, I fell asleep. You seemed to have been awake enough to put your laptop aside and strip out of your pants and work shirt."

He still has an undershirt on, but that's better than what I'm wearing, which is still everything other than my jacket and shoes. I did undo the buttons on my shirt at some point, but that's as far undressing as I got.

Fox hasn't moved over, not even an inch. He's still pressed against me, even if he's not clinging to me anymore. "By the time I was ready to call it a night, you were already snoring. I didn't see the point in waking you to go down the hall to your own bed."

"That might be the sweetest thing you've ever done for me."

"I dunno. Not reporting you to HR was pretty sweet."

"You wouldn't report me. Of course, I didn't know that until recently, but I bet I can answer why you never did."

"If you're about to say anything other than I thought it would have been petty and unprofessional, you'd be wrong."

"Nah, that's not it. You never reported it because it meant I'd stop flirting with you."

"Oh, look, I am correct. You were wrong. Also, if annoying the shit out of someone is how you flirt, you might need a few pointers."

"Flirting, taunting. It's the same thing."

He laughs. "If you say so."

"I do say so. And you know how I know that?"

"How?"

"Because you've been cuddled up to me all night and haven't run away screaming after waking up and realizing that."

Fox lets out an undignified "Pfft" noise. "We've sucked each other's dicks, and you thought I'd freak out at cuddling? Besides, it's not my fault. You took my side of the bed, so naturally, I'd gravitate toward it in the middle of the night."

"Your side of the bed? You were sitting on the other side while you were working."

He nods. "Exactly. That's my work side. My sleeping side is this side."

"And where exactly is your partner's side?"

"I don't have a partner, so why would an imaginary boyfriend get a side?"

I purse my lips. "I'm starting to see why you're single."

"Oh, going to come at me with all the wisdom of another single man in his late twenties?"

"Yup." I roll to face him and make sure we remain plastered to each other. "You're single because you're subconsciously not making room for anyone else in your life."

"Because I want a giant bed all to myself? That's reaching a bit, isn't it?"

"The bed is a metaphor. You are the bed. Or your life is the bed. You're filling your bed with only yourself."

He blinks at me.

"I swear the thought process was processing better in my head," I say.

"Is this how your brain works on little sleep? Because we're going to have problems today if that's the case. We've got a coup to plan."

"Couldn't come up with anything else after I fell asleep?"

Fox sighs. "Sadly, no."

Damn. "I guess we should get up, then."

"Yep," he says softly. "We should." Yet, neither of us moves. Fox brings his thumb to my bottom lip, pulling it out from behind my teeth. "Definitely need to get up."

I can't help myself and go for the easy joke while throwing my leg over his hip and bringing our cocks together. "Apparently, we both already are ... up."

His loud exhale sounds like sex with a little hint of defeat. "We have to be quick."

"If we proved anything that night of the NFL gala, it's that we can be quick, but just so you know, one of these days, I'm going to make the time to go slow with you." I kiss the tip of his nose before pulling away and climbing out of bed.

He reaches for me. "Wait, where are you going?"

"Quick usually means messy, and I only packed one suit for this trip."

"Smart." Fox slips out of bed and ditches his undershirt and then teases me by hooking his thumbs into the waistband of his boxer briefs, but he doesn't tug them down. "Actually, if we really want to be smart, we'd save time and water by showering together. Get all ... fresh for the long day of work ahead."

My gaze and mind are still stuck on his underwear and the anticipation of them coming off that his words don't really register, until I say, "Sounds good."

That's when it all clicks because instead of giving me what I want, a full view of his naked body, he turns on his heel and disappears into the bathroom.

The shower turns on a second later, and I almost trip over my pants as I rush across the room while simultaneously pulling them off.

When I reach the bathroom and Fox's naked form is right there, under the spray with the shower curtain wide open, I'm almost tempted to stand here and enjoy the show, but my dick—and the amount of work we have to get done today—won't allow it.

I am momentarily frozen though, watching him as he lathers himself up and reaches behind him. His hand dips between his ass cheeks, and he sends a taunting glance over his shoulder at me.

"I could do that for you, you know."

His smile widens. "Unless you've got magical fingers that can reach across the room, you're going to have to actually move your feet and come over here. I'm almost clean, and once that happens, it's work time, so—"

Again, I almost trip over myself, this time on my underwear as I try to jump out of them. I should buy cheaper ones. Ones that can tear easily.

Fox laughs, and when I climb into the tub/shower combo, he places his forearms on the tiles in front of him, sticks his ass out, and I swear he even wiggles it slightly. It's the most erotic sight I've ever seen, and it might have nothing to do with his sexy, sleek body and everything to do with his confidence.

Fox has always been to the point with me, but even when he was yelling or getting angry, there was a quiver to his voice. It could have been from pure frustration and emotions running high, but I always saw it as insecurity. Uncertainty.

With the way he's handling Asher's drama, how he takes control when it comes to sex, I'm thinking all my preconceived ideas about Fox were wrong.

Uptight? No, he's efficient.

Insecure? Not at all.

Would look good coming undone? Okay, that one I've always been right about.

And as I approach him, run my hands up his sides and then down the middle of his back, I can't wait to see it happen again.

"What exactly do you want here?" I ask.

"If it weren't for the time crunch, the lack of preparation, and no lube, I'd want you to fuck me right here. Like this." He pushes backward, his ass brushing against my cock. "But seeing as that's off the table, I don't care what else you do to me. Just get me off."

Fucking hell. He can't offer me his ass like that when I can't follow through. It's mean. I may not be able to fuck him, but I can still play him. I can tease myself by feeling the warmth of his hole around my fingers. Explore the rim of his taint with my tongue and bring him to his knees.

I press myself against him, cover his back with my front, and let the water beat down on my skin. I kiss the spot on the back of his neck below his ear. "Tell me if you're not okay with anything I do."

"Specifically now or in general?"

"Now, geez. I don't want to hear the long list you have outside of sex."

"Right. No time for that."

I laugh against his skin and then kiss my way down his shoulder blades and back.

The old shower/bath combo isn't friendly to my knees, but it's not like squatting is an option either. Losing balance and dying from blunt-force trauma after hitting the edge of the bath on my way down is not the way I want to go.

So I endure the hard porcelain on my knees while I massage Fox's back, moving lower and lower until his perfect, round ass is in my hands.

I knead his skin, separating his cheeks and getting quick glimpses of his hole. What I wouldn't give to sink my cock inside him. Another time.

I brush my thumb over his puckered skin, loving how he moans at the slightest touch. The water running down his back prevents me from being able to put my mouth on him, but that's an easy fix. I grip his hips and pull him backward to my mouth, making the water roll off the sides of his shoulders instead.

The first flick of my tongue has him cursing words that don't even make sense, but they sound like "Fuckingly fliberty junk-fuck." Whatever that means.

I lick around his rim, and he arches his back. He's so desperate for it. I want to fuck him so much.

Salvia pools in my mouth, and I let it pass my lips to slick up his hole. With one last swirl of my tongue, I pull back and switch it with my middle finger. I work him slowly and push through the ring of muscle but keep it shallow. His ass sucks me in, warmth surrounding my finger.

I can't help but add my own sound to the mix of Fox's loud breathing. It's a mix of a growl and a moan that rumbles in my chest.

I push my finger deeper and deeper, past the middle knuckle, and then all the way to the base. The lotus tattoo on my hand looks so fucking good between his ass cheeks, and as I pull my finger out and push back in, watching it disappear over and over again hits some kind of bullshit alpha ownership inside me.

Fox's legs begin to tremble, and I stand, keeping my digit deep inside him while I turn my wrist for comfort. The way he's standing, now using his hands instead of his forearms to prop himself up on the wall, with his ass out as far as possible, his torso stretched and arched, it's not something I'm going to forget anytime soon.

He starts fucking himself on my finger, taking over for me, and I let him move however he wants because watching him is an experience in itself.

My cock leaks, and I want to touch myself with my free hand, but I also want to wait it out so he can do it. To prevent my hand from wandering, I wrap my arm around his waist and close my fist over his cock, but to do this, I have to press against his side, trapping my cock against his upper thigh and hip. The friction is glorious as he continues to rock backward.

I begin stroking him, more unintelligible words fall from his mouth, and his hips pick up in speed. He's fucking my fist and my finger at the same time, and I get so lost staring at the side of his face, I practically miss where he comes.

His neck is tight, jaw locked, and teeth gritted, but no noise comes out. Only when I glance down his body and see my fist filling with cum do I flick my gaze back to his face, and that's when

I see it. That glorious look of pleasure where his face is so relaxed. Blissed-out. He's so ... *undone.*

While Fox recovers, I remove my finger from his ass and my hand from his cock and wash them under the water.

He reaches behind him, wrapping his arm around me to grip my ass. "Give me a second, and I'll be functional enough to get you off."

I kiss along the nape of his neck. "I might not make it that long. You're so hot like this." I grind against his side, my cock pulsing with want. I pull back enough so I can reach for myself and relieve some of the fucking need. "Actually, stay just like that." I place one hand over his on the wall and move to stand behind him to see his naked form.

Fox does as I ask, but instead of keeping his head down, he lifts his chin over his shoulder and watches me as I begin to jerk myself off.

"This okay?" I ask.

"Keep going. The idea of you coming all over my back shouldn't be as sexy as it is."

If I wasn't so desperate to come, I'd laugh and bring up all the times he'd come to my office to yell at me or when we'd be in the break room together, and he'd storm out at my cocky attitude.

"I bet past you never thought you'd be here, letting me do this."

"No fucking way. I sometimes still can't believe we've hooked up."

"Your compliments are such a turn-on." My tone might be dry, but his attitude does turn me on something fierce. There's something ... real about the way he says exactly what he's thinking about me. Good or bad.

"Not believing it but still enjoying it is a compliment," he says, and I'm not sure that's any better. "And fuck, I want to see you come." He pushes backward, his ass cheek brushing against my hand and cock.

He doesn't have to wait long. It's been building up, watching him come undone, refusing to touch myself while it happened.

It only takes a couple of minutes before I unleash all over his back and the top of his ass. I keep coming, convinced I'm done, only to come some more. By the time I'm empty, his skin looks like a Jackson Pollock.

Fox eventually slips out from underneath me and washes away my art piece under the spray while I catch my breath.

"You don't have much time to pull yourself together," he says. "We need to get to work."

I'd rather stay in this hotel room all day naked, but he has a point. "Fine."

When he's done, he kisses my cheek. "You finish up, and I'll order room service for breakfast."

No doubt in between preparing press releases and setting up meetings. I don't want to work today, but at least I get to spend the day by his side.

Chapter 29

Fox

Archer paces the long corridor outside the Buffalo locker room. "I wish we could be in there so we knew what they were saying."

He's more nervous than I am about all this. At least outwardly. I'm leaning against the wall, trying not to worry about GMs or coaches getting notified about what's happening down here.

"Kind of defeats the purpose of a 'player only' meeting." I'm so helpful.

"I know, but what if there's a snitch in there and they tell the bosses Dalton was responsible for this?"

I shrug, even if that's a concern of mine too. "Then we won't be in much of a different position than we are now. This Conroy guy hates Dalton, and with the way he's trying to push him out, this issue will probably come down to him or Dalton."

"That's not making me feel better. At all." Finally, Archer stops pacing and faces me. "If we fuck this up for him, can you imagine what Damon is going to think?"

Yeah, that we're terrible at our jobs, and he never should've let the Dalton brothers sign with us. I step forward and approach him, putting my hands on his shoulders. "Breathe. It's going to be okay. Yes, a scandal isn't great, and yes, Dalton doesn't have a great reputation, but at the end of the day, he's an amazing talent. Someone else will pick him up."

"Still won't negate the fact that we've been representing him for all of five minutes, and all the work Damon's done for him means nothing if Dalton loses Buffalo."

I've never seen Archer this anxious before, and maybe this is how he is behind closed doors when it comes to his career. This shouldn't be the takeaway from this, but Archer being comfortable enough to show me his vulnerability when all I've ever seen from him is confidence at work ... I'm tempted to kiss him right here in this hallway.

Luckily, before I can do something I'd regret if anyone walked in on us, I'm saved when my phone rings in my pocket.

I step back and fish it out, seeing Damon's name on my screen and wondering if it's a coincidence he's calling me or if he has a sixth sense and knows when his agents or clients are talking about him.

I put it on speaker. "Hi, you're on speaker with me and Holloway."

"Are you somewhere we can speak freely?"

"Yes, it's just us two here."

"Good. That will save me a second call and allow me to yell. What the fuck is happening in Buffalo?"

Oh, shit. News travels fast. Too fast. If Damon knows, Buffalo management are probably onto us too.

"What have you heard?" I ask cautiously. "And when?"

"That Asher has staged some kind of mutiny in the locker room."

"Mutiny is a bit of a strong word, isn't it?"

"What would you call it?" Damon growls.

Archer takes over the vague answering. "A, uh, polite conversation between teammates about management's mishandling of sensitive team information."

"Nice spin," Damon says.

"I thought so," Archer mutters.

I cut in. "The more pressing matter is how you found out about it, and does this mean it's already leaked to the press?" We thought we were being careful, having each of the players' agents contact them about the meeting, but maybe it was too much to trust that many different people.

"Coach Beauman called me to ask if the rumblings were true and if I had a leash on you two."

That's not embarrassing or anything.

"I thought you could handle this account, but maybe I was wrong. Asher Dalton is too big and too much of a menace for associate agents to handle. I should've passed him off to Xavier."

"What would your solution be here?" I ask because we couldn't see another way other than to give in to everything Conroy wanted. That would've been putting Dalton in a much too vulnerable position for his contract negotiations coming up.

"It was a simple problem, and I shouldn't have to explain to a pair of agents who aren't interns. A public apology would go a long way. It would all blow over."

Damon King is a great boss, and he's really supportive. Usually. Right now, he's making me feel about two feet tall.

"And what about the two-game suspension and anger management the GM is trying to force upon Dalton?" I ask.

"The *what*?"

"We flat out said to Conroy that Dalton will apologize," Archer says. "He wanted more. He originally suggested five games, which we thought was extreme, but it was the anger management that set both Fox and me on edge."

I nod along with Archer, even though Damon can't see us, and add, "Maybe we were reading into it, but it didn't sit right with us mainly because if he agreed to anger management, he would be contradicting his public apology that stated he acted immaturely and on a whim and didn't mean harm. Dalton is adamant his GM has it out for him—"

"Yeah, I remember when he first took over that he had concerns, but I told him to suck it up and be a grownup. Sometimes your clients need that."

"I agree," I say. "And sometimes they need you to listen to them."

Damon's silent for a moment, and I'm trying to think of something else to argue, but my mind goes blank. Or maybe it's now overthinking every moment over the last twenty-four hours and how we got here, staging a coup, and trying to pinpoint the moment we took the wrong turn. I've got nothing.

My gaze finds Archer's icy blue eyes, which are filled with the same blank *don't know what to do* expression.

"Okay," Damon says. "I trust you two to get whatever you need to done, but I want a full report in my inbox tomorrow morning outlining this fuckup. Fix it quickly." Then, before he ends the call, he mumbles, "Maybe having two agents isn't better than one."

The line goes dead.

"Great pep talk," Archer says dryly, but then his face falls. "Oh, shit, that call did end, right?"

I laugh. "It did." But the overthinking from the call still lingers in my head. "This was the right move, wasn't it?"

"This morning, I was certain. Now?" He glances toward the locker room door. "I don't fucking know."

Sounds from down the hall echo in the empty corridor, heavy footsteps only getting louder. My irrational brain tells me that it's Damon, and he can teleport or has been here the whole time, and all of this drama is a test and we failed, but the reality isn't much better.

It's Buffalo's head coach, Beauman, and GM Conroy, along with a few others I don't recognize. I'm assuming it's other coaches or perhaps PR reps.

Archer and I straighten and stand tall, but instead of acknowledging us, they bypass us straight for the locker room.

"I wouldn't go in there if I were you," Archer says.

The group as a whole stop and turn to us. Conroy looks us up and down. "Was that a threat?"

"Nope." Archer pops the *P* sound. "But upper management barging in on a specified player-only meeting wouldn't be a good look for you."

"I'll take my chances." Conroy leads them all inside, behind a wall I know we can't hear through, even if we're up close. I know because Archer tried when the players first started their meeting.

I'm just as nervous as Archer is. However, I refuse to let it show. "On the bright side: this might be about to blow up in our faces, but at least it'll be over with quickly."

Archer tries to suppress a smile, but it escapes. "That's so comforting."

There's a lot of pressure on us to do well, considering this is a client Damon used to represent, but I also knew getting into this that Dalton would be a handful. Of course, I didn't expect him to throw his first spanner in the works within weeks of taking over his account.

Whatever is happening in that room, it takes a long-ass time. Archer goes back to pacing, and I stare at my phone, contemplating doing some more research on other teams' salary caps and thinking of who would be the best fit for Dalton. A lot of teams he'd be comfortable with or are actual contenders for the Cup are already at their cap ceiling. They might be able to take Dalton on through to the end of his contract, but getting another contract at his age after that is no guarantee.

It's over two more hours that we're stuck in this corridor for, and right when I'm about to ask if Archer wants to go get some dinner and come back, the locker room door opens again.

Conroy's red in the face, his brow so far down he almost looks like a cartoon character, and by the sweat running down his forehead, I'd say he's been yelling up a storm in there.

This could be a good or bad thing, but after he charges off down the hallway, not even acknowledging us other than a scowl, it's another half an hour before the door opens again.

Players file out, one after the other, some looking sullen, others smiling and laughing. I want to scream at them and ask for the play-by-play, but then toward the back of the pack, Dalton finally emerges with Zac Moses's arm around his shoulders.

Moses pats him on the back and says, "We owe you, man."

"Damn fucking right you do." Dalton smiles wide, and I finally get the sense of relief wash over me.

I can only hope it's not short-lived. "How did it go? What happened? What do you need us to do?"

"Whoa, slow down." Dalton laughs. "It went about as well as can be expected. No one wants to directly go for the GM in fear of repercussions, but when Conroy barged in with no respect for the player-only rule, the majority swayed in my favor. Coach Beauman quietly got the club's owner on the phone then and told him to listen in while Conroy lost his shit at everyone. It was highly entertaining. Top-notch popcorn-worthy moment."

"So what does that mean for you and the team?" I ask.

"Conroy has been relieved of his duties, and I don't need to go to anger management or be suspended. The only thing Beauman wants me to do is the public apology, and I have those things down to an art by now."

We actually did it? No, we more than did it. I glance at Archer with a mix of emotions: triumph, smugness, but most of all, relief.

"Holy shit," Archer says. "I can't believe they ousted him, but I'm so thankful that these kinds of allegations were taken seriously despite the owner being friends with Conroy."

"Maybe if my teammates didn't have issues with him too, it might have been a different story, but everyone seems happy that jerk is gone."

I frown. "Then why did some of them look like they'd been kicked in the nuts as they left?"

"Really?" Dalton cocks his head. "Who?"

"Rintz and Pahlm," I say.

Dalton waves me off. "Oh, them. They have resting *I'll cut you* face even more than me. They're great guys though. They don't speak a word to me, and I don't to them."

"That ... makes them great?" Archer asks.

"Duh. They're my favorite people on the team. No, possibly in the universe outside Kole and my family. Anyway, we're all going out to celebrate. You two in? This victory is kinda yours too."

"Uh, wow," I say, flattered he'd consider asking. "We'd love to—"

"But unfortunately can't," Archer says. "We should be getting back to LA, plus we have a big report to fill out for Damon. You know ... agent stuff."

While that is true, building a rapport with our new client is probably more important than those things.

Dalton steps closer to Archer. "This wouldn't happen to have anything to do with going out with me and my teammates again, would it?"

Archer pretends to think about it. "That might have something to do with it. I mean, the last time I went out with you all, I basically had to babysit you all, and then I became an accessory to a B and E. So, thank you, but no, thanks."

Dalton laughs and throws his arm around Archer's shoulders. "Come on. Live a little. What if I promise there will be no breaking and entering tonight?" He holds up three fingers on his spare hand. "Scout's honor."

Archer looks to me. "What do you think?"

"I'm in if you are." Hell, I was in before he was.

Archer relents. "Fine. But the first sign of breaking the law, and we're out of there. All of us. Even if we have to drag you kicking and screaming."

"That's what I pay you the big bucks for." Dalton heads down the corridor, whistling, and we follow in step with each other.

"I really hope we don't regret this," Archer says.

"Think of it this way. At least if Dalton does get in trouble, we're here to bail him out."

"Not if we're in the cell next to him."

I was going to say in the figurative sense, but considering the B and E story, all I have is, "Fair point."

But it won't come to that. I'm sure of it.

One look at Archer's worried expression though, and maybe I'm not so sure of it anymore.

Chapter 30
Archer

Surprising the hell out of me, Dalton is on his best behavior all through dinner and even at the bar afterward. They all are.

It's only when I claim they've obviously been taken over by pod people that Moses laughs and gives me the heads-up that the team travel in the morning for a game in Nashville tomorrow night. None of them are going to get fucked-up.

Dalton could've said that as his main selling point for getting us to come out with them, but he didn't, and I'm starting to learn why.

Asher Dalton is an absolute sadist, and even though I want to hate him, I can't. I actually respect the fuck out of him. I'd tell him so, too, if it wouldn't go to his head and he'd taunt me for our whole professional relationship moving forward.

We're at a different bar from the one we were at last time, and this one is much more relaxed. It's a sports bar and obviously a favorite spot of the team, seeing as the walls are basically a shrine to them.

My gaze catches on Fox, who's in line for more drinks and talking to Rafferty Brooker. Like, really talking. Heads close together, laughing and nodding type of talking.

Dalton clinks his beer bottle with mine, breaking my focus. "I think I'm going to like having you two as my agents. Not going to lie, at first, I was worried it would mean having two Damons gang up on me, but you two are kinda all right."

"Kinda all right. I'll take it." I sip my drink, but my gaze strays back to Fox. "Hey, what's Brooker's deal?"

"Where do I start? He's obsessed with his hair, talks to his sticks like they're the ones controlling the puck, and—"

"I meant what is his ... situation. Is he out? Closeted?"

Dalton pulls back. "He's straight. Uh, as far as I'm aware."

I should be happy but looking at the way he's staring at Fox with love hearts in his eyes, I'm going to have to call bullshit on that. Internally. No way would I speculate someone's sexuality publicly if they're not out. "Shit, sorry. My gaydar must be broken."

Dalton follows my line of sight. "Your gaydar or your inner green-eyed monster?"

Bam. Direct hit. "I have no idea what you're talking about."

"Of course not. None at all. Definitely not talking about the way he's chatting up your business partner over there."

"So you agree you think he's chatting him up."

Dalton rolls his eyes. "Not in the way you're thinking. They're probably talking shop. Brooker's agent is ancient, so he's been asking around the team about how to go about finding an agent who will get him the kind of deals and appearances he wants. Like, he's got his own podcast channel thing online where he follows NASCAR, and sometimes the team PR will share the link, so it's getting popular. I get the feeling his agent wants him to stay in his own lane and focus on hockey."

"Did you tell him that we're awesome agents?"

"Was I supposed to when I hadn't even put you to the test yet?" His question sounds so genuine, I can't tell if he's fucking with me or not.

"Please tell me you didn't throw that puck at the intern to test to see how Fox and I would deal with a scandal."

"I can tell you I definitely didn't most definitely do that."

My gaze narrows.

Dalton nudges me. "Come on, man. I'm messing with you. I knew you were the right agent for me when you broke into Ayri

Quinn's house because I wanted to. Those who commit felonies together stay together."

"Actually, what we committed was criminal trespassing, which is a misdemeanor in New York State." I take another sip of my beer. "I looked it up after I got home."

This time when Dalton laughs, it's a full-belly laugh. "Maybe I was wrong about you, then. A great agent would have done it before we committed the crime."

"I didn't know we were committing it until we were already there!"

Even though I know Dalton is going to be one of my headache clients, I can't help but like the guy.

Brooker, on the other hand ... When he and Fox get back to the group, Fox stands next to me, while Brooker hangs off his other side. They're not touching, but still. Dalton can claim they're talking about business all he wants, but there's just something there I don't like. And it has nothing to do with Brooker approaching Fox about representation and not me.

Mainly because I'm sure that's not what they were talking about.

The urge to inch closer to Fox so we're practically against each other is one I know I should fight, but when a barback needs to step into the group's space to clear away some empty bottles and glasses, I seize my opportunity to brush against Fox.

He blinks up at me, cheeks flushed, though I think that's from the alcohol rather than my proximity.

"We should probably get out of here soon," I say. "We still have a report to write and flights to book for tomorrow."

Fox swallows, drawing my attention to his silky smooth neck. I want to nuzzle it, suck on it, and leave a giant fucking mark so Brooker gets the message.

"After this drink." He lifts his beer bottle.

"Deal." I want to ask what he and Brooker were talking about, but that's where my self-restraint does kick in.

We finish off our drinks and say our goodbyes to Dalton's teammates, while Dalton says he'll walk us out.

I don't miss how Brooker thrusts his phone in Fox's direction, though, to get his number.

"See? Totally hitting on him," I say to Dalton when we hit the fresh air. "He asked for his number."

"And Fox gave him a business card," Dalton says. "Don't worry. Brooker's not trying to steal your boyfriend."

I glance back inside the bar and see Brooker using Fox's business card to give him a wave as Fox exits the building.

"Not my boyfriend," I say.

"Maybe not, but you want him to be. I'm not going to tell you what to do, but even I know hooking up with him would be a bad idea for you. And coming from me, you should probably listen when I say something is bad."

Fox is only steps away from us now, so I beg Dalton with my eyes to shut the fuck up.

"What would be a bad idea for Holloway?" he asks.

"Knocking off a liquor store," Dalton says in his Dalton-esque way.

"Yeah, maybe I shouldn't leave you two alone anymore."

I hold out my hand for Dalton to shake. "Have a good night."

"You too." He shakes my hand and then Fox's. "I know I'm not the best at expressing myself—"

"What in the *eat shit and die* are you talking about?" Fox deadpans.

"Exactly," Dalton continues. "But I want you both to know that I do appreciate how you've had my back in all this. Damon is a close family friend, and while he was an absolute killer of an agent and was great at putting out fires, sometimes I felt like he only saw me as Westly Dalton's younger brother and therefore chose the most parental way to represent me. I don't even know if that makes any sense—"

"It does," I say. I know exactly how he feels. Like Damon was micromanaging him. It's how my dad treated all four of his kids when it came to our sporting careers.

"Anyway, thanks again. For seeing me as a professional athlete first and dipshit dickhead second."

I smile at that. "Don't sell yourself short. You're equally both."

I get that genuine laugh from him again that I thought would be rare but comes freely when he's obviously not stressed.

"It was our pleasure," Fox says. "And pain, come to think of it. Do you anticipate any more scandals this year, do you think?"

Dalton rubs his chin. "Are we talking fiscal season or hockey season? Playoffs are getting close, so I could promise to be good until the end of the season. Fiscal year is trickier."

Fox looks at me. "Why do I get the feeling Asher Dalton will be our least favorite client?"

Dalton starts walking backward in the direction of the bar entrance. "Maybe because you're smart?" He turns and disappears inside.

"I don't know how smart we are," I say.

"Why's that?"

"We came out for dinner and drinks when we could have gone back to the hotel to bed."

Fox pats my chest. "Cute you think I wouldn't make you finish off any paperwork before going anywhere near a bed with you again."

"I got you to delay work this morning. I could probably get you to do it again." And because we're in the middle of Upstate New York and there's no one we work with in this vicinity, no one to tattle on us if they see, I step toward Fox and press my chest to his.

"I'm sure you could." This time, he's the one who inches closer by lifting his chin, our lips landing a mere breath away. "But just so you know, if you do, I'll leave writing and proofing the report all up to you."

My tongue darts out because my mouth is suddenly so fucking dry. Doing the report is a small price to pay if it means I get to see Fox naked again sooner.

A car horn blaring behind us makes us both jump.

"That's us," Fox says, stepping back. My lips tingle, craving the contact that isn't coming.

"You ordered a car for us? When?"

"Unlike some people, I can walk and use my phone at the same time. I did it on the walk out here from inside."

"Oh." I turn and walk to one side of the car while Fox walks to the other and gets in.

"Really? No rebuttal? No defending your multitasking abilities?" he asks as he puts on his seat belt.

"You say that like I have any. Have to say, digs aren't super funny when they're true." I buckle up. "I didn't notice you ordering the car because I was too distracted watching Brooker through the glass door looking at your business card like it was his most prized possession."

Probably shouldn't have said that, so I try to deflect away from it by saying hi to our rideshare driver.

He only gives a curt nod and doesn't say a word as he takes off, the hotel already loaded in his GPS. Damn it. Why is the one time I wouldn't mind an annoying chatty driver the one time I get Mr. Silence?

"You sound jealous," Fox says. "Are you jealous?"

"Of you giving Brooker your business card? No." Of him wanting it? Maybe. I stare right ahead between the two front seats and through the windshield so I don't have to look at Fox and pretend that I'm not insanely jealous that I think Brooker could be into him romantically.

"I don't actually know why he approached me."

"Are you being serious?" Does he not see how hot he is? He might not have my over-the-top charm, but he has this way about him that's so damn appealing.

"You're the more logical choice to rep him."

Oh. Right. The "I want you to rep me" line that I don't think is a line at all.

"Maybe Dalton told his teammates about how you handled this situation." Or maybe he wants to get into your pants. And no, I'm obviously not going to let this go. "From what Dalton said, Brooker wants someone who will let him cheat on hockey with NASCAR. His current agent doesn't do that, apparently."

"Right, he was saying something like that. Which is why I think you'd be a better fit to rep him."

Me? I'm pretty sure no athlete wants to be repped by someone who wants to punch them for no reason other than they talked to someone who's taken.

Not that Fox is taken. By me or anyone else. But ... Gah. I wish I had a caveman switch to turn off this line of thinking.

Fox and I have hooked up a total of three times. That's not a relationship. That's not even the beginning of one. I didn't even think he'd want to do it again after the first time, so these feelings of jealousy and claimship can go get fucked. Because that's all this is. It's fucking. Though, without the actual fucking because we haven't done that. Yet. I so wanted to in the shower this morning, and if we had the time and the supplies, we never would've left that hotel room.

"You have a NASCAR client," Fox says, bringing me back out of the runaway thoughts in my head.

"Yeah, the one I stole from you," I point out. "I have no doubt you would've signed Castleberry had I let you meet with him. And then you would have the same experience I have had."

"That's my point though. You do have that experience now, and you've turned a lot of your low-paid athletes into these influencer types so that they have extra streams of income and a future for when they retire."

"That's all pretty easy and learnable. If I can do it, a monkey can."

"Yeah, but you already know it. If Brooker calls, I'm going to tell him to speak with you."

I turn in my seat as much as the seat belt will let me. The world whizzes by us in a blur, and for a split second where a streetlight catches Fox's gorgeous face, I see the same self-doubt I have when I look in a mirror sometimes. Usually when I'm about to meet with a potential big client or someone I desperately want to sign.

"Don't you see yourself when you work?" I ask.

"What do you mean?"

"Take this trip, for instance. Where I was slowly processing everything that happened, trying not to let my blood pressure skyrocket, you got stuck right into what we had to do. You have this calm demeanor that makes you come across so damn confident. You put me at ease a lot today, and I'm sure it's what your clients love most about you. It's ..."

Fox sucks in a sharp breath, and I bite my lip, unsure if I want to or should say this next bit. I'm scared he'll read into it and see exactly what I want to keep hidden: just how deep my feelings for him might be.

"It's what?" he asks softly.

"It's what I admire most about you."

Chapter 31
Fox

Damn Archer Holloway. His words used to make me hate him; now, they make my clothes disappear.

All because he said my calm demeanor in the workplace is admirable. I must be really fucking thirsty for a compliment if that's how I got here, on my bed back in the hotel, naked, with Archer on top of me and me clinging to his back as he grinds his hard cock against mine. I love the feeling of him moving above me, of his strong arms supporting the majority of his weight, and the scrape of his rough beard against my neck and shoulder as he sucks on my skin.

We should be writing that report that Damon needs, but nope, I'm needier.

"I need ..." I breathe heavily.

"Tell me what you need."

I throw my head back. "I need you to fuck me."

He slumps on top of me. "Damn it. I knew I should've brought supplies."

I run my hand through his messy hair and pull his head up to meet my stare. "Lucky one of us is prepared, then."

"Wait ... you brought supplies? To have sex. On this work trip. With me. And we didn't use them this morning?"

I roll my eyes and slip out from underneath him to go over to my bag. "This morning, we didn't have time, and I can't believe you didn't bring any. We'd already hooked up twice. You didn't think it was going to happen again?"

Archer lies on his side, supported by a bent elbow and his head propped up on his hand. "I didn't want to be presumptuous."

I pull out my lube and raise my brow at him. "You?"

"Okay, fine, I didn't want to jinx it."

Of course. "You really are a jock." I open the cap on the lube and get my fingers nice and slippery, and then I toss it over to him, showing him all the reasons why I am not like him in the jock department. It's lucky he even catches it before it can smack him in the head. I'd like to say I was aiming for his head, but I wasn't. "I have condoms, too, if you want to use one."

With my lubed hand, I reach around behind me and get started on working myself open. Generally, when it comes to hookups, I prefer fooling around over anal. It avoids the awkwardness of having to prep and then cleanup and, well, yeah, it's easier to frot or jerk off or exchange quick blowjobs. Plus, the whole condom thing can sometimes ruin the mood. I protect myself by taking PrEP, but that doesn't mean every guy I meet is the same.

"I haven't been tested in a while, but at my last screen, I was good to go. I think I've only been with ..." He looks up at the ceiling, his mouth moving to count something. "One person since? And we didn't do ... this. So it's up to you." He hasn't opened the lube yet, like he's sure I'm going to tell him to put one on.

"I trust you."

"Y-you do?"

I almost laugh, but as I push a finger inside me, my breath gets caught in my throat, and I shudder from the pleasure spreading everywhere. I close my eyes and give in to the sensation. My body lights up in anticipation for what's to come: Archer's cock trying to tear me in two.

Wait ... didn't he ask me something?

"What was the question?" I open my eyes and find him with a

lazy smile on his face while he strokes himself. His gaze is locked on to my cock, which is hard as fucking nails and leaking.

"Wasn't a question. I'm surprised that you trust me, is all. With anything. Let alone your body."

He adds more lube to his cock and goes back to jerking himself slowly to make sure it's spread everywhere. I get stuck watching the motion, mesmerized by how sexy the imagery is. I move my fingers in and out of my ass in time with his strokes, but it's getting to the point where I can't reach any further in this position.

"You want me to finish doing that for you?" Archer rasps.

I can't fucking wait to have that man's hands on me again. Climbing on the bed, I roll Archer onto his back and straddle his waist. He grips my ass in his big hands, and his cock rubs against my butt cheek. I regret giving up the option to have his hard length in my mouth before he puts it in my ass, but it's too late now. Lube tastes gross.

"How do you want me?" I ask.

His fingers dig into my flesh, and he uses his hands to guide me lower so I'm rubbing against him. I'm still too high for our cocks to meet, but from my balls to my hole, I can feel his hard shaft seeking friction.

"I want you just like this while I prep you." One of his hands leaves my ass, but the other encourages me to keep grinding on him. When the first of his fingers breeches me, I still. Not because it hurts or it's bad, but because God fucking damn, it feels amazing.

"Yes, like that," he encourages and pushes his finger deeper.

My breathing becomes deep and slow while he gets deeper than I could before, and I focus on letting him stretch me instead of the sting of it. Unlike this morning, where he took his time, teased me, he's on a mission.

"And once you're ready for me, I would fucking love to see you face down on your pillow, ass up in the air, and for you to let me use your hole. Ruin it. I want to fuck you so hard that you'll be begging for more. Or for me to put you out of your misery and push you over the edge." He adds another finger, which goes in easier.

Either I'm beginning to really loosen up, or I'm so desperate for him to do everything he's promised that I can ignore the uncomfortable pressure in my ass.

"I want that too," I say. "I want it now."

"You're not ready for it yet. Here ..." He removes his fingers, and my hole contracts, seeking that filled feeling. Craving it. Instead of removing his hand completely, he grips his cock and guides it toward my hole. His fat tip sits at my entrance, but he doesn't push it inside me. "You control how much you take. For now. I can't promise I'll last long enough to pound you into the mattress, but I'm going to fucking try. This is all of my fantasies come true. Right here." Archer grips the back of my neck. "With you."

I should get an award for not immediately bouncing on his dick and taking him all until I physically can't take any more. As tempting as that is, I don't want to actually tear my hole open. Only figuratively. So I force myself to go slow. To not replay his sweet words of being his fantasy, that being with me is all he has wanted for so long.

I shake my head and snap out of it.

"You okay?" Archer asks. "We can take our time."

"I'm more than okay. I'm ..." I slowly sink down on him, and when I come back up and repeat the process, I go a little deeper. "I so fucking need this."

He lifts his hips each time I sink down on him, but only a fraction. It's like he's trying to hold himself back from going too hard, too fast. We begin to build a rhythm. I might not be taking him fully, but I'm getting there.

I'm also dangerously close to having it all be over sooner than I'd like. Archer's cock inside me feels so amazing. So right. Even if the sense of wrong still lingers. The part of me that used to hate Archer still can't believe I'm doing this, but the rest of me? It's ready to sing the man's praises. If not for his commitment to his work, then for his cock alone. It should be worshipped.

Fuck me dead, I never want to get off. Actually, get off, yes.

Remove his cock from my ass? Never. I could ride him all fucking night.

While I've been enjoying every second of this, a pained groan pulls me from my bliss. I glance down at Archer, about to ask him what's wrong, but I don't need to ask.

It's obvious. His jaw is set with his teeth gritted, usually how he looks right before he comes, but I get the impression this isn't from that. The sound of complaint is because he can't lift his hips and be buried so deep inside me I see stars. Because I'm not ready yet.

Or so he thinks. I pick up my pace, loving that Archer's face contorts even more.

"Oh God," he murmurs. "Fucking hell." He writhes underneath me, meeting each downward move with an upward thrust of his own, and as we move together faster and faster, I'm for sure certain he's forgotten what he originally said he wanted to do.

I'm about to bring it up to him when he lets out a primal growl. In the next second, his arms are around me, and he rolls us over. His cock slips from my ass in the maneuver, but he still holds me tight.

Warmth spreads throughout my body.

"Time to let me have that ass," he says, his voice croaky.

"Isn't that what you were doing?" I snark.

"I might have gotten carried away for a moment, but I'm back now. I'm levelheaded. I won't be in a minute, though, if you refuse to roll your pretty self over so I can give you everything we both want."

The anticipation is back, and I only hope he can deliver. On already shaky legs, I get myself on my hands and knees and then lower my chest and arms so my ass is in the air, exposed and open for him. There's something about being in this position, about trusting whoever I'm with enough to let them see every part of me. It's not the first time he's been up close and personal with my ass, so when he doesn't immediately fill me up, I get a little self-conscious.

Yet, when I look over my shoulder at him, all he's doing is staring right at me. At my ass.

"You can still grab that condom if you're having doubts."

Archer shakes out of whatever he's obsessing over. "No fucking way. I'm going to feel all of you. I want to be buried so deep inside you that I can feel it on my cock when you come, and when I follow moments later, I want to fill you up."

"Fuck," I hiss. "Do it already. I'm dying for it. I'll even beg if you want me to, though please don't. Give it to me now. All of it. I need your cock." He doesn't even need to make me beg because here I am, willingly doing it. Past me is shaking his head and asking what I've become.

I've become a total cock slut for Archer Holloway's dick.

"What is taking so long?" I complain.

"Okay, fine, but I'm warning you now, if I come in two seconds, it's your own fault for being impatient."

"If you come in two seconds, you better find something else to fuck me with because I neeeeeed it." Now I'm being impatient. "I need it. I need it now. Fuck, fuck, fuck, please." That anticipation is what's really amping this up. It's the best sex I've never had.

Time seems to slow down. It takes an eternity for him to enter me and an even longer time for him to be up against my ass, his cock buried all the way in.

"How you doing?" he asks.

"Like I need you to move, and I need you to hurry the fuck up."

"If you insist."

I don't turn my head again. I don't have to for me to see what I already know is there—his smug smirk.

He starts off slow, and I haven't figured out if it's to piss me off or to keep him back from the edge. Either way, I don't let him play. I push backward on him, taking him deeper and harder, getting faster and faster until I have to fist the sheets and pray my head doesn't go through the headboard.

He does as he promised and turns me out, fucking my hole, pounding into my body, and sounding like a total porn star as he does it. "You're so fucking tight. I love this hole. I'm going to fill you up. I want you to take all of my cum."

I've never felt so sexy and wanted. I've also never felt so used and liked it.

"I'm not going to be able to keep this up for long," he says.

"Keep up or stay up? Forget your little blue pill?" If I actually thought that was the problem, I wouldn't be taunting him. But I can feel how hard he still is with every thrust. So fucking hard.

"Fuck you."

"Kinda already doing that."

My teasing has the desired effect because he only fucks me harder.

He doesn't need to worry about coming before me for long because as he fulfills his promise and uses my hole to get himself off, he pegs my prostate over and over again. I don't even have to reach between my legs to jerk myself off to come. It even takes me a second to realize I'm spilling all over the hotel sheets.

"Oh fuck, I'm coming," I say. "Shit." The trickle of pleasure turns into a roaring fire within seconds.

My muscles begin to ache, and right as my prostate starts to become too sensitive, I feel him when his cock swells inside me and he comes.

Everything inside him tenses. His hands dig into my sides so hard I hope they leave marks, but eventually, his thrusts become slower, his muscles loosen, and then so does his grip.

When he pulls out of me, I give a little wince because my ass is sore, and yet, it still contracts, wanting to be filled again.

Archer flops onto his back, and I slowly stretch out and let my legs straighten out underneath me and turn my head in his direction. He tries to catch his breath as he stares up at the ceiling.

I'm lying in a pool of my own cum, but I don't particularly care. Because that is the best sex I have ever fucking had. I'm relaxed from the roots of my hair to the tips of my toes, and I could easily fall asleep. Cleanup be damned.

My eyes are heavy, ready for sleep, but as I close them, I hear a chuckle.

"Can't go to sleep now. Who's going to keep me awake while I write up this report for us?"

Oh, right. Report. Shit. I push up and realize I'd already been drooling on the pillow, so I wipe my face, only to be pushed back down in the pile of drool.

"You don't have to get up though. I said if we hooked up, I'd do it. Just don't go to sleep yet so you can keep me awake."

"Can't make any promises."

Archer gets out of bed and grabs his boxer briefs on the way to the bathroom. I should really join him in getting cleaned up, but that's too much effort for the current me. Who's boneless.

When Archer comes back out, he says, "Seriously? Are you asleep already?"

"Nope. Can't move."

"Damn. I fucked you so hard you can't walk? You're welcome. If we didn't have to keep this thing between us a secret, I'd be telling everyone."

I huff. "Of course you would be. You'd go around claiming to be some kind of hero for wearing me down."

"Nah, I already claimed that title when I got you to go to a bar with everyone."

I sigh. Loudly.

"Can I ask you something?" Archer's moving about the room, but I haven't shifted an inch, so I don't know where he's at.

I finally make myself roll over, and I find him putting his laptop on the small dining table in the corner and taking a seat. "Depends on if it's a serious question or if you're about to ask if you're the best sex I've ever had and can join a podcast with you to talk about it in detail."

Archer laughs. "Now, there's an idea, but no. It's a serious question. Why have you always been so adamant about not mixing with your colleagues outside of work?"

Why is he bringing this up now? "Because it's smart not to."

"How so?" Archer opens his laptop and clicks on his track pad.

"Because when you spend all day at work with them and then go out afterward, spending that much time with someone is bound to end in making mistakes. Whether it's getting sick of each other

and having a huge fight or ... landing in bed with them. Exhibit A."
I wave my hand over his side of the bed.

"Aww, you broke your rules for me."

"I did. And only time will tell if I'm going to regret it a little or
a lot."

"Ouch. Why do you have to regret it at all?"

Okay, now I'm wide-awake. I sit up in bed and run my hand
over my hair. "Because logic dictates this is only going to end one of
two ways. One, everyone finds out, we're endlessly mocked, and we
end up resenting each other for it. Two, you do something to piss
me off, and I go back to hating you." I'm kind of joking but also
kind of not. I like hooking up with him, and I want to continue to
do it, but I'm still wary of letting my guard down around him. If I
keep telling myself there's an end date, I won't be taken off guard
when it happens. I won't get too comfortable, only to find out my
original hatred for him was valid.

"Hey, what makes you think you won't do something to piss me
off, and I'll end up hating you?" he asks.

"Because you're too much of a good guy to hate anyone. Me
pissing you off is a possibility though. I might steal one of your
clients for once."

"Cool joke. So funny."

"Ah, there's the answer. Your cockiness is what will end this."

"Yeah, that's the most likely scenario." He grins.

Even though we're having a serious conversation, it's good to
know we can keep it light.

I stand and stretch, and Archer's gaze doesn't leave me.

He shakes his head and goes back to looking at his laptop
screen. "Report. Have to do this report."

No one has ever made me feel so irresistible before, and I'm
realizing that's probably why I haven't been interested in anyone
past a few dates or hookups. Because no one has made me think
I'm special enough to pursue.

"While you do that, I'm going to shower, and then I'll come
proof it for you."

"Even though I promised I would do it?"

"That's not why we had sex. I was going to pitch in either way."

"And I remember when your threats used to mean something." He tsks me.

"I guess maybe you really are starting to wear me down." Even if whatever this is between us is doomed, I can't help but let it happen.

Chapter 32
Archer

So much sweat, and I can't even blame the LA heat. It's all nerves. All because of a text I got yesterday from my father. He and my sister, Leila, are in town specifically to see me, which can mean one of two things: they're here to tell me how to do my job or … wait, no. That's it. That's why they're here.

Fox and I only got back from Buffalo on Friday, and both of us spent the weekend apart catching up on the work piling up since we were gone, and now, come Monday, I have to endure lunch with my family. Arguably, my most annoying clients because they don't speak to me like an agent. They speak to me like I'm a toddler wearing a suit and have no idea what I'm babbling about.

Considering the shitshow that was Dalton's scandal, the fact I'd rather be back there than here says something. And that's why I've asked Fox to come with me to this lunch. I need a buffer.

But now that we're outside in the parking lot of the restaurant, I'm realizing this was a bad idea. If Fox ever hooks up with me again after this, it will be a miracle. Maybe I shouldn't have invited him.

"Today is getting weirder by the second," Fox says.

I tilt my head in his direction. "Why?"

"First, you ask me to lunch to meet with one of your clients, and now, as we sit here, not getting out of the car, you look like you might throw up. Just who is your client, and why do you need me as a buffer?"

"Do you remember me telling you about how my dad thinks I'm a quitter because I chose a more stable career over being an athlete?"

Fox's focus flicks between me and then the restaurant and back again. "Wait, are you saying—"

"The client is my sister, but my dad is also here, and I just can't deal with his shit when my workload is piling up on me because of our stint in Buffalo. I figure if I bring in a coworker, maybe he won't go so hard on me, but now that we sit here, I'm realizing that the guy I'm sleeping with is about to meet my dad, and that's not what this was supposed to be about." It's not like Fox and I have spoken about anything more happening between us or that what we're doing could ever be anything more than fucking, but I wouldn't be opposed to something more, and having him meet my dad has a real chance of squashing that.

"That definitely doesn't have to be mentioned at a work lunch," Fox says, but I can read between the lines because I hear the follow-up clear as day, even though he doesn't say it out loud. *Or ever.*

"I just didn't want you to think I somehow tricked you into meeting my dad like ... in that way. When I asked you to be my buffer, I was only focusing on getting my dad to behave. Of course, now I'm not even sure he'll do that."

"Is your sister nice, at least?" Fox asks.

"She's a lot like Dad in some ways. Winning is a big deal to her—"

"So that's a Holloway family trait, then."

"Okay, yes, I like winning too, but I do it more out of necessity than loving the thrill of it. It might have taken me four years to realize this, but there's a lot more to winning than signing that contract or getting that client." I glance over at him quickly before moving my eyes back to the restaurant that seems to get bigger with every glance. Bigger and scarier. "Sometimes winning is about being happy. And if that's the case, I'm winning where it counts."

My admission is a little too raw for me, but he doesn't need to know that he's a big part of that happiness lately. Or maybe it's that I'm getting laid.

"I'll be sure to tell your father you think winning isn't about being number one." His coy smile lets me know he's fucking with me, but just to be sure …

"Please don't. That would be a surefire way to get me kicked off Leila's account."

"She'd fire you over something like that?"

"Not her. Him. Whenever something doesn't go her way, whether it be a sponsorship deal or a magazine spread, hell, even when she doesn't do well in some of her swim meets, he finds a way to tell me he would make a better agent for her because he has lived the industry. He likes to remind me that he let her sign with me because I needed all the help I could get while starting out."

Fox doesn't reply, and for a second, I think he's tuned me out, but when I glance his way again, the dumbfounded look that stares back at me tells me otherwise.

"It's still not too late for me to drop you back at the office," I say.

"I'm good. At least now I know I don't want to put in an effort to make the guy like me."

I almost want to ask him why it would matter if my dad liked him or not, considering this is only a "professional" lunch, but I don't. I tease him a little instead, letting him know exactly where I stand—that I want to sleep with him again. "Eh. If my dad doesn't like you, it'll only make me want you more."

"Wait, what if he *does* like me?"

"Oh, you'll never see me naked again. Guarantee."

Fox laughs. "Then how should I play this? My hostility toward you drew you to me for some fucked-up reason. Is he the same, or should I kill him with kindness to get him to hate me?"

I didn't think it was possible, but somehow, Fox has put me at ease about this lunch. It probably has something to do with him all but admitting out loud he wants to have sex with me again too.

"You wear that to a business lunch?" Dad says as soon as we reach the table, where he and Leila greet us.

Being at ease? It's out the window already. I think that might be a record.

Also, I'm in a fucking suit, but I only wear a tie when meeting with clients. Arrest me for forgoing the tie when it comes to my sister.

"Ah, yeah, lost track of time because of how much work I've been doing, so sorta ran out of the office and forgot the tie." Or was too busy freaking the fuck out to remember to pull it out of my desk. Same thing. I pull Fox next to me. "Dad, Leila, this is Fox. Uh, Lincoln. Linc?" What do people outside of work call him?

"Fox is fine. It's nice to meet you." Fox holds out his hand for Dad to shake, and it takes a second before Dad takes it.

Fox goes to shake Leila's hand when she engulfs him in a huge hug. The thing is, my sister is nice and welcoming and supportive, but if Dad tells her to do something, she's quick to obey. She always takes his side in business meetings, even if I tell her something different. I'm experienced in dealing with brands, but she agrees with him. I can't say I fault her, considering she's only doing what I've always done too—tried to impress him.

"I can't believe Archie didn't tell us he has a boyfriend," she says, and Fox visibly stiffens.

"Not my boyfriend," I say. "He's a work colleague, and I thought it would be good to get a second opinion on your career plan going forward. In case you wanted it."

We take our seats, and I sit in between Fox and my father on the round table with perfectly positioned linen and cutlery. At least with me sitting here, Fox can talk to Leila, and they'll hopefully get to know each other while I endure what I'm sure is a lecture coming from Dad.

Only Dad doesn't address me. He goes right in on Fox. "So ...

Fox. You're a sports agent?" The way he looks Fox up and down sets me on edge.

"I am. I've always loved sports. Never had the talent to do any of them, but mixing that with a knack for stats and data, it was a way of combining what I love with what I'm good at."

"And are you good at it? Being an agent?"

I can already see where this is going. Here come the comparisons between Fox's career and mine. I try to cut this off before it can really get started. "Shouldn't we be talking about Leila instead of grilling Fox?"

"Grilling?" Dad asks. "I'm merely asking so I can figure out if his second opinion is even worth hearing. Would you rather I pretend he's not here?"

When he puts it like that, no. But also maybe?

"It's fine," Fox says. "I am good at what I do, but Archer is definitely the overachiever in our office. He has the most clients and biggest commission checks out of all the associates."

Fox acknowledging my hard work? Yeah, it does something to my insides. But if he's trying to build me up to my dad, it won't work.

"I've seen where Archie lives, so if you're telling me you earn even less than him, you can't be super great at your job."

See?

Beside me, I can sense Fox's stare. He's probably wondering why my dad doesn't know I'm saving up for a nice place. I didn't tell him because there's no point. If something isn't my father's lived experience, he doesn't understand it. Why live in LA and pay California prices when it's so much cheaper to live in the middle of nowhere in a state with no income tax? We've had that conversation time and time again because while there are King Sports employees who work remotely—Lane Pierce being one of them—traveling as much as agents do, we need to be near an airport hub.

This side of him is also why he never understood that while swimming was in my blood, it wasn't in my heart. He thought it was a difficult decision for me to walk away from the sport, but it's the opposite. It was easy. Disappointing him was the hard part.

He had always seen the star athlete as a higher status than those behind the scenes—that being the fastest and strongest somehow equates to power. Even though I have earned more in my few years as a sports agent than he ever did as a swimmer, somehow, he still sees me as the failure. As the quitter. Because standing on a podium with a small plate of gold around my neck means more than being able to put food on my table. Last time I checked, gold wasn't edible.

"Fox is actually excellent at his job," I say. "He might have fewer clients than I do, but we're neck and neck in those commission earnings."

"Ah. So he works smarter than you, not harder."

We haven't even chosen appetizers yet, and Dad is already intent on making today hell.

Fox is about to open his mouth again, but I cut in. Trying to reason with my dad is like shouting into a void.

"So, what's on the menu?" It's a simple distraction tactic, but a successful one.

At least for now.

Chapter 33

Fox

Frustrating the hell out of me really does run in the Holloway family. It's taking all my strength to bite my fucking tongue, but I'm close to snapping. I now have a deeper understanding of Archer and the way he is.

He's competitive because if he's not the best, he's not good enough. I'm actually surprised Archer's not more of an asshole. Yes, that front persona of his is an intolerable jackass, but that's not who he is.

From the outside looking in, I don't understand the type of people who only see the negative in everything. Archer is the highest-earning associate working for King Sports. That's not only in LA either. That's across both offices. Yet, as they talk business, his father nitpicks everything Archer suggests for Leila's career.

"You should be trying to get her big endorsement deals with Speedo or Arena. These beauty product deals you're pitching are a dead end."

I feel for Archer, I really do. Because his dad is stuck in the past, reliving the kind of deals swimmers used to get. He doesn't realize that in this day and age, everything is a brand. Everything has a value. And for athletes who aren't on multimillion-dollar contracts, the best way to supplement their earning potential is with brand deals.

"With all due respect," I cut in. If I can't yell at him for his shitty attitude, I can at least try to get through to him. "Endorsements aren't what they used to be. In a way, it's a good thing because there's a vast market out there, and athletes no longer have to only promote brands that are within their industry. I'm sure as a swimmer, you know how much chlorine can dry out your skin. You use products for that. Or shaving your body hair to glide through the water easier took products too, correct? Why not get paid for it? It's the same for Leila. Why shouldn't she take advantage of brands she's already using? She's wearing makeup. Her blouse is a label."

The thoughts tick over on Dean Holloway's face, but it's impossible to tell if he's pretending or actually taking this seriously. I get the impression he thinks we have no idea what we're doing. I wouldn't be surprised if he's about to tell us to respect our elders.

We would if they weren't so stuck in their fucking ways.

"No," he says. "Doing those types of deals will only label her a wannabe *influencer*, and that will never be her brand. I won't let it."

I've always wondered what banging my head against a brick wall would be like. Now I know.

I go to argue my point more, but Archer doesn't let me.

"Influencer is a horrible term that should die a horrible death. It's seen as such a negative thing when all it means is someone who's a public figure and gets paid to promote products. Essentially, they are athletes without the sport part. This has always been part of an athlete's job, but now there's a bigger scale to take advantage of. But if you're telling me there's no wiggle room here, and Leila doesn't want to pursue other avenues, there's not much else I can do as her agent. I can keep reaching out to swimwear brands, but—" He turns to Leila. "—and no offense here, because I love you, but considering she hasn't had a podium finish in the last year and the Olympic qualifiers are coming up, she needs to pull off something amazing for them to get interested."

"No offense taken," Leila says and bites her top lip. She actually looks like she's about to cry.

She has dark hair, the matching color of the roots of Archer's bleached-blond top. She's really pretty, has a round face and full lips, but if I'm honest, to look at her, she doesn't look like your typical swimmer. I'm definitely not body shaming, and maybe it has to do with the frumpy blouse she's wearing, but swimmers are usually all defined muscle. I get the feeling something else might be going on with her. Leila's the eldest of the siblings, so it's hard to see how she'll be able to keep up competitively when most Olympic swimmers peak mid-twenties.

"If she's not qualifying for these Olympics, she may as well become an influencer," Dean Holloway says.

The way both siblings shrink in on themselves makes me so angry. Parents are supposed to encourage. Support. I'm sure their dad thinks he's being supportive by pushing his kids to be the best, but he's putting too much pressure on them while simultaneously telling them to do it his way or no way.

Archer leans forward on his elbows. "Realistically, this will be Leila's last Olympics, if she can qualify. This is why we really need to start looking at other brand deals." He stares down his sister. "If you agree with Dad and don't want to work with these smaller brands, you're going to have to accept that once these Olympics are over, you're done, and you won't have a million different offers knocking on your door. We can talk about future career prospects like commentating or becoming a sports reporter on the news, maybe working for USA Swimming. But I don't think stepping back and turning down offers is going to work in your favor in the long run."

Her watery eyes are even more prominent now.

Mr. Holloway wipes his mouth with his cloth napkin as he stands and mumbles something about needing a cigarette.

An Olympic swimmer who smokes seems like a walking contradiction.

"He smokes?" I ask when he's out of earshot.

"Took it up after he retired," Archer says.

"Blames us, of course," Leila adds. She puts her face in her hands, and if the way her shoulders shake is any indication, I'm going to go ahead and assume she's finally let those tears fall.

Archer looks like a duck out of water, like he wants to reach for his sister or comfort her but doesn't know how. He looks over at me and mouths, "What do I do?"

I lift my hand in a gesture to give her a few minutes, but he only gives her one.

"Leila?"

She sniffs. "I didn't think he was going to go in so hard on you today. I ... fuck, I wanted to come here alone so I could ask you for your advice. Like real brotherly advice, not agent advice. Though I need that too."

"What's wrong?" Archer asks. "This is your career. It's your choice. If we both tell Dad to fuck off, he might listen."

She lifts her head, her eyes red and her face splotchy. "The thing is, I am ready to take on small brands. Other brands. Outside of swimming. I ..." She bites her lip again. "I also ..." She takes a deep breath. "I won't be going to these Olympics. If I'd known the last one would be my last ... Maybe I would've tried harder for that gold."

"You got silver," I point out. "Two of them, if I recall correctly."

"Wait, you don't want to go to the Olympics?" Archer looks stunned, but if he had been reading his sister anything like I have been, this wouldn't be a shock. She's been checked out for half this conversation.

"It's not that I don't want to. It's that I *can't.*"

Is ... is she saying what I think she's saying?

"Why?" Poor Archer is still confused.

"I'm going to go out on a limb here," I say, "and ask if some of those smaller brand deals you might be interested in could be maternity products?" The baggy blouse trying to hide something, the fuller figure than that of a swimmer ... I'd never say something if I wasn't sure, but it all makes sense.

I've barely gotten through a lunch with Dean Holloway. I don't know how these siblings made it through a lifetime with him. It makes me want to reach out and comfort Archer in a way I never thought I would. Hell, it makes me sympathetic toward him in a way I thought was impossible.

And weirdly, it makes me like him even more.

"How did you know?" Leila asks.

"You're *pregnant*?" Archer shrieks.

It's followed up by a very loud "You're fucking what?" that comes from behind us.

Great timing. Dean Holloway is back.

Chapter 34
Archer

What a shitshow of a fucking lunch.

It takes a million questions, all the who, what, where, when to understand Leila's situation, but it's been difficult to get the answers with Dad doing his disapproving "You've kissed your career goodbye by being stupid."

He's obviously over the moon about becoming a grandfather.

Granted, Leila getting pregnant only a few weeks into dating a guy we didn't even know about isn't ideal, but she's a grown-ass woman. From what she has said, the father is a decent man, they're in love, and they're going to give it a real shot to be together. But it does mean she's giving up her last Olympics. Which means there's a ticking clock on her sponsorship and endorsement opportunities. She needs to be relevant to get the kinds of deals Dad wants her to get.

Maybe this will be the push Dad needs to come around on other types of brand deals.

"What are you going to do now? Be a stay-at-home mother? You saw what that did to your mom, and you're okay with that?"

I grit my teeth. "Mom didn't get burned out from being our mother. She got burned out from being your wife."

It's the first and only time I've ever snapped at our father, but as he sits here berating my awesome sister and putting down our mother, who did nothing but take care of us—alone, I might add, because Dad was always busy training—I'm wondering why I've cared so fucking much about what he thinks.

Leila gasps, Fox's eyes are so wide I can see them out of my periphery, and Dad ... I don't think I've ever seen him stunned.

"What did you just say to me?"

"You only ever focused on your career. That woman raised the four of us by herself, and then once we were all out on our own, she took her life back. She did her time, and she deserves the world. Because you were never there for us where it counted."

"I gave you kids *everything*," he says through gritted teeth.

"No. You gave us the option to follow your rules or fend for ourselves. The minute I quit swimming, you told me I was on my own. You know who gave me the courage to chase this dream? Mom. Because that's what real support looks like." I glance at my sister, who's still teary-eyed. "And I will support you and my nibling in the same way. Because even though I was scared to become a sports agent, and I've spent the last ten years trying to prove that I can be the best at it, it's not until this moment right here that I realize I don't need to prove anything to anyone. The most important thing is that I'm happy." I focus on Fox now. "And I am. For the last four years, I did everything I could to make sure I was the best, including stepping on your toes and not caring that you resented me for it. I want you to know that all those accounts, those extra commissions ... they weren't worth it. You mean more to me than they ever could." Obviously, I've forgotten where I am for a second and who is witnessing my mess of the only apology I've ever given for being the way that I am. "Your friendship and professional relationship, I mean. Obviously. Nothing more."

Except, I actually mean everything more. Instead of working together as a team for four years, getting to know each other on a deeper, more primal level for that whole time, we're basically at square one. My sister only knew her new guy for a few weeks before shit had to get serious between them, and the most fucked-up takeaway from that is ... that I'm jealous.

They're going to give their relationship a real shot. And while

Fox and I aren't talking about a future, and I don't even know if Fox is interested in something more—I'm too scared to ask him—there's no denying it's what I want.

He smiles at me, having no idea what's running through my head. Luckily, because even though Leila has been forced into reassessing everything, I don't want to force anything between Fox and me.

Patience has never been an asset of mine, but Fox is too important to rush this. Even if I'm ready to dive into the deep end.

There's a metaphor somewhere in that about Fox being a pool and going back to swimming, but I can't dive into it—pun intended —while Dad keeps running his mouth.

"I guess that's that, then. You two don't need me. You'll do your own thing, ignore my advice, and then come back crying to me when it all falls apart."

The fact that he could be saying this about his future grandchild sickens me. "Good to know that having kids is the definition of falling apart, *Dad*."

He scowls. "That's not what I meant, and you know it. You were always independent and wanted to do your own thing. You refused to toe the line, and that's why you quit swimming."

"No, I chose to quit swimming because my heart wasn't in it. Perhaps it's because I saw what being at that competitive level did to our family, and that's why I worked my ass off to get where I am today. Where I'm in a position to help Leila keep relevant in an industry she loves while she's still able to have the family she wants."

"You might not regret giving up swimming, but swimming has been Leila's whole life, and now she's missing out because she got sloppy with some random man, and now she's going to have to live with that decision for the rest of her life."

I hate him. Holy shit, I fucking hate this man. I've always known him to be cold and disapproving, but it's generally only ever been directed at me. The latter, anyway. Because my other siblings could do no wrong. They were doing what he asked of them. Now that Leila is stepping out, I'm realizing he's not an asshole so he can push us to be successful. He's an asshole because he's a fucking narcissist.

I lean forward in my seat and reach for my glass of water. I take a sip, put the glass back on the table, but keep hold of it. My moves are slow. Deliberate. Because if this is going to be the last time I see my father, I need to get my words exactly right.

There are so many things I could say. I could keep telling him how he was hard on us, how he has no wiggle room for anything, how he squashes our dreams because they're not his, but instead of dredging up the past, I look to the future and what I want from him. Which is absolutely nothing.

"Seeing as you are determined to act like a typical sports parent, as Leila's agent, I'm going to have to ask you to not be present for any and all future meetings with her."

Dad scoffs.

I look at Leila. "Is that all right with you?"

The way her face lights up, her tears drying on her cheeks, she doesn't need to answer me, but she does with a nod.

"Okay then. It looks like our meeting is concluded."

He stands. "Fine. Turn her into one of those people who sell gadgets and crap online so she can be the laughingstock of swimming." None of us gets a goodbye.

There's a beat of silence where we all watch him leave, and as soon as he's out of the restaurant doors, Fox says, "Wow."

"Is that a good wow or a bad wow?" I ask him.

"It's a ... I can't believe parents like him exist wow." He turns to Leila. "If you need anything, anything at all, we're here for you. You might be nervous about letting go of competitive swimming, but you have nothing to worry about. Your brother is kicking ass with the types of deals he's getting his athletes, and he'll be able to make your transition from pro athlete to whatever you want to be next so easy and stress-free."

Her gaze ping-pongs between us but eventually stays on Fox. "Are you sure you two are only colleagues?"

Fox's mouth opens to dispute any and all connection to me outside of work whatsoever, but then, before any words come out, he reaches across the table and places his hand on top of mine. "Maybe not *only* colleagues."

Vague answer is still vague, but I'm going to fucking take it. I swear I only hear fifty percent pity in his tone too.

I huff. "If there was a chance of anything else ever developing, it's gone now after that shitshow of a lunch. I'm surprised there isn't a Fox-shaped hole in the wall."

"You know I wouldn't do that," Fox says. "One, if I tried to escape through a wall, I would just knock myself out. And two, if I was going to run, I'd still be nice to your face before I got out of your reach. I can't run fast, and you'd be able to catch me easily." He taps the side of his head. "I'm smart."

"Smart-ass, you mean."

"I like him, Archie."

Fox's smile is evil. "Aww, Archie. You hear that? Your sister likes me."

"No. Archie is not becoming a thing."

"Okay, Archie."

"Did you mean what you said?" Leila asks, bringing my attention back to her.

"About what?"

"That I haven't completely screwed myself?"

"Not at all. I've been silently wondering how and when you'd hang up your swimming cap. You're not getting any younger."

"You're lucky this is a classy restaurant or I'd be flipping you off." She looks so innocent and sweet as she says this, it almost makes me laugh.

"Please, we've already caused a scene, why not make it worse?"

She does that thing she always did when we were growing up, where she wants to smile at my antics but turns her lips downward instead. God forbid she admit her little brother is hilarious.

"Seriously though," I say. "Find a time you can come into the office, and we'll brainstorm where you want to go next."

"Thank you."

I stand and go around the table to hug her. The next few months are going to be rough for her. If she's anything like me, she'll spend way too much time trying to find ways to get back in Dad's good books.

She embraces me but freezes mid-hug. "Do you think we've just turned up Dad's pressure cooker on Brandon and Tucker?"

That's exactly what's going to happen, but I'm not going to let her worry about that. "I can handle them." But I'll need to move quickly. I need to get to them before Dad convinces them to fire me as their agent. That might be melodramatic, but the haze of denial I had clouding my vision when it comes to my father has been lifted, and now I'm not going to let anything get past me.

"We need to get back to the office, but let me know when we can get together again. Oh, and I want to meet that man of yours."

She agrees, and when Fox stands, she hugs him too. "It was amazing to meet you."

"You too."

As we turn to leave, my sister's voice makes me stop. "Bye, Uncle Archie."

I have to turn and hug her again.

I'm going to be an uncle, and that is fucking cool. I want to run out and buy all the sporting equipment they have for babies, even though they're not even born yet, but I have more pressing matters.

We pay before we leave, as fast as we can. I need to hurry so I can get in contact with my brothers and come up with a game plan.

As soon as we're outside, I increase my pace, dragging Fox with me. I need to get ahead of Dad, but I'm not going to add to Leila's stress.

In the parking lot, Fox tries to slow me down. "Where's the fire?"

"I have to make sure I get to my brothers before Dad tries to turn them against me."

"Hey," he says soothingly. He tugs on my hand to pull me to him.

My body presses against his, and as much as I want this moment with him, I'm too focused on everything I need to be doing.

"Do you really think that's what he's doing in this moment?"

Fox must be able to tell his words aren't sinking in because he cups my neck. "Your dad left with his tail between his legs because his son gave him some hard truths. And I just want to say that I'm ... weirdly proud of you for what you did back there. I've never seen you with your dad before, but I get the impression you don't usually talk to him like that."

"Never. And that's why I need to get in contact with my brothers before it's too late. I'd rather be proactive than need to be reactive if the shit hits the fan."

"Fair enough. Let's go, then." Fox steps away, and I actually yearn for his touch to come back. I'm going to have to deal with that later, but right now, I need to get to work.

Chapter 35

Fox

All afternoon, the Holloway family lunch runs through my head, and while I might not understand what it's like to have an unsupportive parent like that, I do understand why it has made Archer the man he is.

If anything, that lunch made me respect him more and maybe even fall for him a little. It gives me the perspective I've lacked the entire time I've known him when I thought he was conceited. It's not ego that made him that way. It was his drive to be the best.

Something I see as admirable now instead of annoying.

He disappeared into his office as soon as we got back from lunch, and I've been trying to focus on my own work, but it's difficult when my mind keeps drifting to Archer and hoping he's getting somewhere with his brothers.

The hours tick by, and I try as hard as I can to get my presentation polished, but more often than not, I'm looking at my open office door, waiting for Archer to come knocking.

Not that he said he would, but I was hoping ... Maybe I need to go to him, for once. I tell myself if it gets to 5:30 and he still hasn't shown, I'll go to him, and when the clock slowly ticks over to 5:28, I can't wait any longer. Only before I can stand, that knock does inevitably come.

Archer looks exhausted with bags under his eyes, his usual

smile missing, and his hair messier than usual, like he has spent all afternoon gripping onto it in frustration. He slowly approaches and crumples into the chair opposite my desk.

Even though it's risky as fuck to show affection here, there's no way I can't go and comfort him, so I stand and close my office door, locking it in the process.

As if all his worries are forgotten, his gaze snaps to mine, full of heat.

"Of course you'd think this is leading to sex."

He lets out a small laugh. "I haven't even said anything."

"You don't need to. The way you're looking at me gives you away." I move closer and lean my ass against the desk in front of him.

"Putting your dick right in front of me isn't exactly making me switch back to being exhausted."

I ignore him trying to deflect. "Are you okay?" My question is serious in tone, so he drops the act.

"Like I said, just exhausted. I got ahold of Brandon but not Tucker, and it makes sense that Dad would've gone to Tucker first."

"Why's that?"

"When he's not in the pool, he's studying sports psychology and really believes in that mind-over-matter stuff, so out of all of us, he's the one most likely to listen to Dad. Brandon is a much more go-with-the-flow type of person, so he spent most of our conversation telling me everything will be fine and that Dad will calm down eventually. Having said that though, Brandon's the youngest and closest in age to Tucker, so he's always kind of followed Tucker's lead. So if Dad has convinced Tucker to ditch me as their agent, there's a good chance both will do it."

"I'm sorry."

"It's not your fault."

"I know, but ... it's a sucky situation."

"You got any advice for me?" As he looks up through his lashes, heat still simmering behind his eyes, I realize there might only be one answer to that question that might help. It won't help in the long run because it has nothing to do with his brothers or his dad, but it will help him relax. If I can't fix his work for him, I can temporarily ease the stress from it.

I lean forward and trail my fingertips over the top button of his shirt.

When I twist my fingers to undo it, he says, "Am I still not supposed to be thinking of the thing that this isn't leading to?"

I grip his shirt and pull him up out of his chair so he's standing over me. "Nope. You can think it all you like. You need it."

Instead of doing that whole romantic thing of knocking everything off my desk and taking me right here, he steps back. "Fuck. You have no idea what to do either." There he goes, running his hand through his hair again. He paces toward the door.

"I don't," I admit. I stand from leaning against the desk and go to hold him from behind, but as I do, he spins to pace back the other way, and he slams into me.

He grunts, but I calmly put my hand to his cheek and guide his head up from where his gaze is glued to the floor.

"Other than going to your brother's house and waiting outside until he shows up, there's not much else—"

"He lives and trains in Austin with Brandon."

"Exactly. And unless there are some red-eyes—"

"Edele has already gone for the day. I know because I checked."

"So the way I see it, we can stay on the phones until your brother answers, get in the car, and drive to Texas and arrive there the same time as getting a flight tomorrow morning, or you can let me distract you for the moment." I press against him and wrap my hands around his back. "Let me help you the second way I know how because the first way isn't a viable option."

Archer's shoulders lose some of their tension, but he presses his lips together. "Here? Isn't that against your rules?"

"It is, but some things are more important than rules."

He mock gasps. "Who are you, and where did the real Lincoln Fox go?"

I grab him by his shirt again and walk backward toward my

desk until my ass hits the side of it, and I shuffle my way onto the edge. "I'm right here, and I meant every word. It would suck to lose my position, of course, but the day I chose to have anything physical with you is the day I started choosing you over this job."

"I bet there's a sentence you never thought you'd say." He leans over me and touches his forehead to mine. "How did we get here?"

I get what he means. It's still surreal to be like this with him. The name Archer Holloway still holds an air of resentment, but when I look at him now, I see someone different. Someone I've come to trust. To respect.

"We got here by putting all our bullshit aside and bothering to actually see each other. The real us."

Archer grips my hips. "Speaking of us ..."

My breath hitches, and I don't know what he's going to say, but I worry if I let him say it, it's not going to be the thing I want to hear. So I don't let him finish that sentence. "I want you to fuck me. Right here. Against my desk."

He drops his head to my shoulder and murmurs something I can't understand. I think he's about to back off again, maybe not wanting to force me to break my rules, so before he can protest, I cup his head and lift it to bring his lips to mine.

That's when he breaks.

That's when he lets me distract him and take him away from everything. It might only be temporary, but now that he's let go of any self-restraint he had, there's no stopping us.

Chapter 36
Archer

With our pants around our ankles, Fox's work shirt scrunched up to his shoulder blades while he bends over his desk, sinking inside him is like living an actual dream. One I'm sure I've had before. It's not his tight ass that's giving me déjà vu; it's his office. His desk. It's the risk of other agents and employees being right outside Fox's door, hearing what we're doing in here.

With high risk comes high reward though, because fucking damn, he feels so good. I keep my movements slow but hard, slamming into him.

He moves his forearm and accidentally knocks the desk phone off its receiver, but he doesn't care. It's lucky we're doing this in his office and not in mine. My desk is covered in contracts, sticky notes, and energy drink cans. I'm chaotically messy, physically and mentally.

Not Fox though. Fox's office is as tidy and buttoned up as the rest of him. Except for in moments like this. Where he's barely hanging on. Where there's sweat around the back of his neck, his warm skin is clammy, and he's moaning like he's getting paid for it.

My grip on his hips tightens. "As much as I love the sounds you make, if you keep going, someone might hear." It might be past five o'clock, but sports agents don't always keep usual office hours.

Fox moans again, but it sounds more like a complaint. "It's impossible to stop."

"I know one way I can make you quiet, but it involves getting louder first." I pull almost all the way out of him and then push back inside without letting him breathe in between.

Gone are the long, hard, and slow thrusts. I take his body in a way I haven't yet. We've done the quickie blowjobs, I've fucked him slow, fast, and everything in between, but we haven't done this.

This is primal. The kind of sex that leaves bruises. I'm conscious enough to make sure this is good for him but not strong enough to be able to keep going without coming too soon.

But that's the point. Two bodies, slapping together, chasing that point of nirvana. We're both running toward bliss, and this is one race I don't want to win.

"Touch yourself." It's supposed to sound like an order, but I can hear the begging in my voice.

The second he does though, one of the loudest moans yet falls from his mouth.

"Fuck," I hiss. "You're so loud."

Fox turns his sweaty head to the side, staring at me over his shoulder. His eyes are hooded, his lips slightly parted like he needs to breathe through his nose and mouth to get enough air, and he grits out, "Can't help it. I'm being turned out on top of my desk. Professional Fox has left the building."

And this is possibly what I like most about him. When he lets go like this, when he falls apart in my arms, I can't even begin to describe what it does to me.

He trusts me enough to be stripped back to nothing but a human being with desires that need to be filled, and he wants me to be the one to fill them.

To fill *him*.

Fox starts to moan again but leans on his elbow and bites down on his fist to muffle it.

He's still jerking himself, and because he's only using one arm for balance, each hard thrust almost sends him flying across the desk. He's so hot like this, ass freely taking every inch I give. I move in and out of him so smoothly, and every second of it sets my body on edge in the best possible way.

Am I going to come, am I going to cramp? Honestly, it could be either. But all of my focus is directed at making sure Fox gets there first. Then I'm going to fill his hole and make him go out to dinner with my cum dripping out of him.

"I can't ..." Oh, shit. "No, no, not yet." I'm going to blow this.

"Come."

I think that's what he says. It's hard to tell when he's biting his knuckles.

I might not have heard him, but my body did. I freeze, my muscles locking up as all of my strength shoots out of the tip of my cock. I hold him right where he is while I begin to unload.

The loud "Fuck"—louder than any noise Fox has made—that falls from my mouth snaps me out of my own selfish release because there's no way Fox has come yet.

Even though my legs are jelly and threaten to fall out from underneath me, I push my hips forward, hoping I can reach his prostate while I'm still hard. It won't last long because any second now, my dick is going to catch up with the rest of me that's ready to fall into a heap on the floor.

He strokes himself faster, breathes heavier, and when I move inside him again, he whispers, "Finally," and that's when I see cum fly across the desk.

Fox collapses, chest lying right where the cum is, while I give in to the urge to crumple to the ground and fall, landing on my back with my pants still around my ankles.

Fox straightens up and pulls up his pants. "That looks really comfortable." He's still panting, and so am I.

"It is, actually."

"That might have sounded sarcastic, but I'm being for real. It looks way too comfortable and way too tempting. I worry if I let myself join you down there, we won't get up, and I don't want to spend the night on the floor of my office."

I hold out my arms. "Come on. Live a little."

He doesn't need much convincing. "Fine, but at least pull up your pants in case someone comes in." He drops down beside me and curls into my side.

"Isn't the door locked?"

His hand comes out of nowhere to playfully slap my chest. "Don't logic me while my shirt is covered in my brains."

I try to follow what he's saying. "Did ... did you just call your cum your brains?"

"Yup. Feels like it after I've blown my load. No brain cells left. Only cat memes."

"Wait, wait, wait. You're ... a cat person? This is never going to work between us."

That earns me another slap. "Shut up."

I roll onto my side to face him. "All joking aside though ... I ..." Fuck, why can't I say it? The words are right there on the tip of my tongue, but would telling him I want something more—something official—scare him off?

What if it's only a cloud of lust making me think I have real feelings for him?

"You, what?" he asks.

Say it. Just fucking say it.

My message tone breaks the growing silence where I'm trying to find the right words when there aren't any.

"You should check that," Fox says, the light dimming in his eyes. "It might be your brother."

Shit. He's right. I pull away from him and sit up, fishing my phone out of my pants pocket and checking it as I stand. The words are clear as day, in black and white, but I'm sure I'm hallucinating or that trying to redress myself shakes my vision as I read.

"Was it your brother?" he asks.

I have to read it a second time to be sure, but the words are still there. I lift my head to look at Fox, confused as fuck but excited nonetheless.

"Archer?" he cocks his head.

"Uh, yeah. Sorry. It's Tucker. He ..." It's entirely possible all four of us have been trying so hard to earn Dad's approval that we've developed nothing but resentment for the man. "Here." I flip my phone toward him.

It's only two sentences, and I wasn't expecting it, but I'm more than fucking thankful for what it says.

I already told Dad to fuck off. You're our agent and always will be.

I get to keep my brothers. My sister.

I might have lost my dad, but that doesn't seem anywhere near as daunting as I thought it would. If anything, working with Fox, being with him, learning from him ... he's the one who has made me see something in myself that I didn't know was there.

I am enough.

Normally, the sporadic hooking-up schedule would be perfect for me. I've always been too busy with work to think of anything else, let alone invest time in something that could turn into a relationship. But ever since Fox was there for me with all the shit that happened with my dad and my siblings, helped me by distracting me when there wasn't anything else he could do, I haven't stopped thinking about him as something ... more. More than a hookup. More than my colleague.

When he took my hand and told my sister we were more than that, I wanted to ask him to clarify then and there, but I didn't, and the more time that passes, the more awkward it would be to bring up.

The number of successful relationships I've had in my life is exactly zero, so statistics are not on our side, and working together adds another layer of reasons why we shouldn't go any further.

Yet, for whatever reason, with Fox, I'm beginning to want everything everyone else wants: a future with someone.

Logistically, it's a nightmare. On the outside, it doesn't make sense. But somewhere, deep down inside, Fox is everything I've never wanted but do now. I want him. It's that simple. I want him to be my boyfriend, but how in the fuck do I bring it up?

It takes me way too long to bring it up.

Weeks, even. Most nights, I end up at his apartment. He always welcomes me with a smile, and once we're behind closed doors, we blow each other's minds by blowing other body parts. He doesn't ask me to stay the night; I just don't leave, and he doesn't stop me from staying. He even makes me breakfast in the morning and makes me coffee without asking if I want any. He just knows I do.

It becomes a bit of a routine, and every time I'm at his apartment, I'm tempted to say something but ultimately back down.

But tonight ... tonight, I'm going to do it.

I'm going to ask Lincoln Fox to be my boyfriend.

I want us to start telling people. Yes, it means we'll lose the bet, but in the big scheme of things, it's a stupid bet. One we have no skin in.

I buzz his building for him to let me up, but it only occurs to me on the climb upstairs to his apartment that I should've brought flowers. Or something. What do you give a man who has the potential to gut punch you in the heart?

Fox is standing at his open door waiting for me when I reach him, and at the sight of his undone business shirt with no undershirt today, and his work pants that are unbelted with the button popped, I can't help thinking it will be so much easier to have this conversation after we make each other come.

"Hey." He steps aside to let me in, and in all the times we've done this, in our little routine that I both love and hate, we've never kissed each other hello.

Sure, most of the time, the second the door closes, we're on each other, but a simple kiss on the cheek is so small it might be the right thing to do in this situation to let him know I want more.

So with a minor hesitation hovering by him, I lean in and press my lips to his cheek.

"Hey," I reply.

He freezes for a moment, either taken off guard or trying not to recoil at the tiniest amount of non-sexual affection.

I'm hoping for the former but can't rule out the latter.

My palms are fucking sweaty, and my heart is in my throat, making it tight. I shove my hands in my pockets and enter his apartment with him following me behind.

I stand in the middle of his living room, no doubt looking like a lost little lamb, but let's face it, that's exactly what I am.

I don't know how to bring it up. I don't know how to—

Arms wrap around me from behind, but where I expect them to reach for my clothes and to strip me naked, all they do is hold me close. Fox's forehead lands on my shoulder, and his breath tickles my skin even through the material of my black button-down shirt.

I usually come here still in my work suit because that way I can recycle it the next day. That's one good thing about men's clothing, I suppose. It's harder to pick out who's doing the walk of shame when a lot of suits look the same. But today, I wanted to make some sort of effort. I realize now that a suit might have been the way to show effort, but he sees me every single day in one. So I dressed down. Casual but nice. Dark button-down and faded jeans. I put on a generous amount of cologne and took thirty minutes styling my hair to make it look exactly the same as it did before trying to fix it.

And I'm about to find out if going to this effort was worth it or if he's even noticed it.

Fox lifts his head. "Are you okay?"

It's not the first time in the last few weeks he's asked me, but it is the first time I haven't dismissed it with an excuse like "I'm tired" or "You know, work is work."

I turn in his arms and pull him against me in a hug. "I've never been better. I just ... it ..."

He steps back, a furrowed brow marring his gorgeous face. "What's wrong?"

"I'm nervous as fuck because of what I have to say."

He steps back again, putting purposeful distance between us, and the smart part of my brain tells me that this is my answer. This is how he feels. If I tell him I want more, all he's going to do is keep moving away from me.

"What did you do?" There's anger in his tone that he hasn't used on me in a long time now.

"Wait, I tell you I have to say something, and you immediately assume I've done something wrong?"

He throws up both hands. "Well, when you come in here looking all depressed with low energy and tell me 'I have to say something,' what do you expect me to think?"

I huff because, yeah, okay, he has a point. "This is not ... that. Or maybe you will see it as a fuckup. It's hard to know."

"Tell me before I think the worst in my head, where there's no coming back from those kinds of insecurities."

"I'm worried you're going to laugh at me."

"I won't. Whatever it is."

I take a deep breath and then let it out in a rush. "I like you, okay?"

"But?" he says, dragging the word out.

"That's it. I like you. I'm in serious *like* with you. That's the whole thing. I thought you should know."

His gaze narrows. "Have you been ... hate fucking me this whole time or ..."

"What? No. That's not what I mean. Ugh, I suck at this. Would it help if I got down on one knee and said I really like you? Like really, really like you? What if I write it on a piece of paper with the question, 'Will you be my boyfriend?' and then you can check a yes or no box? I don't know how to ... How to ..." I wave my hand around aimlessly because I don't know what else to do to show him what I mean.

And then Fox does the one thing he promised he wouldn't. He *laughs*.

My neck feels hot, and in the next second, that heat rises to my cheeks. "What happened to not laughing?"

He somewhat pulls it back, but it's still there on his lips. I can practically see the laughter trying to escape. "I'm sorry. Sorry.

Truly am. I'm not laughing at you, if that helps. Or what you said. I ... I like you in that way too."

"Y-you do?"

"*Reluctantly.*" He grins. "I only laughed because I thought that was a given, so you freaking out was all kinds of cute."

"I'm not cute," I protest. I might even pout.

Fox closes the gap he put between us only moments ago and wraps his arms around my back. "Just so you know, I'm not the type of guy to sleep with someone he doesn't like."

"Okay, so if we like each other ... what does that mean?"

He purses his lips. "Exclusivity, for one, but I was doing that anyway, so no real change there."

"Same." That's not the thing I was worried about to begin with though. "What about telling people. HR? Damon? I know we don't want others making money off that stupid bet, but I'm not sure sneaking around forever is the answer."

"I agree. Maybe we should go to HR first, at least. And then if people figure it out, they figure it out after that. It's only going to be a big deal if we let them make it a big deal."

"We could always get married and take the pot for ourselves," I joke.

And it is a joke. But Fox says something completely out of left field. "You might be onto something there."

"Uh, what?" My voice cracks. Did he not see how hard it was for me to say I like him? Now, suddenly, he's proposing?

Now, he's laughing at me again. "Not the getting married part, but how do you feel about manipulating that situation to go in our favor?"

It's a no-brainer. "I'm listening."

Chapter 37
Fox

It's showtime.

This whole sneaking around and scheming behind people's backs is actually really fun, and I can see why Archer used to get a kick out of it.

There are lines, however, ones I won't cross, and that's fucking with someone else's career. I'm going to fuck with their money instead. Money they put on the line because their penchant for gossip outweighs any sense of morality.

Still bitter about the bet? Little bit. But in the big scheme of things, with how it's all played out, with who my *boyfriend* is, I can't be too bitter. Mostly, I'm pissed everyone was right.

I might not have known where Archer and I were headed after that first hookup, but becoming boyfriends was way down the bottom of the list of possibilities. Some mornings when I've woken up next to him, I still can't believe we're together. Not fighting. My resentment toward him nothing but a memory.

My envy toward him was the main source of my resentment, but I didn't think acknowledging that would be what led me to free-fall into his arms.

Until last night, when he turned up on my doorstep and fumbled over asking me to be his boyfriend, my feelings toward him were hesitant. Like I told him, they were reluctant. Now that I know he's in this for real, that he wants to be with me, walking into the break room, where he's sitting with Buck and Luca, the good ol' dude bros of the office who came up with the stupid bet, it's difficult not to blow our cover.

We'll be letting everyone know about us soon enough, but we have some money to win first.

I walk over to the coffee machine and get it ready to make myself a nice cup of karma. On the way past the group, I give an up-nod. "Buck. Luca." Then I give a pointed glare at Archer.

They immediately take the bait.

"Uh-oh, trouble in paradise already?" Buck asks. "Working together not going so well for you two?"

"He likes to pretend he hates me," Archer says, "but he can't help loving me. I'm his favorite person in the world."

Weirdly accurate.

"You should've seen him when we were dealing with all that Asher Dalton drama. He couldn't stop telling me how awe-inspiring I am. Said he wouldn't know where he'd be if it weren't for me. It was a nonstop love fest."

That's laying it on a bit thick, but whatever.

He keeps talking, keeps spewing cocky bullshit, but I press the button on the coffee grinder, drowning him out. While it does its thing, I turn to them with a smile.

"Sorry, couldn't hear that over the machine."

"I was saying—"

As soon as he starts, I push the button on the coffee machine to run some water through it, which is also loud as fuck.

I put my hand to my ear and mouth. "What? Can't hear you."

Buck and Luca laugh, and my groundwork here is done.

I finish making my coffee while the chatter goes on behind me, Buck and Luca asking Archer what he did wrong this time and basically ribbing him about how much I hate him.

Yes. Hate. I hate him. Am definitely not fucking him on the side and am dangerously close to falling for him wholly and completely.

Once outside the break room, I can't help but hang back, leaning against the wall so the people inside think I'm gone.

"How does someone make another person hate them so much?" Buck asks.

"It's a gift," Archer says. "But in all seriousness, we do work well together. He's just trying to save face and not admit he likes me."

One of them scoffs. Luca, I think. "Sure."

"I'm serious."

"How serious? Enough to put into the betting fund?" Buck taunts.

Oh, Bucky boy, you didn't just take the bait. We got you hook, line, and sinker.

I leave figuring the bet details up to Archer and Buck to work out and head back to my office with a triumphant smile on my face.

When Archer and I make our way into HR the following day, no one bats an eye. They're probably not even surprised. They will be surprised when it turns out we're disclosing our relationship instead of filing complaints against each other, and I can't wait to see everyone's faces when we tell them we're a couple. Boyfriend and boyfriend.

One day soon, that won't feel so weird. Until then, I'm going to keep reminding myself exactly how I got to this point with Archer while simultaneously trying to ignore that voice in the back of my head saying we could have had this long ago if my insecurities hadn't consumed me for the past four years.

Yes, let's not remind ourselves of all that wasted time. Though logic would dictate I needed this time to grow up and, as Archer puts it, open myself up to letting someone in.

He was right about that, but I hadn't noticed the barriers I had put up around myself until he pointed them out.

This still might be new between us, but it's not like anything I've had with anyone else before. Archer and I might not have gotten off to the best start, but he has always made me grow as a person. Sometimes with career focus, others while testing my self-restraint, but he pushes me to be better. To do better. Even if it's only so I can beat him at something for once.

I glance over at him as we walk side by side. He's still the same old Archer, his appearance unchanged. His bleached blond hair has grown out a bit, and he's due for a re-dye and haircut, but other than that, he still looks like the man I once hated. Yet, from the second he showed me something real, the moment he allowed himself to be vulnerable with me, each feature I used to hate has become more attractive.

The way he styles his hair went from trying too hard to appear trendy to inviting me to run my hand through it. His tattoos that spread from his neck down his chest and arms I used to think were his pretentious way of trying to make him seem cultured are now the very things I like to trace with my tongue. Especially when he's impatient. Then I only do it slower.

"Having second thoughts?" he asks as we get to the tiny corner of the office where all the evil HR people are banished.

Banished, voluntarily hiding from all the shit us employees put them through. Same thing.

"Not at all. I was thinking about what we're going to do with the money we win. Fancy dinner tonight, followed up by me inspecting your tattoos again. I really need to commit them to memory and not forget every inch of your inked skin. You know, for identifying purposes in case you were to ever show up dead in a river."

Archer stops in his tracks. "While I love it when you inspect my tattoos, that last part sounded more like a threat than you looking out for my safety."

"As if I'd volunteer to identify your body if I was the one who killed you. You're so illogical."

He laughs. "Right. I'm the illogical one here."

"Yep." I go to continue down the hall, but Archer grabs my

hand and gently tugs me back. Yet, when he can't find his words, I begin to doubt where his head is at. "Wait, you're not having second thoughts, are you?"

"No. I ... I want to say something before we go in there though."

That tone doesn't fill me with joy. "Which is?"

"I can't promise that I won't fuck this up between us, and it's not like I have a ton of experience with relationships."

"We're both in the same boat there."

He nods. "Which only makes what I have to say even more important, and that's thank you."

"Thank ... you? For what?"

"For even giving this a chance. For trying. I wish I could be confident that this is going to work out, that maybe one day we'll be able to promise each other more than a 'let's see what happens,' but for you to take this step with me ... it's more than I ever thought I'd get, so I want you to know that I'm grateful."

It's possible I melt on the spot. "If I wasn't so worried about being seen and ruining our plan, I'd lean in and kiss you right now."

Archer tilts his head. "The bet's already been made."

"Fair point." I lean in and kiss him. It's soft. Quick. It's nowhere near enough. But that can come later.

"Ah, so this is what our meeting is about," Rita says. She's standing in the entryway to the HR offices, but she doesn't look surprised. Or even all that bothered.

"Yep," Archer says confidently. "We're going to need to sign one of those pieces of paper. You know, the one Damon pretends doesn't exist because he says fraternization between employees isn't allowed, but has them anyway because he knows telling people not to do something only makes them want to do it more?"

"You mean the consensual relationship agreement?" she asks.

"Yeah. The one that says we won't hold the firm responsible if Fox breaks my heart."

Like that will happen. If anything, he'll realize I'm the same old uptight person I know I can be and I'm too boring for him.

Archer is light in between his moments of being cutthroat. It's almost as if business Archer and boyfriend Archer are two different people. The only difference is I'm no longer in his crosshairs professionally.

Rita steps aside to get started on this paperwork, but I can't help thinking about how this is going to end. Because even though I want to see where this can go, I'm still confident the answer is nowhere.

Chapter 38
Archer

With that form officially signed, we're free to do whatever we want. Wherever we want. Whenever we want. Sorta. Okay, not really. We're still expected to be professional in the office. Apparently, kissing in a hallway is not considered professional.

Now, all we have to do is let everyone else know. We haven't decided how we're going to do it yet, but according to Fox, a big song and dance—literally, I suggested a good old-fashioned flash mob—will make him break up with me. That, and hiring all those backup dancers, would eat all our profits from winning this bet. So that's out.

I try to come up with an idea as we walk out of the HR office.

Right about now, Rita from HR will be scanning our signed "Consensual Relationship Agreement" and emailing copies to our managing partners here, Cam and Xavier, and to Damon King. So if we want to do this ourselves, we're going to have to keep it basic.

"We could walk out there into the middle of the bullpen and make an announcement," I say. "Or invite everyone for after-work drinks?"

He gasps. "In the middle of a workweek?"

"Oh. Right. Antisocial dude is antisocial, especially during the week."

"Hey, last time I agreed to go out with you, I ended up drunk dialing the CEO. You can see why I'm hesitant."

I lean in close to his ear, with my hand going to the small of his back as I say, "If I recall, the last time we were out together, you pulled me into a very public bathroom and told a random stranger exactly what we did in there. Gotta say, both are great memories."

I love the way Fox's cheeks pinken.

When we turn the corner, going back onto the main floor of the office, I remove my hand from his back and put a foot of distance between us. Until we can agree on a way to announce it, I'm not going to push him into it. As much as I want to hold his hand in this moment and tell everyone how smitten I am with him.

"Smitten" isn't a word that was in my vocabulary until recently, and the only reason I can say I've experienced it now is because of Fox. It's exactly what I am when it comes to him.

I've always had a bucketload of respect for him, even when it wasn't reciprocated, but finding out he has this whole other side to him outside of work that isn't so buttoned up and proper is the real draw.

I can't say the last four years have been wasted by continuing our feud—pissing him off on purpose to get a rise out of him—because I don't think I would have been ready for this level of feelings while having something to prove, but I don't want to waste any more time without him.

So I'm hoping if he doesn't like my ideas on how to tell everyone that he at least has some ideas of his own.

"You two are dating?" The loud voice of our boss Camden makes us jump apart and has the entire office looking our way.

That's one way to announce it, I suppose. It's not as grand as I would like, but it's quick and to the point. Like ripping off a Band-Aid.

I glance at Fox beside me, silently asking how he wants to play this.

He puts his arm around my back. "Yeah. We are."

Buck pops his head up from the bullpen. "Bullshit."

I laugh. "You've been saying all along you thought we'd hook up. Now that we have, you're calling bullshit?"

"There's no way you work that fast. You only placed the b—uh, never mind."

"Placed the what?" Cam asks.

"Nothing," Buck says, trying to cover his ass.

"Oh, were you unaware of this office bet where people were putting money on whether or not Fox and I would end up together?"

Cam rubs his hand over his face, and it sorta reminds me of how Damon does it. I saw it a lot while interning in New York for him. "There's a what?"

"A bet. So, naturally, I bought into it on the condition that if I could snag him within a month, I'd win the whole pot. That means I win, right? Took me less than a day."

Fox elbows me in the ribs. It's supposed to be playful, at least I hope it is, but it stings like a bitch. "Could you not make me sound so easy?"

"You played us," Buck says.

"You bet on us!" Fox's growl is something I'm used to from him. Though it's usually directed at me.

Cam stands between us and Buck, his gaze ping-ponging back and forth.

Through the other side of the bullpen, leaning on the doorframe to his office, Xavier's watching this all unfold. He straightens up and approaches. "Okay, this is what's going to happen. Buckley, pay Archer and Fox their winnings, and then I want everyone in this office to promise they'll never bet on another coworker ever again. We don't do that shit here. If we find out any of this is going on, everyone involved will be written up and sent to HR for sensitivity training." Then he turns his sternness on me and Fox. "And you two ..." He hesitates as if still contemplating what to do with us. "My office. Now. Cam, you as well."

"What did I do?" Cam asks, heading in Xavier's direction.

As we pass Buck, he's unlocking his bottom desk drawer, and he pulls out a thick envelope full of cash. "Here."

I lift it to my nose and breathe in the scent of what is probably a whole lot of bad bacteria. "Smells like victory."

"Smells like a scam," he mumbles back.

I love the feeling of triumph, and by the look of it, so does Fox. We walk into Xavier's office with an air of smugness surrounding us, but as soon as Cam closes the door behind us, the fun is sucked from the room.

"Sit." Xave gestures to the seats across from him. Cam rounds the opposite side and leans against the edge of Xave's desk.

"Are we in trouble?" Fox asks.

If we were, it would be a tad contradictory of our bosses, who are also a couple, to have anything to say about it.

"Not in trouble," Xavier says. "But we do need to go over some ground rules if this is actually happening. Unless you want to tell us it's all a big trick like Buckley seems to think it is."

"It's not," I say as fast as I can. It's entirely possible I'm worried Fox will take the out if given the option. As if finding out this won't be as easy as we'd hoped and there's some red tape to get through first would be too much for him.

It's entirely possible I'm more insecure about how new this is than I thought. Like I'm waiting for that other shoe to drop, and Fox is going to realize he has always been right about me. But I'm not going to let myself sabotage this.

Fox smiles over at me. "It's real. Weirdly ... we work. Don't ask me how because I'm still not sure, but being with Archer is nothing like I'd expect it would be and everything I didn't know I was missing."

My heart does a weird double beat and twinges. Hearing that makes me fall for him a little more while also amplifying that voice in the back of my head saying I'm going to fuck this up.

This is too important to fuck up.

"In that case," Xavier says, "we're going to go over the advice Damon gave us when we first got together."

"Do we have to do the daddy voice?" Cam asks.

"God no," Xave says. "That was like getting the sex talk from a parent."

"Can confirm, it was not fun," Cam adds.

"Aww. Now I want the daddy voice," I say.

Fox rubs his temples. "Sure. Because this situation needs more awkwardness."

Xavier leans forward in his seat. "Nope. This is going to be quick and to the point. One, don't let this interfere with work. If you two are in an argument at home, don't bring it to the office. Obviously, don't get clients involved. Because you share the Dalton brothers, you have to work together no matter what's going on at home."

"Understood," I say.

"No PDA at work," Xave continues. "I don't want to hear about someone walking into your offices and getting an eyeful of something they shouldn't see."

Fox laughs like there was no chance of that happening anyway. I mean, if the door was locked, why would anyone be letting themselves in?

"There needs to be a separation between work and home," Cam says.

I snap my fingers. "Is that why you two have offices on complete opposite sides of this floor?"

"Exactly," Xavier says.

Fox glances over at me. "I thought that was obvious?"

It was? "Here I was thinking it was because they couldn't keep their hands off each other and had to be separated."

Cam puts his arm around Xavier. "Sometimes it's because of that."

The moment has me thinking. "Can I ask a serious question?"

"In my experience, you can't," Fox snarks.

"No, for real. I'm sorta wondering if it really is difficult working with your partner. Like, are we shooting ourselves in the foot here?"

"It's not always easy," Xavier says. "You have to learn to communicate extremely well."

Oh, fun. Considering neither of us is great at that ... It only took us four years to even say out loud we were attracted to one another. Yeah, we might be fucked here.

"For Xave and me"—Cam squeezes his partner's shoulder—"it was make it work or face the alternative where one of us had to give up our dream job at our dream firm and go work for someone else. Somewhere that might not be as welcoming and safe as King Sports. So even when we have disagreed, we've always worked through it. It's important to be partners both inside and outside of the office, but the trick is knowing how to still keep them separate. Soooo good luck?"

Wow. Thanks, boss. How ... reassuring?

Chapter 39

Fox

"Glass of ... what's your most expensive wine?" Archer asks our server.

"With your tasting dinner tonight, each course will have its own wine pairing for you, but we can start you out with a glass of a 2017 Morey-Saint-Denis, which is two hundred dollars a glass if you like red wine or a 2020 Beaune Blanc if you prefer white for the same price."

My eyes must be comically wide because Archer smiles at me, hands the server the wine list, and says, "We'll have one of each. Thank you."

The server walks away, and I lean in to whisper because I feel like I'm being watched, "Are we really going to spend all the money we won on us on one dinner?"

The restaurant Archer chose is dark and moody, and servers basically line the walls, waiting for someone to call them over for something.

"Yep. We deserve it." Archer's hand reaches for mine on top of the table. "Besides. This is technically our first date. We should make it memorable."

"Having a heart attack when seeing the check costs more than rent will be memorable, I guess."

Archer doesn't falter. "Not our money. Think of it this way:

everyone in the office was so adamant we'd end up together that they've funded it. It's *free money*."

"That we could have donated to charity or split it to get ahead of our bills or for you to put away on that down payment on a place."

"Aww. My super-serious boyfriend is on this date. Where's my fun boyfriend? I want him here."

"First date and you're already calling me your boyfriend? You're so obsessed with me."

"There he is! But it's true. I really am, and that makes us even. You're just as obsessed with me."

I snort, but I can't deny it.

To think this is technically our first date is weird because we've been hooking up for so long already, but as I think back to the times that we've been out together, it's always been for work functions or that disastrous lunch with his dad, which I refuse to call a date.

This is the first time it's only the two of us without an agenda behind the meal, like a strategy meeting or takeout for the sake of sustenance before sleeping together.

Our wine arrives, and when Archer lets me pick which one I want first, I take the white one.

For two hundred dollars a glass, it tastes just like every other white wine I've ever had, but I pretend to savor the taste.

"You know, if this is the bar you're setting for our first date, you might never be able to afford to buy real estate. I might become accustomed to this standard of living."

"With how you've been handling your career, I have no doubt you'll be able to fund your own fine dining standards soon enough."

"Dalton's commission is definitely helping with that, even if it's only fifty percent of what it could have been had you not immedi-ately chased after him." I take another sip of wine to hide my smile. Hey, he wants his fun boyfriend to be here, and there's nothing more fun than pointing out how he used to steal my clients.

"Will I ever live Jeremiah Castleberry down?"

"Never. He's going to be my trump card forever. You don't

clean your dishes when you're at my house? Jeremiah Castleberry will be brought up. We both go after the same client again? Jere. Miah. Castle. Berry."

Archer laughs and puts up his hands. "Okay, okay. I get it. You'll use him as an excuse to win any argument in our relationship. I can live with that."

I won't actually use it, but that's not going to stop me from messing with him over it.

When he puts his hands back down, he reaches across the table again to hold mine. "As long as you know I will do everything in my power to make you happy and that if I do ever steal a future client, it'll be because they obviously have a thing for you and I can't allow you to work together, then we'll be all good."

I laugh. "Why do I foresee every single potential client having 'a thing for me' in your eyes?"

"Because you have a very jealous boyfriend."

"Jealous or the type of guy to manipulate situations to make sure the outcome is the one he wants?"

Archer lifts his red wine, pausing halfway to his mouth. "Is there a difference?"

If it weren't for the slight twitch of his lips before the rim of the glass covers his mouth from view, I'd question if he was being serious.

He must feel the need to clarify, too, because he says, "That was a joke, but I did mean what I said about doing everything I can to make you happy. If that means giving you every single one of my clients, I'd do it."

I narrow my gaze. "No you wouldn't."

"Okay, no I wouldn't, at least not on a whim, but ..." Archer averts his gaze. "But if finally cutting my father out of my life has taught me anything, it's that my career shouldn't be my first priority. It's important, yes, but family—my brothers and sister—and my relationship with you should be equally important. So if it came down to a choice between you or my clients, I'd choose you. Simple as that."

I'm lucky the chairs in this restaurant are solid because I could easily fall off mine right about now.

The idea of Archer Holloway saying these things to me is absolutely unfathomable, but here he is. Saying them.

Making me fall for him even harder and faster.

It's as if the switch has been flipped from casual hookup to boyfriend, and now we're in a freefall. I only have to hope it will be a soft landing when we get through the other side.

I've finally had a chance to sit down with Rafferty Brooker—Dalton's teammate from Buffalo—and this meeting is going well. At least, I think it is. His team is in town for an away game, so he's come into the office, and I've gotten a good vision of what he wants for his future.

I know exactly what he wants out of his career, and I'm excited to build a plan to make it happen. There's only one thing niggling at me, and that's as I sit here and listen to Brooker talk about what he needs out of an agent going forward, I can't help thinking that Archer would be the perfect agent for him. Not me.

But I want this so badly.

A few months ago, I wouldn't have even given it another thought. I would've been adamant that I'm the right person for the job purely because I wouldn't want Archer to steal it from under me. Now, it's really difficult to stop my inner voice from yelling Archer would be better for this case.

Archer said on our first official date that he would give up any potential client for me if he had to, but it's not like he's had to do it to prove that to me. As much as I try to tell myself it was only lip service and he wouldn't actually do that, I'd like to think I know him well enough now to know he was telling the complete and honest truth.

So can I really sit here and sign Brooker when there's someone better for him on this same floor?

"You're pretty much the only agent I've met with who hasn't immediately told me to finish out my hockey career and milk that cash cow for all it's worth before looking into this switch," Brooker says.

I lift one shoulder. "King Sports might be known as the"—I use air quotes—"'gay sports agency,' but we're so much more than that. It is our literal job to make our clients happy, and we mean it when we say that. I don't know who else you've met with, but by the sounds of it, you've been meeting with the type of agent who doesn't care so much about the client but how much their commission check will be. There's no question that staying in the NHL for another two-to-five-year deal will be more financially beneficial, but what's the real cost of putting your body through another few years of arguably the most grueling sport there is?"

"Arguably? I'm one tear away from a knee replacement."

"You hockey players do put your bodies through a lot. My point is, we understand that as much as you love your job and what you do, you also need to look to the future. I will put your needs before that of King Sports, and that motto has always been this firm's mission statement."

He's nodding along as I talk, all the while that stupid voice inside my head is screaming Archer's name.

"In fact ..." I hesitate because what I'm about to say makes a lot of sense, but none at the same time. "If you'll excuse me for just a minute. I want to introduce you to another agent, but I need to talk to him first."

I pick up the desk phone receiver and hit Archer's extension.

"Miss me already? It's been a whole two hours since we parted ways at the elevator this morning."

Thank God I didn't put him on speaker.

"Have you got a minute to drop into my office? There's someone I want you to meet."

"Uh, okay. I'll be right in."

I hang up and turn back to Brooker, but he's frowning at me.

"Are you saying you're not willing to take my case? Already palming me off after spouting how you're not like the other agents I've met with?"

I can see where he'd come to that conclusion, but I'm trying to be the bigger person here. "No, no, not at all. I would love to be your agent, but to prove to you that I'm actually a team player and looking out for your best interests, the kind of transition you're looking at would be better suited to a colleague of mine who has experience with repping content creators. He handles a lot of sports where the majority of revenue comes from endorsements and sponsorships, and while I'm certain I could do it, he already has done it with other clients. If you're happy for me to take on your case, I will happily do it, but from a professional standpoint, Archer is your guy."

Speak of the devil. Archer knocks on the door, and I tell him to come in. I stand to introduce him to Brooker, and Brooker stands as well to shake his hand.

"I think you two met when we were in Buffalo, but officially, Archer Holloway, this is Rafferty Brooker."

"Call me Raff," Brooker says.

We won't, and as if reading each other's minds, Archer and I share a glance that says as much. The whole last name in sports is a sacred thing. It's why everyone calls me Fox. Archer hardly ever gets Holloway, but after meeting his father, I can see why he wouldn't encourage the use of his dad's name.

"I'm going to cut to the chase here." I gesture for them to sit in front of me. "With Brooker gaining some traction in NASCAR circles, he's beginning to think of the end of his hockey career."

Archer knows all this because I've spoken about it with him, so I don't go into too much detail.

"And as much as I'd love to represent him, you have more experience. You already rep someone in NASCAR, you know that world, you know the world of sponsorship contracts ... So ... I'm offering him to you. Or at least setting up a meeting with you so he can choose."

Archer cocks his head. "You're ... suggesting he go with me? You. The guy who used to complain if a client chose me over you."

"Unlike you, I am doing this as a professional courtesy because also unlike you ..." I pause, glancing at Brooker. "The old him," I clarify. "I can admit when there's someone out there better than me."

Archer gets a look in his eye, and if we hadn't gotten past all our shit and we weren't dating, I'd think he would be scheming something. But I trust him, and I wait for whatever idea he has to come out his mouth.

He doesn't disappoint. He leans back in his chair but turns his head toward Brooker. "How do you feel about having two agents?"

We share matching smiles. As much as me offering this to him is an abnormality, Archer offering to share it goes to show exactly how much we've grown together.

"Can I ... do that? Is it double the percentage for me or ..." Brooker asks.

"We split the agent's percentage," I say. "Dalton and his brother have the same deal with us. We rep them as a team. I don't think it would take much for our higher-ups to approve this."

"I'm willing if you are. I haven't been able to find one agent interested, and here you are telling me there's two for the price of one? Sign me up."

The sense of accomplishment I always get when signing a client fills me with happiness that's hard to contain, but I manage. "We'll get those contracts drawn up and sent to you."

We all stand together, Brooker shakes both our hands, and as he walks out the office door, Archer rounds my desk to join my side.

"Before we do this, there's probably something you should know."

My breath gets stuck in my throat, and I don't know why I immediately jump to he's cheated on me when he's given me no reason to suspect that, but at this point, I would probably accept that more than what I think is likely going to come out of his mouth which is that he signed one of my clients from under me. After I invited him in on this one.

It's possible old habits die hard, but as I look into his eyes, yes, there is worry there, but there's also something else. Something that looks like love. And if I'm honest with myself, he's made it so easy to fall for him that I don't know when I did, just that I have.

My heart races because I'm hoping I'm reading him correctly. If the next words out of his mouth aren't those three little words that are at the tip of my own tongue, I might die a little inside.

"I realized yesterday, in this very room," he starts. Stops to swallow. Talks again. "That ever since that night you admitted you were attracted to me, I've been riding an avalanche of emotion I haven't been able to identify."

Oh shit. It's happening. I think ... "You can't really ride avalanches."

He grunts. "I just mean everything has moved so fast, and I've barely been able to keep my feet on the ground. After you got me through the rough patch with my family, the answer became obvious."

Could he drag this out any longer? Say it.

He does. In a rush so fast it sounds like one word. "I'minlove-withyou. If that changes your mind about signing another client together—"

"I'm in love with you too." I can finally breathe again. "And no, it doesn't change anything."

Archer's shoulders sag like he'd been holding his breath that whole time. Even with that relief, he's still cautious. "Are you sure we're not pushing our luck?"

I shake my head, never sure of anything more in my life. "Nah. If this was going to go to shit, it would have already. You're stuck with me."

He grips my hips and pulls me against him. "It's not a bad place to be stuck."

Chapter 40
Epilogue
Archer

This year's King Sports Achievement Awards is being held in an event space with different themed rooms. This year, Damon went with the exposed brick and pipes vibe with dark pillars that make it look gloomy. Paired with the sophisticated lighting though, it's giving trendy LA.

We stare out at the filling ballroom, at the grandiosity of it all, and I'm ninety percent sure the King Sports Achievement Awards is an excuse for the firm to throw a massive party and get a major tax write-off, but at the same time, it does boost morale.

I throw my arm around my man's shoulders. "Another made-up award ceremony, another chance for public bathroom sex."

"You wish. That was a whole *I shouldn't but want to* fantasy. I couldn't have you, so doing it was a feat. I already have you now, so only boring sex from now on. It's, like, the law of relationships."

"In that case, can we break up, have breakup sex, then go home and have makeup sex?" I say *home* like we live together, which we practically do, but it's not official or anything. I'm at Fox's apartment more than my own. It'll happen one day, but we've been together for less than a year, things are going extremely well, and I don't want to push it too hard, too fast. Having a serious relationship is new for both of us, so there are ample chances for us to fuck this up.

"While you know I love drama," Fox deadpans, "I'm not going up on stage tonight in cum-stained pants."

"It really is true what they say, romance dies off so quickly."

"Because nothing screams romance like cum stains."

I nod seriously and say, "You get me. But also, it's cute you think you're winning anything tonight. Haven't I always taken out the awards you've been eligible for?"

"You've won two awards. Two. Calm down."

I laugh. In the last four years since finishing my internship, I won a Rising Star award in my first year as a junior agent and an Associate of the Year at the last awards. The other two years, the award at our level went to New York employees. Fox has yet to win one, but I wouldn't be surprised if this is his year. Or maybe not because we broke the no-fraternization rule Damon tries to impose. Tries but fails. A lot. My argument is if it's really forbidden, why have paperwork ready for when it happens?

Yeah, neither of us is going to win tonight.

Which is a shame because ever since Fox decided to stop having a one-sided competition with me, he's been thriving. We continue to learn from each other, and who knows? In the future, like way, way down the road when we're in our forties and we're still working well as business partners, we might be able to open up our own small firm between the two of us. Nothing like King Sports, of course, which is taking over the world, but an agency we run together and share our clients ... I've been thinking a lot about that lately.

We both have skills the other doesn't have experience in, like me with content creation and him with his take-charge confidence in a crisis. By taking on the Daltons and sharing Brooker's account, we're learning from each other as we go.

"The Daltons are here," Fox says.

I turn my attention to the entrance of the ballroom. Asher and Emmett Dalton are so different from one another. In appearance and attitude.

Asher is broody with dark hair and piercing green eyes. Emmett, with blond curly hair and blue eyes, is less confident but always has a warm smile on his face. They both look good in black tie.

Each agent gets to invite their clients along to this shindig, but I never have until this year. I don't know why, and for someone who's known for being competitive, it does seem weird I haven't. The only reason I did this time was because Fox convinced me to by saying it would be a good way to introduce Jeremiah Castleberry to Rafferty Brooker and give Brooker that contact with someone who's actually involved in NASCAR. I've always seen inviting clients as a way to boast or show off if I won, and despite what everyone might think of my competitive side, it was never about gloating for me. It was about proving I was the best with the results speaking for themselves, not me shoving it down people's throats. Fox sees this awards ceremony for the amazing chance it is —a networking opportunity.

We're so similar but have very different mindsets. It's why we work.

It's why we'll continue to work well together, hopefully well into our graying years.

We move to greet the brothers and thank them for coming, when another client steps in front of me.

"I hope you know I don't get dressed up like this for just anyone." Jeremiah Castleberry's smooth Southern accent brings a smile to my face.

I hold out my hand for him, which turns into one of those handshake-slash-one-armed hugs. "I'm happy you made it out here." I pat his back and pull away. "And I think you should dress like this more often. Race in it, even. You might find yourself a man if you raced in a tux."

"Or I could die in a fiery car crash because this wool is basically tinder for flames."

"What's romance without a little risk of bursting into flames?"

Jeremiah clutches his head. "Well, if that doesn't bring me back to all them Sunday school lessons about why I'll burn in hell."

Coming from Louisiana, Jeremiah is a one-of-a-kind type of man. From growing up in the homophobic Deep South to joining what might be one of the most homophobic, toxic masculine sports in the world, he's a living legend for being himself. His world might be trying to reject him in every possible way, but he gets up every day and fights.

"Jeremiah, I want you to meet my boyfriend and partner, Lincoln Fox."

Fox smiles. "It's nice to finally meet you. I was supposed to a few years ago, but someone canceled our appointment so he could steal you as his own client."

The corner of Jeremiah's lips turns up, and his gaze flicks between Fox and me. Then he reaches for Fox's hand to shake. "And you're now his boyfriend?"

I wrap my arm around Fox's shoulders. "What can I say? My charm wore him down. I'm that irresistible."

"So irresistible it took me a good four years before I had a nice word to say about him."

I shrug. "Still counts. Doesn't matter if I moved slower than a turtle in mud. You're mine now."

"I can't tell if that's romantic or some kind of bestiality fantasy where you're a turtle and I'm—"

"Mud?" Jeremiah asks.

"Wow. This conversation went downhill really fast. Good one, babe." I kiss the top of Fox's head.

"Yes. All my fault."

My gaze catches on Brooker approaching Asher Dalton, stopping him and his brother halfway between the entrance and the open bar. It reminds me of the plan Fox and I had when it comes to Jeremiah.

Whether Fox saw him and is reminded too, or he's just on the ball—it's probably the latter—Fox says, "While we have you, there's something we wanted to discuss with you. We have an NHL client interested in building more momentum with his NASCAR content, and we wanted to know if you'd be interested in going on his podcast."

Jeremiah's gaze narrows. "NHL player. NASCAR podcast. Why do I get the sense those two don't really mix?"

"I dunno about that," I say. Both sports are predominantly full of white cis men, both have had their share of toxicity when it comes to gay rights and acceptance ... but that's not really a selling point.

"How so?"

Yes, Archer. How so? Because now I'm not so sure what my argument was going to be.

"Even other athletes enjoy sports outside of their own. Just meet with him," I say. "He's right over there." I point behind him.

"Wait, he's here? Now? Does this have anything to do with you saying I could find a man in a tux? Is this a setup? Do I look okay?"

Jeremiah's panic is cute but unwarranted.

"This isn't anything more than a professional setup," Fox says. "As far as we know, Rafferty is straight, and with him knowing King Sports' reputation for repping queer athletes, I'd like to say with confidence that he's an ally."

"You'd *like* to?" Jeremiah asks.

"I would assume he's an ally, considering his teammate is in a same-sex relationship and his two agents are gay, but to be honest with you, sexuality has never been a topic of discussion."

I agree with Fox. "If he had an issue with it, he wouldn't have signed with us." Right?

"Okay, so it doesn't matter if I look like a swamp monster in a suit. Let's do this."

As Jeremiah turns on his heel, Fox leans in close and whispers to me, "Does he really think he looks like a swamp monster? He's ..." He stops himself.

"You're allowed to say he's good-looking. I have eyes."

"Right?"

Jeremiah has silky golden hair and rough stubble, but it frames his face and lessens the harshness of his square jawline perfectly. He's only around five-nine-ish, and being a NASCAR driver, he's not exactly stacked with muscles. Good things come in small packages and all that. Bottom line is he's gorgeous, but I'm not going to say that out loud when he's my client.

On our way through the crowd, we pass Brady, Thad, Thad's

baseball-playing partner, Kelley, and Thad's baseball client, Frederik Zaka.

I have no idea what they're talking about, but Thad's voice is loud over the growing noise of chatter as he says firmly, "No, Zaka. He's too young for you."

Zaka laughs.

I'll get the newest office gossip later. Ever since Fox and I became a couple, I'm sure there are new rumors everyone is gagging over. Though after a sternly written email from Damon King prohibiting the betting over the personal lives of King Sports employees, it won't be as much fun to speculate.

As we reach the Daltons and Brooker, we interrupt their chat with someone I don't recognize until he turns toward us to welcome us into their circle.

It's Lane Pierce's husband, Oskar Voyjik, retired manwhore ... I mean hockey player. But they're another King Sports couple who broke the no-fraternization rule.

Considering Damon is adamant this firm isn't a matchmaking service and that fraternization isn't allowed or is at least highly frowned upon, I think it's obvious as we glance around this room that he's a romantic at heart and can't hold a grudge against any of us who have broken the rules. Hell, by the time he found out about us, it wasn't so much a lecture on being in the wrong but a resigned sigh of defeat. He's totally a romantic.

"Oskar, these are our new agents, Lincoln Fox and Archer Holloway," Asher Dalton says.

Oskar smiles, crinkling an old scar near his eye from his playing days. "I've heard stories about you two."

That's not vague or remotely terrifying. Without telling us explicitly what he's heard, he leaves us with that.

Our eyes must match—widened in fear—because Dalton laughs. "He's talking about how you two basically ousted our GM. I tell everyone I meet how epic that was. Even if they don't ask."

"Y-you're ... you're Jeremiah Castleberry," Brooker says.

"He is!" I pat Jeremiah's shoulder. "We brought him over here to actually talk to you."

"I ... I ..."

Aww, Brooker's stammering is cute for a six-one hockey player.

"This is Raff Brooker," I say to Jeremiah.

Brooker finally finds his voice. "I would love to pick your brain about ... well, everything."

A little unsure, Jeremiah looks to us, and we give him an encouraging nod.

"Go. Talk," I say. "I promise he won't bite."

"Hard," Asher mumbles.

Brooker nudges him.

"I'm joking. The biggest threat you have when it comes to Brooker is him fanboying you to death."

"Dude, that isn't any better," Brooker says.

"Since when have you known me to make anything better?" Dalton asks.

"True. Why don't you two go get a drink and talk? Away from this brat." I point at Dalton.

Emmett laughs. "Holloway sure has you pegged."

"He wishes he could peg me." Asher Dalton is extra ... Asher Dalton-y tonight.

"Yes. So ... true."

He ignores my dry tone. "Knew it."

Damon King gets up on the small stage at the front and taps the microphone on the podium. "If you could all take your seats, we'll get this night started."

Unlike the NFL awards we went to, where the seated dinner and the awards were in different rooms, this ballroom has large round tables we'll be sitting at and being fed while they hand out the awards.

Because the Daltons, Brooker, and Jeremiah are on my client list, they're all at the combined table for Fox and me.

We take our places, and Damon starts with a speech about how amazing we all are and that we're helping build not only his legacy but the legacy of queer athletes and the allies who dare stand up with us.

Beside me, Fox looks nervous.

I lean in. "You okay?"

"Is it stupid that these awards don't really mean anything, but I want to win one anyway?"

"It'll happen. One year. Might not be this year because of me, so I'm sorry if you don't win tonight. You deserve to win one though."

His shoulders relax. "You're right. There's no point hoping for one this year."

"I could be wrong?"

I'm not wrong.

Unsurprisingly, Brady takes out the Rising Star award I was once given. With a mentor like me, of course he was going to win it. Yup. It had everything to do with me and not the fact that he's already outearning Fox and me combined because he represents his NFL quarterback brother. It's all me. Naturally.

"I'm such a good mentor," I say.

Fox snorts.

"That wasn't supposed to be funny, but okay." My grin lets him know I'm not completely delusional.

Associate of the Year goes to a New York agent, and Senior Associate of the Year goes to Merek Lynn, also of the New York office.

I knew Merek back when I interned, and he was always a great agent. But when Brady and Thad both signed contracts with clients of Merek's, transferring accounts, Merek apparently started worrying it was the beginning of the end of his career. Apparently, he's spent the last year getting his groove back, seeing as he's taking out this award.

I put my fingers in my mouth and whistle even harder than I did for Brady when he won.

Damon's right. This company that he has built from the ground up is more than a sports talent agency. It represents our queer identities in a world that is often flipflopping when it comes to their views of us. Just when we think we're making progress, we regress. I'm so proud to be a part of Damon's dynasty.

I feel so sorry for Fox though. It's obvious he's disappointed he didn't win an award again, but he's trying not to show it.

"Before we wrap everything up, there's a new award that I'd like to introduce this year." Damon pulls out another award.

The design of the awards changes for each ceremony. This year, the award is what looks like a giant glass jelly bean. Or a miniature Cloud Gate in Chicago.

"This award," Damon continues, "is to recognize adaptability to change, innovative ideas, and embracing that this business sometimes relies on teamwork."

My heart rate kicks up a notch. Teamwork? Like a team of agents? Fox and I lock eyes, the same thought most likely going through his head.

"And that's why," Damon says, "this year's Future of Sports Management award goes to ... Lincoln Fox and Archer Holloway."

Holy fuck.

The room erupts in applause, but we're too stunned to immediately get up. It's only when Asher shakes my shoulder from my other side that I stand on shaky legs and offer my hand to Fox.

That's how we take to the stage, hand in hand, to accept our joint award.

Shit. This is a surreal moment.

Fox gestures for me to talk first, but I had no idea this was going to happen. Not even an inkling. I have nothing prepared. Going off the fly will have to do.

"Uh," I start. "If you had told me that this would happen at last year's award, I would've told you to stay away from the open bar."

There are snickers all around, but then I realize that this is my chance to put it all out there. To take this seriously and acknowledge how much work both Fox and I have done. From burying the hatchet to falling in love and becoming a team, we're not the men we were this same time last year.

"The most important person I have to thank would be Lincoln Fox. Of course." I glance over at him, to our award in his hand, before turning back. "I owe a lot to that man. It's no secret we weren't each other's biggest fans, but it turns out if we both swallowed our egos and started listening to each other, we were more alike than we'd realized. I'm with Fox because he pushes me to be better. He encourages me to go for the things I want. I owe my achievements this year to him. I admire his smarts, his intuition, and his drive. But most of all, I love him for being him."

He steps up to the podium and leans over to speak into the mic. "All of what he said. But, uh, about him. Not me."

There are more chuckles around the room.

We might have won a joint award tonight, but being with him is the real prize.

Out of nowhere, Maddox O'Shay, Damon's partner, jumps up on stage and shuffles us aside as he takes to the podium and mic. "I guess there's only one question left to ask. Whose house will the trophy live at?"

In unison, we both say, "Mine."

"Uh-oh. I told Damon he really should have gotten two trophies." Maddox is giddy, as if waiting for drama to unfold right in front of him, but Damon gently moves him out of the way and gestures for us to go back to our seats.

He thanks everyone for coming out tonight and tells us all to enjoy the open bar until ten, when we all need to be out of the event center.

Before we reach our table, I pull on Fox's arm. "What if the award lived at *our* place?"

"Our place?"

"I'm at your apartment nearly every night anyway. I've been living in a run-down, cheap place, saving for a down payment. We could buy a place. Together."

Fox's mouth gapes. "I ... uh, that's a big commitment."

"But I'm ready for it. I love you. All of you. We make an awesome team, and I want it to continue to be awesome."

"I want that too. I keep waiting for something to happen. Like a deal-breaker to pop up. It hasn't. I fall more and more every day."

I didn't realize how much I needed to hear that until the words were out there, and I feel lighter than a feather. "Let's look for a house or a bigger apartment that we can buy and move in together."

Fox hesitates for a split second before agreeing. "Okay, let's do it. Though it's entirely possible this could totally blow up in our faces."

"Possible but unlikely. We're stuck with each other, remember?" Whether Lincoln Fox likes it or not, he is my future, and I'm going to do everything in my power to keep him. "I'd bet on us."

Thank you!

Thank you so much for reading *The Office Bet*.

This book ended up being longer than anticipated which means during the editing process, a fun little scene was deleted. If you want to read about Fox and Archer going for after work drinks and the fallout of everyone finding out about them, join my Patreon! The deleted scene is available to all tiers, including the FREE tier.

Read it here: patreon.com/EdenFinley

King Sports has been an idea floating around in my head ever since I finished writing the Fake Boyfriend series and knew Damon was going to take on the world.

Damon's origin story, back before he had gray hairs from stress, is titled: Fake Out - Fake Boyfriend book 1

Because King Sports has been years in the making, we've met a lot of side characters before. So if you want any of their stories, here's a list of books that currently exist in the Damonverse:

The Backup Plan - King Sports book 1 (Thad and Kelley)

Twincerely Yours - FU2 book 8 (Emmett and Jonah)

Line Mates & Study Dates - CU Hockey book 4 (Asher and Kole)

Clueless Puckboy - Puckboys book 5 (Quinn and Vance)
Can't Say Goodbye (Brady, Kit, and Prescott)
Football Royalty - FU book 8 (Peyton and Levi)
Blindsided - Fake Boyfriend book 4 (Talon and Miller)

Where will King Sports go next? Your guess is as good as mine.

Also by Eden Finley

FAKE BOYFRIEND SERIES

Fake Out

Trick Play

Deke

Blindsided

Hat Trick

Novellas:

Fake Boyfriend Breakaways: A short story collection

Final Play

FAMOUS SERIES

Pop Star

Spotlight

Fandom

Encore

Novellas:

Rockstar Hearts

FRANKLIN U: multi-author shared world series

Football Royalty

Twincerely Yours

MIKE BRAVO OPS

Iris

Rogue

Atlas

Zeus

BOOKS COWRITTEN WITH SAXON JAMES

Power Plays & Straight A's

Face Offs & Cheap Shots

Goal Lines & First Times

Line Mates & Study Dates

Puck Drills & Quick Thrills

Egotistical Puckboy

Irresponsible Puckboy

Shameless Puckboy

Foolish Puckboy

Clueless Puckboy

Bromantic Puckboy

Forbidden Puckboy

Possessive Puckboy

Stubborn Puckboy

Up in Flames

The Bastard and the Heir

VINO & VERITAS *Sarina Bowen's True North Series*

Headstrong

STEELE BROTHERS

Unwritten Law

Unspoken Vow